W9-CPF-734

Kenneth Royce is one of Britain's best, most compelling and respected adventure thriller writers and the creator of television's *The XYY Man*, *Strangers* and *Bulman*, which ran world-wide for a record ten years. All three series are now being re-run on SKY. His books have been translated into eighteen languages.

GHOSTMAN

Jones boasted that he never forgot a face.
When he was found dead outside the
National Gallery it was assumed he had
remembered one too many. The man he
had claimed to have identified had been
publicly executed in Moscow some years
before. The presumed look-alike was called
Mirek and his background stood up. The
Security Service calls in Willie 'Glasshouse'
Jackson — Jacko — as they realise that there
is a more sinister aspect. Jacko and his
assistant begin to unearth commercial and
political corruption in which life is cheap and
profits vast, as the killing machines swing into
action.

KENNETH ROYCE

◆

GHOSTMAN

Complete and Unabridged

ULVERSCROFT
Leicester

First published in Great Britain in 1997 by
Severn House Publishers Limited
Surrey

First Large Print Edition
published 1999
by arrangement with
Severn House Publishers Limited
Surrey

British Library CIP Data

Royce, Kenneth, *1920 – 1997*
    The ghostman.—Large print ed.—
    Ulverscroft large print series: mystery
    1. MI5—Fiction
    2. Suspense fiction
    3. Large type books
    I. Title
    823.9'14 [F]

    ISBN 0–7089–4063–3

Published by
F. A. Thorpe (Publishing) Ltd.
Anstey, Leicestershire
Set by Words & Graphics Ltd.
Anstey, Leicestershire
Printed and bound in Great Britain by
T. J. International Ltd., Padstow, Cornwall

This book is printed on acid-free paper

To all my wonderful friends in
the village of Abbots Ann

Publisher's Note

Kenneth Royce died at his home
in the late summer of 1997.

The final page proofs of this title
were beside his favourite armchair.

1

Tommy Jones entered the foyer of the Brook Park Hotel as two other men left. They hardly saw each other but it was enough for Jones. Never strong on emotion he now suffered a peculiar feeling, almost disturbing as he suddenly turned and followed the two men outside. It was not that his reactions were slow, rather that the other two men were in a hurry. By the time he reached the pavement they were already climbing into a taxi. He caught another glimpse of the man who interested him most as he sat down in the cab. And then it was pulling away.

Jones stood there in the bitterly cold wind until the taxi was out of sight. Even then he did not return to the foyer immediately. He stood with head slightly cocked at an angle and tried to probe his own feelings. He was definitely disturbed, not a new sensation to him, but this one carried a vague sense of apprehension.

Tommy Jones did not see people, crowds around him, he saw faces. The world was made up of faces, each differing more than fingerprints, more identifiable even when aged or altered. Fundamental structure was a key and ethnic differences actioned keyboards in his mind that could connect a face with a particular country and sometimes with a particular part of that country, no matter how far flung. It was a gift, like painting or orating, for he seldom had to apply himself too much; a face, any face, simply imprinted itself on his mind without conscious thought. A useless and sometimes embarrassing gift as he saw it, until the Security Service saw that it was not and yanked him through its doors to supply him with a desk and files to look at, and a modest income supplemented by appreciation and praise.

Jones was in his mid-thirties, of average height with an almost permanently bland expression aided by large framed glasses. A slightly serious air rode on him easily and the odd thing about him was that he seemed not to notice anyone. That myth was exploded the moment he entered the hotel and passed the two men. He was satisfied that he had just seen Vadim Bykov.

Jones's memory for events was not quite as good as his ability to identify faces. He still felt that something was wrong but could not put his finger on it until he returned to MI5 after lunch where he reported to his boss Derek North.

The experienced North listened to Jones's report as he sat behind his desk in a cold office; the heating system was playing up and he quietly smiled as he tapped a pen against his desk. Everyone had known it would happen. Some had placed bets on it. One day the infallible Jones would slip up. North's smile widened and he was now wishing he had taken a bet himself. 'You sure it was Vadim Bykov?'

'Absolutely.' Jones appeared pained, not used to being challenged since his early days here.

'Vadim Bykov was publicly executed a few years

ago. The world press was there. It was important that the warning to others came through.' North grinned. 'Whoops! Not this time, Jonesy.'

Jones stood in front of the desk gazing quietly down at North, for whom he had a great respect. North was clever and efficient and moving up the tree. Jones felt no rancour and simply said, 'Then it was his twin I saw.'

'As far as I know he had no brothers, although he did have a sister and a wife. I'll check.'

Jones smiled. 'You've been waiting for this to happen, haven't you?'

North chuckled. 'Some of them have. But only in the friendliest way. They haven't your gift, you see. Don't worry. You can't win them all.'

'I realise that. But this is not the one I have lost. It was Bykov and I would like it on record that I reported it.' Jones drew himself up and adjusted his glasses. 'I'll put in a written report.' He left the room leaving North thinking it could not be Bykov, but if not who? Yet he supposed that even Jones could be wrong. Two hours later Jones supplied a written report and North, who was always overworked, accepted that he would have to follow it up. He sent for Jones and told him to sit down.

'Is this guy staying at the hotel? And what were you doing there anyway?'

Jones pushed up his glasses, knowing that North still did not take him seriously. 'I've no idea. It was all so quick. And I was having lunch with a friend. It was a coincidence; they do happen.'

'Your report means I've got to action it which

3

you well know or you wouldn't have put the bloody thing in. Find out if he's staying there and if so for how long. If he's not there then there's not much we can do about it. We can't afford too much time on a very iffy sighting.'

'It's not iffy to me. What you're asking isn't really my job, is it?'

'Not normally but as you're the only one who has seen the bugger I think it a reasonable request, don't you? You know what you saw so you'd know him again.'

'I'll do my best.' Jones still sat there and seemed uncomfortable.

'And?' queried North, hoping Jones would go and find nobody resembling Bykov.

'Didn't he work for us? Before my time? Before the Soviet Union broke up?'

North smiled, feeling slightly sorry for Jones. 'You could say that. You could also say that was a pretty good reason why he was shot dead in front of so many. He was the best thing that happened to us since Penkovsky. But he belonged to Six, not us.'

'Should I tell them?'

'Don't you dare. This is our patch. We'll handle it if there's anything to handle. Do it as quickly as you can.'

'What's the best way of setting about it?'

North stared unbelievingly. Then he relaxed. Perhaps he was being too hard on Jones. It was easy to see that Jones was no longer in his element. He was basically a desk man and carried hundreds of images in his head. Field work, even minor field

4

work, was foreign soil to him. 'Take Ryan with you. I think he once met Bykov.' Ryan was near retirement and was padding out time. 'He'll know what to do. Any problem refer him to me.'

In fact the very experienced Ryan was only too glad to leave the building. Knowing of his imminent retirement he had been given odd jobs to eke out his time. He did not think early evening was a good point to return to the hotel. It could be busy and although more residents might be around, he wanted a quiet word with the manager first. So he made an appointment for early the following morning. Meanwhile he borrowed a mugshot of Bykov from the files.

Jones and Ryan arrived at the hotel at nine the next day. They were shown into the manager's office where Ryan provided formal identification; it had the effect of commanding attention.

Ryan produced the mugshot and laid it on the manager's desk while Jones tried to study his technique. 'Is this man staying here? He'll be a few years older now but I believe his hair is still thick and dark.'

The plump manager, an Italian by his faint accent, picked up the photograph and studied it. 'He doesn't come to mind. But this is not the tourist season. Stays are usually shorter at this time of year; mainly businessmen here for an appointment and then off again. Unless there's a conference, of course. But in any event I cannot be expected to know every guest.'

'Of course not. There was just a chance . . .' Ryan shrugged.

'I can show this to the reception staff,' said the manager, trying to be helpful. 'All the staff if you have enough prints. If it is that important. Of course, he may have been just using the bar or the restaurant.'

Ryan reached out and took the mugshot back. 'I'd rather you didn't show this around. If he is here he might find out that we are enquiring if too many people become involved. Is it possible to see the registrations, say going back a week?'

'Certainly. But what name would you be looking for? A particular name might ring a bell with reception.'

Ryan smiled. 'I wish I knew. I'll know it if I see it.'

Half an hour later, still in the manager's office, Ryan had carefully checked through the hotel bookings while the manager left them to get on with his work.

'There's no Bykov entered,' Jones said.

The older Ryan shot him a scathing glance. 'Did you expect it? He's dead but even with a resurrection he's unlikely to return under his own name.' He made a note. 'Jan Mirek,' he said. 'The only eastern European name I can find.'

'That's Polish, not Russian.'

'Bright boy.' Ryan scratched his grey hair, his rugged features noncommittal. 'If he's here, or someone like him, it could be any one of these entries. Surprising number for out of season.'

When the manager returned Ryan asked about Jan Mirek and was promised that he would be looked into and a description provided as soon as he had one. And then: 'Have you had breakfast, gentlemen?' He glanced at his watch. 'There is just about time, or perhaps just a coffee?'

In the near-empty restaurant Jones had his second sighting of the man whom he believed to be Vadim Bykov, and more importantly Ryan had his first. 'Stop staring, you bloody fool,' Ryan hissed across the table.

Ryan was shaken, which in turn unsettled Jones. Ryan was a rock; been there, seen it, done it. His experience was vast, his service record impeccable, if not outstanding. A man not given to obvious emotion, a man to be relied upon especially in a crisis. Right now he was trying to steady his hands holding utensils above his plate and Jones was staring at him because he could not understand the reaction. But then, Jones had never met Bykov, even briefly as Ryan had many years ago.

Ryan steadied down and managed to get some food in his mouth, aware that he had shown his shock and annoyed that he had. He belatedly realised that he should have taken Jones's claim more seriously. Suddenly he was no longer padding out time to satisfy Derek North and Jones but found himself on an important job that baffled him by the very presence of the man the other side of the restaurant. He considered it lucky that there were two men and that they were engrossed in conversation.

Ryan continued to eat and think and wished that Jones would act as normally instead of watching his every move as if he would learn some great lesson in espionage. Ryan realised he had been flat-footed and had to make the best of what he had. He ate slowly and said, 'I want you to inform North that I substantially back your story but that I need to be sure. Tell him to get a team round here straight away to wait outside and to follow a man who looks like Bykov, an absolute double. Tell him that he might have noticed us, particularly your first gawping, and we need to know if he moves to somewhere else. This is uncanny.'

When Jones pulled out his mobile phone Ryan almost threw his plate at him. 'You stupid bastard,' his lips barely moved, the accusation just audible to Jones yet unmistakable, the rage well masked. 'You should be chained to a desk. Just make your excuses to me, get up normally and walk slowly out. Make your call in the manager's office whether he's there or not. Can you remember that? Don't come back. I'll stay here.'

Jones did his best to appear casual. To the watching Ryan the act was overdone and he was glad that there were few witnesses. The two men across the room were still deep in conversation and the man who looked like Bykov was at an angle to them, with his back partly facing them. It was a lucky break. Jones was more convincing when crossing the floor and Ryan hid his relief when he finally went beyond the double doors. He had to hope that Jones got the message right.

Ryan now had a better chance of observing the two men without having to worry about Jones giving the game away. If Derek North had taken Jones more seriously it wouldn't have happened. If the Bykov lookalike had seen Jones's first reaction he would know of the interest in him. Or perhaps his companion would have noticed it and passed it on. The real Bykov would have shown no reaction anyway; he had lived in acute danger for so long and knew all the tricks of the trade. He had been caught because quite simply he had been betraying his country for too long. He should have got out earlier and was not helped by the British SIS who were squeezing the last ounce of information from him. Greed for knowledge on the one hand and overconfidence on the other had been his ultimate downfall. But he had been executed; it couldn't possibly be him.

That was the logic of it. But Ryan had seen that face before a few years back; only briefly but it was enough. Ryan had been working for the SIS at the time, had spent two years with them before going to the Security Service. It had been in the Moscow Airport transit lounge while waiting to reboard the Air India flight to New Delhi. He had collected information from a waste bin drop at a nod from Bykov who had been standing at the bar talking to the fat barmaid who had been serving warm beer. As soon as the signal was given and understood Bykov disappeared. Not long, not an actual meeting, but memorable and enough.

Having finished his breakfast Ryan called for more coffee and a copy of *The Times*. Without Jones it was more difficult to justify a long stay at the table. He had been annoyed with Jones's lack of experience but had to admit that he would not be sitting there now, surreptitiously watching a man who possessed a remarkable likeness to

Bykov, had it not been for Jones's aptitude for recognising faces.

Waiting was always tiresome and difficult to do, particularly when the objective was sitting in the same room. The animated conversation between the two men had died down and the second man was beginning to gaze round the restaurant. There were now only three other tables occupied and Ryan was the only person alone. He began to take more interest in the second man. If there is such a thing as a typical top civil servant then this man was it: neat suit, straight tie, hair brushed back, and the odd word that drifted over to Ryan was uttered in a public school accent; he seemed to be vaguely worried.

The Bykov lookalike was more stolid. The cut of the suit was not good enough to be the best of British. The face was pale, as Ryan remembered, the hair thick and black and slightly unruly. He spoke fast but so softly that Ryan could detect no actual words, and very little sound. It was impossible to pick up an accent.

Ryan glanced at his watch. He could not stay there forever and people at one of the other tables were leaving. The two men were now silently drinking coffee. Ryan thumbed through *The Times*, folded it neatly, finished his coffee and was about to push his chair back when the other two men rose almost in unison. Ryan stayed where he was and gazed at the headlines of *The Times* once again. The two men were coming his way.

Ryan was dying to get a closer look and glanced up as the two men approached. They all exchanged polite 'good morning's' and smiled, and then the two were heading for the door. Ryan remained where he was. Neither man had shown a flicker of recognition which meant nothing. He did not think that North would have had the time to get a team down here although he might have called on help from the police. Ryan did not think there was anything more he could do for he could not now follow them. He briefly wondered what had happened to Jones. He pushed his chair back unhurriedly; it was now in the hands of others if they arrived in time.

He strode out of the dining room and walked down the short corridor to the foyer where he immediately saw the two men enter one of the lifts. He went to the manager's office which was empty and he now wondered more seriously what had happened to Jones. He went back to the foyer and sat as far away from the doors as he could but facing them, *The Times* ready to become a shield.

The two men, now in topcoats, appeared a few minutes later and left the hotel. Ryan waited. Where the hell was Jones and had he made the call? Ryan pulled out his phone and rang through. Yes, Jones had reported in and a half team was on its way which was the best that could be done in the circumstances. North doubted that they would have arrived by now; it took time to get a team and for them to arrive. Then North said, 'I had to accept Jones's word that the instructions were from you. You know how screwed up he is about this. He doesn't like being wrong.'

11

'He wasn't wrong,' Ryan said tersely. 'I saw the guy. It gave me a very nasty turn.'

'But we both know it can't be.'

'Not any longer.'

'Then Bykov has a double. Everybody has, so they say. For Christ's sake, Sam, let's be logical about this. And if by some miracle it is Bykov would he put himself on open show like that?'

Ryan had had more time to think it through than North. 'Everyone might have a double but you're pushing coincidence beyond the limits if they both came from the same part of the world. Leave it until I get back while I make further enquiries here. Has Jones returned?'

'Not yet. Why?'

'I don't know where he's gone. He made the call in the manager's office and hasn't been seen since. He's hopeless on this side of things. I'll come back as soon as I've wound up here.' He pocketed the phone and crossed to reception. He spoke to the head receptionist. 'The two men who just went out, I wonder if you could tell me the name of the darker one?'

The manager came up as the receptionist hesitated. 'It's all right, you can tell him.'

'That was Mister Mirek, sir. The other man is just a visitor.'

'Thank you.' Ryan took the manager aside. 'Do you think I can look in his room while he's away?'

The manager wanted to be helpful but did not like the idea and was hesitant.

Ryan said, 'I understand your feelings. I could

get a search warrant but it would take some time. I won't take long and you could be there all the time. I don't intend to take anything but I do need to know more about this man.'

'I really haven't the time. And I am answerable for what happens here.'

'I know. You could cut me short any time you like. A few minutes, no more.'

'All right. Follow me.'

They entered the lift and rose to the top floor. As they left the lift Ryan said, 'By the way, have you seen anything of my colleague? He went to your office to use his mobile.'

'No. The last time I saw him was with you.'

They approached a room at the end of the corridor and the manager opened the door for Ryan to enter.

Ryan worked quickly and expertly. Bykov had not brought that much with him. A large suitcase and a document case were on the luggage rack but Ryan first went through the various drawers and found nothing that most visitors would not have. 'Is his passport downstairs?'

'It would have been returned to him. Perhaps he carries it with him.' The manager was now caught up with the speed and thoroughness with which Ryan worked.

Ryan tried the document case to find it locked with a triple coded number on each catch. The combinations were too many to try; it could take all day and he did not want to force it open. He picked it up to test its weight, shook it slightly. It seemed to be empty, so why lock it?

'Is this man dangerous?' asked the manager, becoming slightly worried.

'We don't know. He reminds us of someone we once knew. We simply want to know what he's doing here. He may be completely harmless. In any event he would not be a danger to you or your hotel.' Detecting a growing concern and signs of impatience Ryan added, 'We are really grateful to you for your cooperation over this. I'll put it in my report.'

Ryan turned to the large suitcase which turned out to be unlocked. Nor was it empty. Among a few items of clothing was a Polish passport confirming Mirek's name. There was an empty wallet, presumably a backup, and a card for a London restaurant. Ryan made a note. He tidied everything up and then went into the bathroom.

An American dry multi-voltage shaver was on the glass shelf. There were no powder marks of any description. A bottle of pills, orange coloured with the label typed in Polish and a month-old date. Ryan tipped one out and slipped it into his pocket, and as the manager was about to protest said, 'Well, that seems to be that then. I'm most obliged to you.'

They went down to the manager's office and as there was still no sign of Jones the manager offered to put a call out on the pager asking Jones to report to his office. There was no response.

Ryan shook the manager's hand, offered to pay for the breakfasts, thanked him profusely and finally asked him if he would ring him if and when Mirek returned. He passed over a number.

Ryan returned to his office a rather troubled man. Like Jones he knew what he had seen and was not only deeply puzzled but disturbed, too. Maybe Mirek was just someone who bore a remarkable likeness to Vadim Bykov. It could happen. And as everyone knew Bykov had been shot dead. But if that logic was removed then something much more sinister presented itself. Yet Mirek was on open view which made a nonsense of it all.

Ryan reported to North who now took more notice; Ryan was not a man given to fancy, he was a tough, seasoned operator who had once seen Bykov, no matter how briefly. Later that day a message came through that Mirek had returned to the hotel and a team was now in place to pick him up when he left. But what the hell had happened to Jones?

They knew later that day. North received the call at home and he rang Ryan at once. Jones had been found dead on the steps of the National Gallery. He had been sitting at the top and leaning against one of the pillars until someone had brushed past him and he had tumbled down the steps to the pavement. There was a small bloodstain on the back of his topcoat and when the paramedics arrived they discovered he had been shot in the back and was already dead.

2

North and Ryan returned to HQ. Once there North checked with the police on the latest developments and made it known that Jones was an MI5 man, which took the enquiry beyond the realms of a normal murder enquiry.

The police had virtually nothing to go on except one dead body. To pick up witnesses in so public a place at a time when most people were in a hurry to reach their destinations made it very difficult for them. It meant they would have to appeal for witnesses through the media. Trafalgar Square was a high-density area, but not so much in the middle of winter on a miserable day when observation would be at its lowest. There had been no reports in, no phone calls.

'Pros,' North observed, brushing back his hair.

'Why the plural?' The heavily built Ryan seemed to be uncomfortable in the seat the other side of the desk from North.

'A manner of speaking.' North gestured, his good looks soured by his expression. 'They weren't seen because they chose their moment. One occupies him in talk, the other shoots him and they both gently lower him, pat him on the head and tell him to sober up.'

'You're still plural. Because we were watching two men? You think they did it?'

'Don't you? Who else would want to? And what

the bloody hell was he doing there?' North stared across the desk not expecting Ryan to answer and thinking that they both knew but did not want to voice it. North rang a number and murmured into the phone, 'Anything happen?'

'No, he's still in the hotel. Just left the restaurant and gone up to his room. No visitors.'

North put the phone down. 'Come on, let's say it. Jonesy decided to follow them on his own initiative because both you and I ridiculed him. He was going to show us. He'd been right from the start. He identified Bykov or someone remarkably like him and we took the piss. He'd have given himself away in minutes and all they had to do was to choose their moment. Poor sod. He did not deserve that.'

'Let's use the name this guy is registered under, the one in his passport, Jan Mirek, which may yet turn out to be absolutely correct. You're suggesting that when they left the hotel Jonesy was waiting for them and then followed. They killed him and then Mirek had the cold nerve to return to the hotel as if nothing had happened?'

'What else could he do? To flee would have been admission. As it is the police have nothing to go on, as yet. If they did the job properly what have they to worry about? If by some miracle he is Bykov, he would have one hell of a nerve just coming here. All he has to do is to keep that nerve. That would be nothing new to him. How can we find out definitely whether or not he's Bykov? We've got to start from there. Until we do we're groping in the dark.'

Ryan said, 'Do you think I can have a drink?'

North smiled slightly. 'You remind me of George Bulman when you say that. The only difference is he would have said it before starting work.' North opened a cabinet and produced whisky and glasses. 'You'll have to get your own water if you need it.'

Ryan reached for the glass. 'I hate drinking on an empty stomach. So how many people actually knew Bykov? I suppose you'll have to contact the SIS?'

'He was their contact, as you well know. Just how sure are you that this Mirek is actually Bykov and how could it have happened if he is?'

Ryan said, 'We just go through the routine.'

'You didn't answer the first part of the question.' North smoothed back his hair again. 'I'll contact Moscow. They might even agree to exhume the body — if anybody knows where it is. He was their traitor after all so it's in their own interests to know what has happened. They might even come up with a quick answer.'

The two men exchanged glances; neither believed Moscow would provide a quick answer even if they had one, even though the Cold War was long over; they probably had their own agenda.

'He had a wife,' said North. 'I'll contact Ian Marshall of Six and see if they can help us. We are obliged to do that anyway.' North finished his drink. 'Let's go home. I don't think we'll get anywhere tonight.' He gazed at Ryan in some despair. 'If the surveillance team had arrived just a few minutes earlier this would not have happened.'

'You're blaming yourself? Don't be ridiculous. Jones broke the rules and paid the price.'

North was not convinced; he felt he should have given his supernumerary more credit. And he did not like the way a gun had been introduced so easily and effectively; someone had a great deal to hide to justify that action.

★ ★ ★

They met in Ian Marshall's office at the new SIS HQ. 'Nice,' said North as he sat down in a comfortable armchair facing Marshall's rather large desk.

Marshall was quite friendly; the SIS had always considered themselves as the superior service, even after the horrific scandals that had come their way. He was a grey man — hair, complexion, clothes — and carried a slightly supercilious air, grey, piercing eyes peering above bifocals. As the more down-to-earth North related his story Marshall's thin lips parted into a disbelieving smile until he heard about Jones being murdered. That could not be ignored.

When North had finished Marshall reacted as they all had: 'But Bykov was shot dead in front of witnesses, for God's sake. We lost the best inside man we'd had in years.'

'So Jones was shot for nothing. No reason? Nothing to hide?'

'I don't know. This fellow Mirek would hardly go back to the hotel if he'd just shot someone.'

'I think that's exactly what he would do. As if nothing had happened. Besides, it might be imperative for him to stay there for whatever

19

reason. He obviously has contacts to meet. How many of your people actually met Bykov?'

'Very few. Very few indeed. Once he was recruited contact was largely done through drops or a complicated system of messengers.'

'Who recruited him?'

'That's classified.'

'Balls. Our man has been murdered. We need someone who really knew Bykov to have a look at this man while he is here.'

Marshall hesitated, then gave the impression that he was doing North a huge favour as he said, 'Rimmer.'

'Peter Rimmer? Well, could he take a look at this guy? It might solve all the problems.'

'Peter died a few months ago.'

'I had no idea. Of natural causes?'

'Of course of natural causes. He was killed in a car crash in Holland. Never came out of a coma and died three weeks later.'

'And you call that natural causes?'

'There was no one else involved. He ran into the pylon of a bridge. He'd been having trouble at home and was depressed. That's what the inquiry threw up. He'd also been drinking but we managed to keep that quiet; he was dead, poor blighter.'

'So he was married?'

'No. But he left a girlfriend and two kids.'

'Must be tough on them?'

'We looked after them as best we could. It was his problem not ours. How does it concern this matter, anyway?'

'So, is there anyone else who can actually point the finger?'

Marshall sat back and considered the question. He took off his bifocals, showing hard eyes. 'A difficult one, that. I never met Bykov. There'll be file photos of him, of course. You probably have your own for whatever reason.' He suddenly sat forward, 'Look, I'll have to speak with the father figure and even that won't be conclusive because we've had two heads since Bykov was executed. There is, of course, your bloke Ryan who did a spell with us. But I believe he hardly saw him.'

'How long does a trained man need for recognition? As we all know people forget faces very quickly indeed. Police line-ups are too often a lottery. But Ryan is an old pro and he thought he saw a ghost and that was from an original stance of high scepticism. So those who actually knew him this end really are thin on the ground. What about his wife?'

'What about her?'

'If she's within reach I'd like to have a word with her.'

'The last I heard was that she had remarried and was living in Paris. And that's our patch, North. Lay off. Bykov was our man and the enquiry will be under our auspices.'

North bit back a sharp retort. Calmly he said, 'And you'll take over the murder enquiry of our man Jones, will you? I'll notify the police and the Home Secretary that it's now all in your hands.'

'There's no need for that.' Marshall put his bifocals back on and peered over them again in an effort to appear more benevolent. 'Of course the police must continue with their enquiries.'

'And so too will we. Paris may be your patch but make no mistake that this is ours.' In a quiet tone he added, 'Do you think we can be less departmental for a while and really try to find out what the bloody hell is going on here? Bykov was your man. If we turn anything up you will, of course, be advised. I hope you will do the same for us.'

'Okay.' Marshall gave it some more thought before adding, 'We're probably both be wasting our time. Bykov can't be alive.'

'I wonder if Jones thought that before he took a bullet in his back.'

★ ★ ★

Back at his own office North rang a friend in the French Sûreté Special Branch. After that he rang Willie 'Glasshouse' Jackson at his theatrical costume warehouse in an undeveloped patch of London's dockland and asked if they could meet on any soil that 'Jacko' chose. He had to be far more careful with Jacko than he had with his friend in the Sûreté for Jacko would be suspicious from the start. Jacko would meet him at the Hot Pot in Soho if North paid. North would have paid anyway but it was Jacko's little way of being in control of a situation he knew he far from controlled. In any event Jacko was not short of money.

The Hot Pot was a meeting place for many of London's top villains, and had been refurbished a couple of years before to include air-conditioning. The food was excellent, the chef himself an old lag, and the wine cellar second to none. Jacko was already seated when North entered and the whole place went suddenly quiet as the stranger crossed to Jacko's table at which point conversation picked up again.

'Nothing's changed,' said North as they shook hands. 'I would have thought they would have remembered me. You're looking well.'

Jacko grinned. 'Some of them will remember you. That's why they stopped talking.'

'Whoops! How's business?'

'Don't you know? You're the one who keeps tabs on me.'

The banter went on for a while. It was as if both men were on a refresher course as they had not been in contact for a while. North opened his menu, gazing across the table at the man for whom he had a tremendous respect. Jacko had been an SAS sergeant before being slung out after a spell in a military prison following a period when he had gone berserk as a result of the death of his brother in an air crash some years before. His brother had been carrying drugs from Holland but the plane was never found — it was too far down in the North Sea. Jacko had always blamed himself for not keeping a better eye on his younger brother. Above medium height, Jacko was solid right through. And a marvellous shot. His features were lean, uncompromising; his eyes were sharp. When he smiled it was like looking at a different person.

'You've got nothing left to bribe me with,' said Jacko with a laugh. 'So what do you hope to get me for this time?' Before North could answer he added, 'You kept your word and expunged my record so I owe you an ear if nothing else. But that's the only reason I'm here.'

'That hurts me to the quick, Jacko. I thought it was my company you liked.' When Jacko did not rise to the bait North said, 'You've lost some hair, you're a little thin on top.'

'It's worrying about conniving blokes like you. So what is it this time?' Jacko always put business first; the lunch could wait.

North gazed round the room; he'd never seen so many recognisable faces of villainy in one place. Most had been wanted at some time, and some still were. 'I can't tell you here. There are too many people trying to listen in. I just wanted to establish your availability.'

'I'm not available.'

North appeared surprised. 'I heard that business wasn't so good.'

'That's right. I suppose one of the theatre producers told you. But it's good enough. I'm far from going broke and it will pick up anyway. I can always do a bit of stunt work if I need to.'

'I know you keep yourself fit. What about the gorgeous Georgette? Everything okay there?'

'You really do spread it around, don't you? Georgie's okay.'

'And her law business?'

'It's not her business, it's a partnership. She's doing all right.'

24

'And are things all right between the two of you?'

Jacko gave North an icy stare. 'Is this your way of gaining my confidence?'

'I heard that things were strained between you. That she's struggling a little. Where is she now?'

'In Cyprus. She's building up the international side of things. You're on very dangerous ground. I think you'd better back off then we can have our lunch and I can bugger off and forget we ever met.'

'I'm sorry.' North put feeling into the apology. 'My intention is to help, not annoy you. Supposing I could put some business her way without her knowledge so that you could get the credit.'

'Who are you kidding? The Security Service have their own lawyers, all good sworn-in members.'

'This business would be overseas. I can supply some contacts who would be under a little pressure from me. Nothing sinister. The rest would be up to her. Wouldn't that help to get matters back on an even keel?'

'So you're trying to get at me through her. That's typical.'

'I have to use what I've got, Jacko. I know you won't help me for the love of it. I know you don't need the money even if it is in shorter supply. And I know you'd like to help Georgie whether you are still with her or not. You shouldn't blame me.'

'Why don't you use George?'

'Bulman is on one of his rare holidays. But this calls for more specialised skills. Look, may I suggest we have lunch and then you come back with me and we'll discuss it in my office.' It was the craftiest ploy of all but North remained bland.

'You mean you are going to let me inside the portals of the Security Service? Sign me in? Have an ID tag on my lapel? Well, well, you are desperate.'

'But can you resist it?' smiled North.

'Let's order,' Jacko smiled back. He understood the line North had cast, and North was right, he could not resist it.

'And there's someone I want you to meet. She might persuade you to work for me.'

Jacko looked up from the menu, intrigued. She? He said nothing more but was well aware that North would only use him when it was impossible for him openly to use his own personnel. So who was the woman working for?

★ ★ ★

Jacko was not impressed with the apparent lack of security when he entered the portals of the Security Service but guessed it was there just the same. The only open evidence were the TV scanners but entering with someone of North's stature was no different from any business block. They took the lift to the third floor and walked the short distance to North's office.

North pointed to the chair Ryan had used, as being the most comfortable. Jacko took everything in, the scrambler phone if they still used the same colours, the fax, the computer, the clear desk and the cabinet with the bar sealing unit.

'Comfy,' Jacko remarked. 'Your everyday security office. You've left the door open.'

'It's stuffy in here. The heating system is playing up.' North winked. 'And we can see if anyone is trying to listen at the door. We've had to cut back on bugs.'

Jacko smiled. He actually liked North; he was straight as security men go, and most people who worked with him liked him. 'So we've had the bullshit, what's next?'

'An odd tale. Now listen.' North related the strange story of the apparent resurrection of Vadim Bykov and the murder of Tommy Jones. He gave it straight, partly because of Jacko's aptitude for detecting omissions and partly because this was not the time to play silly games. A man was dead and he felt responsible. Without mentioning names he covered his contact with the SIS and their opinion of the strange affair. He had no need to elaborate to obtain Jacko's full attention.

Jacko had listened in silence and when North had finished queried what had been bugging him from halfway into North's narration. 'What has any of this got to do with me?'

'An obvious question.' North sat back and intertwined his fingers, peering over the arch they formed. 'There are some interdepartmental problems. Sometimes they are tedious and even childish but they exist nevertheless. Bykov isn't our man but this fellow who we know as Jan Mirek is on our patch and has killed one of our men. It's our problem. The SIS won't see it like that. If there is anyone around who remotely looks like

27

Bykov they will want control.

'If a less obdurate person was handling this at the SIS we would obviously work something out between us. Bykov was extraordinarily important to them; their most important source of information since poor old Penkovsky. I can understand their stance only too clearly and they have a strong case. At the end there may be nothing in it at all but meanwhile they don't want us to cock anything up.'

'So why not leave them to it? What's the big deal?'

'But for Tommy Jones we would not even be discussing it. He made the ID and I scoffed at him and then gave him a job he was not really qualified to do as a result of which he got murdered. I should not have sent him in the first place, he is simply not trained for that kind of work.'

'But he had this guy Ryan with him.'

'Ryan could have done it on his own and he would not have been so stupid as to follow Mirek or whoever the fellow is. I was trying to punish Jonesy for being so stupid. Bykov was shot dead. Jones was a bloody fool. But he wasn't, was he? I was.'

North unclasped his hands and Jacko could see that he was having difficulty in controlling his feelings. He supposed he would have felt the same. Yet he still had not received an answer. 'What can I do that you can't?'

'You can operate outside the organisation for me. All I want you to do is to go to Paris and locate Bykov's wife. She's the only one who can really identify him. If she can't, nobody can.' North went to the fax machine in the far corner. He brought back some sheets. 'I can now tell you where she lives.'

'You mean you want me to operate outside the organisation so that you can wash your hands of me if the SIS find out?'

North nodded. It was no time for deceit. 'That's about it. You only have to contact her and ask if she would fly over to see if she can identify this man. All expenses paid, of course. It has to be done quickly or Mirek might move on.'

Whatever Jacko had expected it wasn't this. 'One of your men has been murdered and you want me to pick up where he left off and you say, 'That's about it.' I don't think so. Anyway she would never come, she knows her husband's been executed.'

'I'm not going to argue the point. I'll leave that to someone who should know something about how a woman might react. Can you spare me another half hour?'

Jacko glanced at his watch. 'I must phone the office first.' He used his own phone, explained he would be late, switched off and closed the flap. 'I wonder what Cheltenham made of that,' he quipped. 'Okay, what happens next?'

'You go to the scene of the crime. You can't mistake the area, the police have it sealed off. At the top of the steps will be a young lady who will introduce herself as Paula Ashton. You take it from there. Let me know what you decide.'

'Paula Ashton. Does she know all about this?'

'There wouldn't be much point in meeting her if

she didn't. I spoke to her before contacting you.'

'Is she casual labour, too?'

'She's not a full-time, paid-up member but there's nothing casual about her. She operates much as you do but more frequently; she does need the money.'

'I see. I hope she knows I'm on my way.'

'She will do by the time you've left the building.'

Jacko rose and stared down at North. 'I'm not guaranteeing anything, Derek. You only bring me dirty problems. And I'm not forgetting you left us in the shit in Switzerland.'

'Then you had also better not forget that I supplied the contact that kept you safely under cover while the heat was on. George kept in touch; I knew what he was doing.'

North was already tapping out a number as Jacko made for a lift.

* * *

It was not instant recognition but as Jacko climbed the steps of the National Gallery and saw the slim figure of a woman standing under the canopy he had a vague recollection of having met her before. She was dressed in jeans, a belted raincoat, and flat heels. Her fair hair was blowing in a sharp, bitter wind, her eyes screwed against the cold. By the way she watched him approach he thought that she too must have experienced some recognition.

The police tape was roped right down the steps from top to bottom and as he neared the top he could see the patches of dried blood on each step. Detective were still scraping away for the forensic boys.

'Paula Ashton?' he said as he reached her.

'Jacko?'

He found that kind of familiar for a first meeting. Only friends called him Jacko. Close up he was less sure of having met her before. She seemed to be rather amused at seeing him and her grey-green eyes were slightly mocking, her lips itching to smile. They shook hands formally rather than warmly. 'Have we met before?' asked Jacko on the defensive.

'You don't remember? Some years ago? A pub in the Falls Road? I was a brunette then.' She was almost laughing at him as she put an arm through his as they went down the steps towards Nelson's Column. He suddenly stopped and turned to face her as bloody recollection came back. 'I thought you were dead,' he said at last.

'So did a lot of people. It seemed best to let them think that at the time.' She tugged at his arm. 'Come on, it's too cold to hang about, there's a decent pub up St Martin's Lane where we can talk.'

He remembered again. 'Yeah, you knew quite a lot about pubs, didn't you?' He wasn't sure how he felt about the presence of Paula Ashton, if that was her name. He suddenly felt uncertain and uneasy.

She squeezed his arm. 'This is what this is all about, isn't it? People coming back from the dead?'

31

Jacko was too unsettled to reply. He did not like the way things were going. It was as if he had suddenly lost control of his own destiny and he was frantically trying to remember more about the woman on his arm.

3

The warm air hit them as they entered the pub. Paula Ashton insisted on getting the drinks which he found strange as North would pick up the tab anyway. A scotch for him and a G & T for her. They gazed around; all tables were full but they managed to find a fairly secluded place at the far end of the long bar.

They stood quite close together, raised glasses then sipped at them. There were far too many people around for Jacko's comfort and he believed Paula Ashton thought the same but it was far too cold outside to stand around talking. They fell into a low key way of speaking which just carried sufficiently for each to hear; it was a practised way of speaking above noise without substantially adding to it. And they stood close together, almost like lovers. As he caught a faint whiff of her perfume another memory came back. She was very used to this kind of situation and was well versed in acting the lover.

'You know he wants us to go to Paris?' asked Jacko, gazing round the busy bar.

'Oh, yes. Assume that I know what you know, it will save time.'

But Jacko was still trying to recall what very little he knew about this woman. 'Falls Road?' he queried. 'Go on from there.'

'And break the Official Secrets Act? Jacko, how could you?'

'Cut the bullshit. You're one up on me. I need to know who I'm working with.'

Paula sipped her drink gazing round warily. She moved a little closer and almost whispered in his ear. 'I was with Fourteen Int.'

'Det? The Detachment?' He should have realised as 14 Int was a special unit known as Det, which itself was an abbreviation of Detachment, and which was run by B Squadron of 22 SAS. This rather attractive young lady now sipping her gin and tonic was fully entitled to wear the grey beret of the SAS. They had done, and were probably still doing, a marvellous job, often acting as lovers in bars and clubs, but they could handle the weapons too and gunfire was far from unknown to them. They were very highly rated by the men they served with.

He smiled at her, feeling the respect she deserved. 'That explains a lot.'

'It might if you actually believe me. We must have trust.'

'What you've said is checkable. And I will check which you would expect.' He was more relaxed now. 'I check anything from North as I'm sure you do. I like the bloke, but it's duty first with him and we're dispensable.'

'So why do we do it?'

'We can't help ourselves. It's in the genes and he trades on it.' He eased to the bar to call for more drinks. 'He and I go through a pantomime every time he needs my help during which he finds some way of blackmailing or bribing me into doing a job for him when we both know that eventually I'm going to do it anyway because it beats hiring theatrical clothes to the film and stage people.'

'You think we're so predictable?'

'He does. And he's right, isn't he? Oh, he throws the odd acceptable bone and has done me an important favour but he's single minded in getting what he wants.'

'Aren't we?'

Jacko gave it some thought. 'No. Not in the way he is. We wouldn't throw anyone to the wolves to get what we want. Now what about this Paris trip? I don't think this bloke's wife will come over. It's too tall an order. She won't want to be reminded.'

Paula took the fresh drink from Jacko. 'She would want to be certain. I know I would.'

'She must believe he's dead. It would have taken her a long time to get over it. If he's alive and wanted her to know he would have contacted her. If we go over there she'll be reminded of the whole sad business. It's not playing the game.'

'But if there is a possibility of him still being alive, no matter how remote, don't you think she'd want to be sure? It would be on her mind forever if she didn't check.'

'What about checking fingerprints? I wonder if North has tried that? There must be plenty in his room. It would be easy to do.'

'Did you mention this to North?'

'It's all happened so fast I've only just caught up with it. I know he faxed certain people. That's how he got the wife's Paris address.'

'It's not something he'll have overlooked. Or any other forensic possibility. Jacko, if we're going to

35

go we'd better do it quickly before this man moves on.'

Jacko drained his drink. 'Okay. I've got to pick up my passport. I suppose you have yours.'

As they left the pub and took the full blast of an east wind Jacko said, 'Why the two of us? You could easily have done this on your own.'

Paula took his arm again. 'I don't think you're that dim, Jacko. With one man already dead.'

'In that case, Paula, are you my bodyguard or am I yours?'

★ ★ ★

Derek North read the fax he had received from Moscow. No files for Vadim Bykov could be found. This was an incredible piece of mismanagement for the KGB. Given that there had been interdepartmental chaos after the collapse of Communism in the Soviet Union a case could be made that there had followed administrative mishaps but North would not swallow it. If files were missing then their absence was deliberate. He faxed a separate source and hoped to fare better. He checked with Ian Marshall at the SIS who confirmed that there were no fingerprints of Vadim Bykov on file. That was more understandable; there would be no reason to have them; direct contact with Bykov had always been avoided. North had also checked with the Polish Police the details of Mirek's passport which Sam Ryan had obtained from Mirek's room. The answer to that was that it was bona fide.

Meanwhile, Scotland Yard's Murder Squad was

investigating the shooting of Tommy Jones in the same way as they would any other murder. From North's point of view it would look very suspicious to the man called Mirek if routine enquiries did not proceed. It was a delicately balanced situation.

With the help of the hotel management Detective Superintendent Matthew Simes made a call on Jan Mirek the evening after the murder and the interview took place in Mirek's room. Simes had Detective Sergeant Andrews with him. There were two chairs in the room so Andrews stood while the other two faced each other across the foot of the bed.

'It's good of you to take time out to receive us,' said Simes with well practiced conviction. 'We shall be speaking to all the guests but are particularly interested in those who were in the dining room at breakfast time yesterday. I believe you were one of those, sir?'

The face below the dark, bushy hair was lined and sunken at the cheeks, the flesh slightly loose as sometimes happens with someone who has been on a diet. Mirek's gaze was sharp. 'I believe you are enquiring about a missing person?' The accent was barely noticeable, too slight to pinpoint.

The burley Simes apologised at once. 'I'm sorry, sir. I thought the manager might have mentioned it to you. It's about this man.' Simes produced a photograph of Tommy Jones and passed it across. 'Do you recognise him?'

Mirek took the print, barely glanced at it before handing it back. 'He was in the dining room yesterday morning. He's missing?'

37

'Murdered, sir. We wondered if you know anything about him? Had you ever seen him before, for instance?'

'Murdered?' Mirek slowly shook his head. 'Here? In the hotel? That surely can't be?'

'No, not in the hotel. You were quick to recognise him.'

'Yes, of course. I recognised him at once. But I know nothing about him. I have never met him. He was simply having breakfast with another man, big, rather like yourself. He must have left at some point. I did not see him leave but when I left the big man was on his own and we exchanged greetings.'

'You were alone?'

'No. I had a business aquaintance with me. We left the hotel together then went our separate ways.'

'Where did you go, sir?'

Mirek was sitting quite comfortably in his chair but now his hands tightened on the arms and he half rose then sank back again. His bright eyes were suddenly piercing. In a very controlled voice he said, 'I find that question offensive. To use your own vernacular, Superintendent, it is none of your bloody business.'

Simes was not put out; he had encountered every gesture in the book. 'This is a murder enquiry, sir, and it is very much my business. If it's any consolation I shall be putting the same question to every guest. It's a fair question though I fully recognise that from where you are sitting, it is not.'

38

Mirek appeared uncomfortable. 'I'd rather not say.'

'That's your prerogative, sir. Would you like to call a solicitor?'

'What would I need a lawyer for? I've done nothing wrong.'

Simes said nothing, letting it hang in the air and guessing that Mirek would follow up.

'I went to a strip club.' He looked up in a self-derisory kind of way. 'I was a naughty boy.'

'Which club was that?'

'The Blue Palm.'

'That's a pricey place,' said Andrews, tired of saying nothing.

'Any witnesses, sir?' Simes took over again.'

Mirek shrugged. 'Anyone who saw me in there. I had to pay to get in, and I bought drinks at outrageous prices. Someone should remember me. You can check.'

'We'll do that, sir. Have you a snapshot of yourself that we might borrow? If not, Detective Sergeant Andrews is a dab hand with a camera. And were you alone at this club?'

While Mirek was thinking where he might have a spare passport photo Andrews produced a miniature camera and took a shot of Mirek while he was looking at Simes. Mirek was startled by the flash and said tetchily, 'I thought you were supposed to get permission to do that.'

'I thought we had, sir,' Simes replied smoothly. 'It's only a snapshot. When we've finished with it we'll give it to you. And after the club, sir, where did you go then?'

'You want me to give you an hour by hour account of my whole day? When did this murder take place?'

'The pathologist isn't absolutely sure, sir, but probably before one; that's a qualified guess.'

'And how did he die?'

'I thought you might know that, sir.'

The gaze was hard again but this time there was a warning. 'Don't play with me, Mr Simes. Why should I know?'

Simes appeared surprised. 'It was in the evening and morning papers and on TV and radio. You must have heard or seen something about it.'

Mirek shook his head. 'No. If I heard or saw something it went straight through my head. I did not connect it with the man I saw at breakfast. Is that all?'

'What about your visitor?'

'What about the man who was having breakfast with the murdered man? Shouldn't you be looking for him?'

'He's already helping us with our enquiries, sir.'

Mirek considered the request. 'I don't like bringing someone else into an enquiry like this. He is one of your own civil servants.'

'Can we have a name?'

'I can lose his goodwill if I give it to you. He has nothing to do with this matter. We were talking business.'

'With a civil servant?'

'Have you not heard of your own Department of Trade and Industry? Please don't involve him.'

'We probably won't but at least he can add

strength to your recognition of the murdered man. Every little helps. A good upright civil servant will be only too pleased to help. Just his name. We may not follow it up.'

Mirek rose and wandered over to the window. 'I don't like this. It's bad for business and trust.'

'What is your business, sir?'

'It's of a technical nature. Computerised machines. Anything to do with microchips. It's specialised.' He turned to face Simes who was still sitting. 'Your DTI has been most helpful but it's a two-way trade. I feel I must make a stand against this. This man has done no wrong. And neither have I. I've cooperated fully. It is no fault of mine that I happened to be having breakfast in a room with a man who was later killed. You are more than verging on harassment.'

Simes inclined his head. 'I'm sorry you see it like that, sir. I can't force you to give me his name but we can set up enquiries in a different direction which will produce his name but will take longer.' He paused then added quietly, 'If we have to check through the whole staff of the DTI we'll come up with a name. But if we do it that way won't it be more damaging to your association with him than if you simply tell us?'

'You want him to confirm that the man in the snapshot is the one we both saw?'

'That's about it. We don't really believe that a presumably high-ranking civil servant shot someone in the back on the steps of the National Gallery. He'll understand.'

'Shot in the back?'

'You really haven't been following the news, have you, sir?'

'His name is Jeremy Clarke.'

Simes showed no sign. 'And he did not go to the Blue Palm with you?'

'I told you. We split up outside the hotel.'

'Perhaps he recommended it to you?'

'Perhaps he supplied me with high-class call girls as well. That would depend on whether he wanted something from me or vice versa. I already knew of the Blue Palm as I'm sure many foreign visitors do. It is a well-run club.'

Simes glanced at his sergeant. 'Well, I guess that's about all for now.' Simes rose. 'You have been most helpful, sir, and I do understand your reluctance to involve someone else. How long will you be staying in London?'

Mirek turned away from the window. He shrugged. 'That will depend on how well the business goes. A week or two. I might take an extra week just to look around.'

'May I compliment you on your English, sir. There can't be many Polish gentlemen who speak it so well. Did you learn it here?'

Mirek smiled, more relaxed now. 'No. In Poland and Denmark. I have been here before but for no great time. English and Japanese are the two great commercial languages, wouldn't you say?' He held out a hand. 'I hope you didn't find me too awkward.'

Simes smiled warmly. 'A pleasure to meet you, sir. I hope your business goes well, and I am sorry you were caught up in this enquiry.'

On the way down in the lift Andrews said, 'You were spreading the oil a bit there, sir.'

Simes chuckled. 'When you are dealing with such an accomplished liar as Mirek what else can you do.'

'You don't think he went to the Blue Palm?'

'Oh, yes. If he said he did then that's it. He'd expect us to check. But it would be an in and out job, just laying a trail.'

They reached the ground floor and crossed the vestibule. As they walked towards the waiting police car, Andrews said, 'Do you think he did it?'

Simes climbed in and sat down. 'I haven't the slightest idea, but I think we should find out more about him.'

★ ★ ★

Detective Superintendent Matthew Simes had been advised of the Security Service interest in Jan Mirek and reported to North who agreed to come over to New Scotland Yard. The two men had briefly met before and whatever feelings Simes had for the intrusion of MI5 he did not show it and his handshake was warm.

'So what do you think?' asked North as he sat down in Simes's office.

'I think he's a dab hand at answering questions. Maybe he's had practice?'

North smiled grimly. 'If he is the man Tommy Jones thought he is, then he's had immense experience of answering questions from the KGB when they were at their worst. Top that, old boy.

The problem is the man has been officially dead for a few years.'

'Awkward,' said Simes, apparently not impressed. 'Did the fellow you think this chap could be live in England for any length of time?'

'Not as far as I know. What's your gut feeling?'

Simes gazed phlegmatically at his desk. Then he shrugged his heavy shoulders. 'My gut feeling is that he expected us to call, was well prepared but on occasion liked to give the impression that he was not. I'm checking on his background with the Polish police.'

North did not say that he had already done that with Polish Intelligence. 'You think he might be involved?'

'I've no idea. He offered a red herring which made me wonder why. Of course he may have other things to cover, totally divorced from the murder. He's doing business with, or taking advice from, one of the DTI people, a bloke called Jeremy Clarke. Have you heard of him?'

'Oh yes. A toiler, really does try. I can't see him involved in murder, particularly one of ours.'

Simes spread his hands across the desk. 'That's about as much as I can tell you at the moment. Are our enquiries running tandem with yours?'

'Our motives are different. You want a murderer and so do we but we are interested in Mirek for other reasons so we branch off. If we keep each other informed of progress or even lack of it, the wires should not get crossed. Shared information.'

Simes could not recall ever having received shared information from the Security Service. 'You know,' he observed after a little thought, 'if this joker is the man you say he can't possibly be, you've got to hand it to him for nerve. To hang around can't be easy.'

'To do a runner would have declared his guilt. On the assumption that he's risen from the dead, he was between the devil and the deep blue sea. His motives for staying must be very strong, and for killing in the way it was done, even stronger. We've taken steps to try to make a more positive identification. Once we're sure one way or the other, life might be easier.'

Simes passed over the snap his sergeant had taken in the hotel room. 'Is that of any use to you? I'll get extra copies run off if it is. It was taken today.'

North studied it and then pushed it back across the desk. 'Thanks, but we have file copies.'

'Won't they be out of date?'

North did not want to admit to having a team on Mirek and that they had already taken his photograph leaving and arriving at the hotel, shots which had been taken from a special observation delivery van with holes drilled through the sides. It was too late to admit it now so he said, 'Judging from that snap he hasn't changed much in a few years. But we must remember that our file copy is of the real man; your snap is of Mirek. We have yet to connect or dissociate the two.'

North studied Simes's impassive reaction and suddenly smiled. 'Oh, ye of little faith. I really will keep you informed.'

Simes grinned and said nothing, thereby conveying a lot.

Jacko and Paula Ashton took an early morning flight the day after meeting. They sat side by side on the aircraft and Paula said, 'I would still have preferred the Tunnel.'

Jacko shook his head once again; she had tried to persuade him to go under the English Channel. 'I was in South Armagh buried in a field near this farmhouse. A dog found me and I knew I was in deep trouble from then on. I could hear voices from the farmhouse and the dog started to bark and the voices came nearer. The only thing I could do was to keep still; there were too many to try to gun down and lying prone with earth wrapped all round me was not the best position to try it. Instead of rooting me out they brought up a digger and piled earth on top. I was being buried alive and the weight was too much to shift.'

Jacko leaned back and gazed at an air vent, his eyes glazed. 'It was not a nice way to die.'

Paula turned to watch him relive it in his mind. She grasped his hand. 'And in a single bound — ' she said.

Jacko shook the memory off with difficulty and realised that he had never talked of it since that day. 'It wasn't funny, Paula. I had a back-up watching me through glasses and he called up a chopper with a detachment on board. There was a lot of gunfire, deep thuds under the earth like shock waves, before they started to dig me out.' He turned and tried to smile but there were beads of sweat below his hairline. 'I prefer it up here. I enjoyed the para jumps.'

'So it's a psychological hang-up. You have to get back in the saddle.'

'Be buried again, you mean?'

Paula took one look at him and decided to drop the matter. He had probably had nightmares about it and perhaps still did. 'I'm sorry, Jacko. I didn't mean to be flippant.'

When they landed at Charles de Gaulle they summoned a cab outside the airport and Paula gave the address, having a few words with the driver. They sat in the back of the cab and Jacko said, 'So that's why North chose you? You speak fluent French.'

'One reason among many.'

'I said you could do it on your own. You'll be doing all the talking when we get there. And good luck. I don't fancy any of it.'

It had been some time since Jacko had been in France but he was not getting the kick out of it he might have expected. The whole idea of the reason for the visit was preposterous. He was glad then for Paula's presence.

The address was on the north fringe of Paris, about three miles out and still fairly rural. It was a chateau which had been divided into luxury apartments of generous proportions and set in beautiful grounds with a snaking tree-lined drive to the impressive double doors of the entrance.

They climbed out, Paula paid off the cabbie and the two crunched across the thick layers of gravel to the open doors of the huge porch. Inside were similar glass doors which were closed against the weather. They could see a desk and a concierge behind it. They went in, very silent and uncertain. Again Jacko thought the mission was crazy and wondered at their reception.

Jacko let Paula take over. At the desk she asked for Irina Janesky; an appointment had been made through the French Sûreté. They were directed to the west wing of the chateau reached by a long, thick-carpeted corridor at the end of which was a walnut door which might well have been an original. The bell was modern. Paula rang making Jacko feel inadequate. A maid answered, Paula gave her name and said they had an appointment with Madame Janesky. She apologised for being late. They were shown into a huge drawing room which was straight out of mid-nineteenth century France. Expensive rugs, satin-covered period furniture, gilded side tables; Irina Janesky was not short of cash.

A log fire burned in a massive open fireplace with ornate marble surrounds and they were shown chairs either side of the fire. It was quiet in the room, the window drapes hanging in broody folds of rich brocade. The view of the grounds through the huge windows was at once relaxing, even in its winter setting.

Jacko sat on the edge of his chair and felt intimidated. He was quite wealthy himself but there was something museumish about this place that not only spoke of wealth and taste but in his mind he could see the 'don't touch' signs, and indeed there was one roped-off area. It was magnificent but without a lived-in atmosphere to it.

Neither knew what to expect but when a door

opened and a tall, elegant woman entered the room they both believed correctly that it was Irina Janesky. She had high Slavish cheekbones and her features were almost gaunt, but her eyes were bright and alert and she held herself well. She fitted into the room exceedingly well in spite of her fashionable designer clothes.

Jacko and Paula rose as Irina Janesky approached.

'Please sit down.' A long-fingered hand gestured towards the chairs and Madame Janesky sat between them. 'Jacque Verrat of the Sûreté told me you would be coming. I agreed to meet you very much against my will. I believe it's something to do with my late husband.' She spoke good English but the accent was not French.

Imperious was a description that sprung to Jacko's mind. And totally in control. She had thrown out a challenge as icy as her expression; she did not want them here and her attitude made it clear that they did not belong. She looked to Jacko for leadership but it was Paula who spoke.

'We think there's a possibility that your husband may still be alive.'

Madame Irina Janesky did not flinch or show emotion of any kind. Yet the atmosphere was suddenly as glacial as her gaze. She sat quite still and so did the others as if she had control of them. And at that moment she did; a formidable figure with an aura of disturbing strength. They waited for her to speak.

4

The silence was painful. Jacko and Paula were waiting for some verbal reaction but none followed. Irina Janesky sat upright on her chair, hands clasped, gazing on the log fire. Jacko was watching the hands for some sort of movement, restlessness, anything, but there was nothing. He wondered if she had gone into shock.

Paula, too, was waiting for a tangible reaction and wondered if she had handled it badly; there was no easy way to tell a woman that her husband might still be alive. The silence in the room was increasingly uneasy, more than that, there was a kind of menace about it. The fire suddenly crackled and sparks flew out and seemed to have more effect on Irina Janesky than Paula's words.

Without a quiver in her voice Irina said contemptuously, 'How ridiculous. My husband is dead.' And that seemed to be the end of it.

Paula said, 'You are probably right. But a man remarkably like him has been seen in London.'

Irina Janesky broke from her icy pose and turned to gaze at Paula. 'You mean to say that you've flown from London to tell me that there is someone who looks like my late husband. You think that is something I would want to know?'

'No, Madame Janesky. There are some in London who knew your husband and have seen this man and believe that he is Vadim Bykov. Apparently files in

Moscow have been mislaid or destroyed following the break-up of the Soviet Union so there is no technical way, so far, to establish whether or not it is he.'

'I don't need technicality. I know precisely what happened.' Suddenly Irina showed more emotion and her expression turned to scorn as she said with great emphasis to Paula, 'Whoever you have seen it is not my husband. That is quite impossible. And I deeply resent being disturbed in this way. The whole idea is preposterous.' She lifted her head high and gazed at a point above the massive mantelpiece. 'Would you like me to give you the location of my late husband's grave? I am supposed not to know as he was buried with dishonour but I still have a little influence.'

'It would be more satisfying if you could take a look at this man.'

Jacko was pleased with the way Paula was handling a very difficult situation.

'Take a look at him? What on earth for?'

'To satisfy yourself. To remove any doubts.'

Irina gazed scornfully at Paula. 'Why have they sent someone so young? What could you possibly know about the death of my first husband?'

'I'm just the messenger with my colleague here. Neither of us have seen or know anything about this man. But you would. At a glance. And that would be an end of the matter. Naturally all expenses would be paid.'

The snort was derisory and a bitter smile touched her firm lips. 'Are you suggesting that I go to London?'

'He's there at the moment but we don't know for how long.'

The ramifications were coming through as Irina absorbed what she was being told. 'You are, of course, British Intelligence. Your police would send policemen. Why should I try to satisfy an organisation who were directly responsible for my husband's execution? You must be mad.'

'It would satisfy you. One way or the other.'

'Don't be absurd. I am already satisfied. Really, this is all too ridiculous. You've had a wasted journey and I find I cannot feel sorry about that. Please go and do not come here again.'

Jacko rose slowly but Paula remained seated for a little longer before rising. Paula gazed down at the impassive figure of the woman who was probably in her middle to late forties.

'I'm sorry we have disturbed you. We just felt it needed clarification, particularly as you remarried.'

Irina rose and stood with the poise of a model. Throughout she had shown no real emotion except perhaps a touch of anger or exasperation. There had been no sign of shock. 'The difference between us,' she said, 'is that I *know* my husband is dead and where he is buried. The problem is yours, not mine. You had no right to come here.'

'We had to come,' said Paula. 'I understand what you say makes perfect sense, but the fact remains that a man who met your husband in Moscow says he recognised him two days ago in London. He is a man of considerable experience. We realise he can be wrong and everything points to him having to be. Yet the doubt remains and we thought you could clear up the issue once and for all.'

'I've done that. I have no doubts.'

'You will have the moment we leave here.' It was a bold move but Paula was holding her ground well.

'That comment shows how little you know about the whole affair. There can be no doubts about a certainty. I'm sorry you've wasted your journey. Don't waste another.'

Paula glanced at Jacko and he accepted that she had failed. He gave her a smile; she had tried hard but was up against a very self-assured woman who perhaps did not give a damn whether or not her first husband was alive or dead. Perhaps Irina Janesky wanted no complications with her present marriage. And yet as he turned his attention to Irina he believed he saw the first sign of uncertainty. Had a seed of doubt been planted and she did not want to be haunted by the possibility of Bykov's survival, no matter how impossible it seemed?

'Stranger things have happened,' said Jacko almost flippantly.

'I know of only one resurrection. I don't think Vadim was that holy.' The reply was not quite as icy as the others.

They crossed the room to the door and the maid appeared as if on a hidden signal but Irina dismissed her.

'May we use your phone to call a taxi?' asked Paula as they entered the spacious hall.

'I'll get my chauffeur to run you to the airport.'

'That's very kind of you. I hope we have not upset you too much. We simply had to approach you in the light of the evidence in London.' Paula was genuinely concerned. 'It was not easy for us either.'

Irina stopped in mid-stride. She stood quite still for a while and then asked, 'Have you a photograph of this man?'

'No. Not yet.' Jacko filled the breach as Paula hesitated. 'I believe efforts are being made to get some. But it has to be a good snap to get a good likeness. Visual contact can pick out small mannerisms, stance and so on that a photograph cannot.'

'What exactly was it you wanted me to do?'

'Simply fly with us back to London. The man who calls himself Mirek has most of his meals at his hotel, certainly breakfast each morning according to the management. Take a look at him and confirm whether or not he is your first husband. If you don't want a confrontation that can be arranged; you see him but he will not see you. Accommodation will be arranged for the night at a top hotel.'

'And when would this happen?'

'Now if you like. We could catch a flight back, hope that he's at breakfast tomorrow morning and you can fly straight back or as you wish.'

There was a long silence as they stood in the hall, the front door just feet away and Jacko was thinking that Paula had swung it after all, but was holding his breath.

'I could not possibly go now. I would have to explain to my husband and he might not like the idea at all.'

'We could catch a late plane. If we leave it until

tomorrow you would probably miss the breakfast session and perhaps have to stay an extra night.' Paula hastened to add, 'That's no problem for us but it might be for you.'

'We could fly over later tonight in my husband's plane. He would have to have time to arrange with air control.'

Jacko held in his feelings. So she was coming after all. There was still no emotion about her, no warmth.

Paula asked, 'Will your husband come?'

'No. I doubt that he would fancy the idea. But he will have to make the arrangements.'

'Thank you, Madame Janesky. It should clear the matter up once and for all.'

'You had better stay here while we sort things out. You can rest in one of the guest rooms.'

Jacko was uneasy about that. The whole business was strange and it was getting no clearer from his point of view. He did not like the idea of staying here but would have been hard pushed to give a reason except a warning born of experience. But to arrange anything else would be complicated; they needed to be in touch. And they needed to contact London.

The maid took them to a guest room on the first floor, a splendid room with a small sitting room attached and where they ate the light luncheon which was provided.

A wary Jacko sat in a comfortable armchair and when Paula sank down opposite him he said, 'What made her change her mind?'

'Doubt can eat away at you. Once we had gone

she would start thinking and wondering. And if it turned out that Mirek is Bykov then she is at present bigamously married. Neither she or her husband would think much of that.'

They sat pondering before Jacko said, 'You did extremely well. She was far from helpful.'

'Thanks, Jacko. I'd better ring London.'

Jacko nodded his agreement but wondered who might be listening on an extension.

★ ★ ★

In London North had being trying to push Ian Marshall into providing more names of people who had actually met Bykov at some time. The lack of actual physical contact was far from unusual — the less contact the better. Nor was it so unusual to receive secret information from people who were just contact names. Those at high risk preferred no contact at all with their clandestine masters. Nevertheless there had been personnel in the SIS who had met Bykov at some time, no matter how briefly. Marshall had provided the name of the dead Peter Rimmer but had now come up with the name of Oliver Brittan who had retired two years ago. The only serving official was Sam Ryan who had switched from MI6 to MI5 and as North well knew had not actually met Bykov but had very briefly seen him some years before.

Armed with some shots his own people had taken of Mirek North drove down to a little village near Horsham in Sussex. Although it was still bitterly cold the snow had held off and the roads down were clear. Once he had left London and the roads were less busy he was more relaxed and wondered whether he had got caught up in a frantic wild goose chase. What did it matter whether or not Bykov was alive or dead? Who cared?

North had already decided that he cared very much indeed from the moment poor old Jonesy had been murdered. There had to be a powerful reason for that which surely exceeded recognition. It was almost lunchtime by the time he reached the village pub and obtained final directions from there.

The cottage was a nineteenth-century, roses-round-the door, kind of dwelling; pretty, peaceful, and fairly isolated on the fringe of the village he pulled up outside, opened the white paling gate and went down the uneven path to the front door protected by a low porch. He hammered on the old-fashioned knocker.

A grey-haired lady with kind blue eyes answered the door; North introduced himself and asked if he could have a few words with Oliver Brittan.

The blue eyes clouded but still managed to take in North as he stood stooped under the porch. 'Are you from the Firm?'

'No, the other lot. You must be Mrs Brittan?'

'You'd better come in. You'll need a drink of some kind if you've driven down from London. May I take your coat?'

North sat in a chintzy armchair by the inglenook fire and was wondering where Oliver Brittan might be. When Mrs Brittan returned with a tray of tea she told him. She put down the tray and said,

'Oliver died almost a year ago. I thought you people would know.'

North silently cursed Ian Marshall for not doing his homework properly. He took the proffered cup. 'I'm so sorry. I had no idea.' He judged her to be in her late fifties and was loathe to ask the manner of the death.

'So you've had a wasted journey, Mr North. I'm sorry too.'

'Not wasted. Pleasant company and a super cup of tea cannot be described as wasted.'

'Was it something about his work? Perhaps I can help?'

'It's about someone he once knew. In Russia.'

'Then I can't help. A pity. Life is very lonely without him.'

'It must be difficult for you. Have you children?'

'A married son in Australia and a daughter in Canada. The whole family seemed to have this urge to travel. I certainly expected Oliver to last longer than he did but it's impossible to legislate against accidents.'

North, sipping his tea, glanced at her over the top of his cup. Cautiously he asked, 'What kind of an accident?'

'Oh, the usual kind, Mr North; a car accident. He simply ran off a motorway, crashed through the central barrier and was hit head-on by a passing truck.'

North thought he had better not raise questions, then realised that she needed to talk about it. He was about to probe when she said, 'He was never a heavy drinker and was a bloody good driver.'

58

'Maybe he dozed at the wheel. It happens with the most experienced of drivers.'

'Perhaps. Many reasons were put forward by the police, none of which I can accept. They even suggested the brakes were faulty. It had just passed its MOT.'

'What did they say was wrong with the brakes.'

'Oh, they trotted out a lot of technical jargon which went straight over my head. Oliver loved cars and always looked after ours.' She put her cup down and looked across at North, hands twined together. 'We'll never know will we? Accidental death was the coroner's verdict.'

'You don't think it was?'

'How can I know? He had retired so it could not have been work connected. I have to accept what they say.'

'But you don't agree with it?'

'We'd been married for thirty-eight years. Oh, I knew what his work entailed but never the detail. I am not a fool and he did not take me for one. He was as honest with me as the Official Secrets Act allowed him to be.' She spread her hands in acceptance. 'I just have to live with it. But being alone offers more time for thought.' She suddenly brightened. 'I'm prattling. It is not your problem.'

North was thinking it might be but there was nothing he could say to her that would not sound trite or dishonest. 'Have you got everything you need?'

'Oh, I'm not poor. Oliver was never very clever with money but I'm all right.'

North chose his moment to rise and said, 'I'm sorry I intruded, Mrs Brittan.' He pulled out a snap of Mirek and held it up before her. 'I don't suppose you've ever set eyes on this man?'

He expected an immediate denial but she gazed at the snap for some time before taking it from him, putting on her glasses and studying it again. 'Yes, I've seen him before but I can't remember when.'

'Here or abroad?'

'Oh, Oliver did most of the travelling. I'm sure it would be here.'

North continued to let her hold the snap and then she handed it back and took off her glasses.

North said carefully, 'Forgive me for stressing this but are you absolutely sure, Mrs Brittan?'

'Oh, yes. I've a fairly good memory for faces. That does not mean I cannot be wrong but, yes, I've seen that face somewhere.'

'In a magazine or newspaper perhaps?' As far as he knew Bykov had never appeared in a British publication but he had to make sure. And the snap he had shown might not be of Bykov.

'Perhaps. But that was not my recollection. I'm sure I've seen him around somewhere.' She gazed up at North and added, 'Is this what you wanted to ask Oliver?'

'Yes. Oliver knew him or had at least met him if it's the man we think it is. I did not expect you to have recognised him.'

'Well it's a distinctive face. Not your average Brit. Looks like an eastern European. Not easy to forget.'

'You've been most helpful. And thank you so much for the tea. If you do remember when or where you saw this man could you please let me know?' He passed a card over. 'Would it have been recently do you think?'

'That all depends what you call recently. Months rather than years. But you know how difficult it is to judge time.'

North drove back to London thinking that it was not entirely a wasted journey. Few people this side of the Balkans had actually met Bykov and two of them were dead: Rimmer and Brittan. Ryan, who had had maybe something more than a glance of Bykov but some years ago, was still alive but he had moved from the SIS to the Security Service. Jones, who was sure he had seen Bykov judging from the old file copies, had been murdered. Had they all been murdered? Anyone this end that he had been able to find out about — and it was accepted that there were precious few who had actually met Bykov — were now dead with the exception of Ryan.

Another thing that began to concern North was what was a mugshot of Bykov doing at MI5 in the first place? He had never been their pigeon. Someone must have put it there some years ago and there must have been a reason. North called headquarters on his car phone and asked for Ryan to wait for him in his office. He made good time getting back to London because the flow of traffic was flooding towards him as people hurried home.

Ryan was reading a news-sheet when North came

hurrying in. He put the paper down and stayed seated as North waved him down. North went to his desk, produced a bottle of scotch and glasses and realised how much he missed Bulman when there was a bottle around. He passed a heavily charged glass of whisky across the desk and raised his own in salute.

'I needed that.' North put down his glass. 'How did we get a mugshot of Bykov in the first place?'

The hefty Ryan looked surprised. 'I don't know. Jones was the one who found it.'

North fiddled with his glass. 'I wondered if you brought it with you when you left the Firm. Maybe amongst some others?'

'Why would I do that? If Six want to pass some shots over they would do it, and vice versa. Common interest in certain people.'

'So far as I know Bykov posed no threat to us. He was only here once and very briefly. I doubt that any of our people got anywhere near him at that time. All the action was in Russia. Strange. Do you think Peter Rimmer or Oliver Brittan could have sent it over?'

Ryan could not see where this was leading. 'I barely knew Rimmer. I ran into Brittan from time to time but he was in the position I am now with you, on the verge of retirement. I think he retired before I crossed over.'

North smiled at the unfortunate phrasing. 'They are both dead,' he said flatly.

Ryan stirred. 'Rimmer died soon after I left. I did not know Brittan was dead. What point are you making?'

'It's obvious isn't it? They both knew Bykov. And Jonesy thought he had seen him. All dead. A bit of a coincidence, isn't it?'

Ryan was thoughtful and was taking his whisky much more slowly than North. 'Are you saying anyone who knew Bykov is being knocked off?'

'I'm suggesting the possibility. We know there weren't many.'

'That's a bit far-fetched isn't it? I'm still around.'

'For how long?'

The shaken Ryan considered that and then finished his whisky in a gulp. 'Shit, sir. I don't like what you're saying.'

'Neither do I, Sam. I can barely spare the time to go to young Jonesy's funeral; I don't want any more.'

Ryan looked North in the eye. 'I did move from the Firm to here which might have confused some people. And I saw him for the shortest of times. Still?' He put down his empty glass. 'Had I followed him it could have been me couldn't it?'

'No. You are far too experienced. You would not have done it. They won't find you as easy as Jonesy.'

'Steady on.' Ryan reached for the bottle uninvited and charged his glass. 'You're talking as if it is going to happen.'

'I'm pointing out the dangers. I think you should take time off and go away for a while. Give your wife a well-earned holiday.'

Ryan considered it. 'Don't you think there's an awful lot of assumption here? We don't know for sure that it's the same guy. How did Rimmer and Brittan die?'

'Never mind them. How did Jonesy die? That should be enough. As for identification Bykov's wife is flying in from Paris in her present husband's private jet. We're putting her up at the Ritz and hopefully tomorrow she'll be able to pass judgment on Mirek; yea or nay. That should settle it.'

Ryan perked up. 'Thank God for that. Private jet, eh?'

'Apparently her second husband is a wealthy Polish businessman who has spent most of his working life in Paris. She landed on her feet all right. When our people offered to pay the expenses she spurned them. Meanwhile watch your back, Sam. There's too much about this business I don't like at all.'

★ ★ ★

Jacko and Paula never got to meet Irina Janesky's husband. They didn't see her again until it was time to go. The maid came to their room to tell them the car was ready and they went downstairs with the overnight bags they had brought with them. Irina was already in the car.

They all sat in the back, Irina facing them on the long rear seat. A glass partition separated them from the driver. Permission had apparently been obtained to fly out of Orly and that scrap of information formed the only conversation on the way to the airport. It was ten-thirty before they took off and again the Janesky influence was evident in the way the car was allowed to go straight to the plane where a crew of two were already on board. Jacko suspected that Jacque Verrat of the Sûreté had played a big part in smoothing things over.

At Heathrow they were met by two of North's men and again they bypassed Customs and Immigration and were taken straight to an official car which sped off to central London. The arrangement in the back was the same as in France, just the three passengers; North's men comprised the driver and a link man. An atmosphere of mystique was building up as if this was some desperate life-or-death mission. And Jacko felt the analogy was not far wrong. Like North he was picking up vibes which ostensibly were out of all proportion to a simple mission of identification. He wondered if Paula was feeling the same and when he turned to glance at her in the poor light of the car she was gazing straight ahead. She must have been aware of what he was feeling, however, for a finger came out to touch his hand on the seat. There was something so unnatural about the whole business. Irina Janesky had made a strong contribution with a strange behaviour which could be partly understood, except for the continued lack of all emotion.

It was the longest car journey Jacko could remember. Irina showed no interest in talking. She sat rigid the whole way to the Ritz and that did not encourage Jacko and Paula to converse in front of her. It was a miserable journey and the Ritz was reached with some relief. At this point Jacko and Paula handed over to North's man who escorted Irina into the hotel. They had arranged to meet her the following morning at eight-thirty and a car would take them to the hotel in Kensington. Their inclusion for that part of the mission was apparently on the insistence of Irina. She preferred them to officials she had yet to meet.

Jacko and Paula stood outside the Ritz and gazed down towards Piccadilly at the distant lights, marvelling at how quiet London could be during the early hours of the morning. Not for them an official car, which had already left, but the hotel staff had telephoned for a taxi and they shared the same cab, to Paula's flat first and then on to Jacko's home. They were too tired to talk much but found a great relief in each other's company after the restrictions they had just suffered. Before she climbed out Jacko gave Paula a peck on the cheek and said, 'Well done. I'll pick you up in the morning in my own car.' He leaned out of the cab as she was about to mount the steps of the house. 'Tomorrow's the great day. I don't know about you but I'm dreading it.'

'So am I, Jacko.' Paula was about to move away when she added, 'I've convinced myself about the doubt she needs to settle but there is something else there I can't fathom.'

Jacko called through the open cab window. 'We've done, well you have, what they wanted of us. It's now up to them.'

'Is it?' Paula pulled up her jacket against the chill breeze. 'Then why haven't they signed us off? Don't you get the feeling that this isn't the end but the beginning?'

'Let's just see what happens tomorrow. Should be interesting. At least.' But his gut feeling told him something different.

5

When Jacko reached his house in Notting Hill there was a fax advising him that a car would collect him at eight in the morning. It had been sent while he and Paula had been in the taxi. So he would not need his own car; he wondered about Paula but it was far too late to ring her. And, as he saw it, it was too late to go to bed. He sat in an armchair with a cushion behind his head and dozed the rest of the night away. He was awake early, showered and shaved, and was ready long before the car came ten minutes late.

Jacko climbed in next to the driver. 'Where are we going?'

'Kensington.' The driver was a regular and did not know Jacko but suspected he was not of the same ilk; a part-timer. Small stuff.

Jacko who knew the form and the thinking only too well had expected to be taken to the Ritz first. It was also clear that they were not picking up Paula. He sat back and dozed, knowing the driver would not be communicative and also knowing that only those beyond the pale would sit with the driver rather than in the back.

Jacko was dropped off at the hotel where one of North's men approached him and guided him to the manager's office in which North and Paula were already waiting with Irina Janesky and another man Jacko assumed to be one of North's. It was warm in the office and tea and coffee were available with the compliments of the management. It was also very quiet. Nobody wanted to talk and when they did they did so in whispers for some strange reason. Nobody was looking forward to what was about to happen and the strain was evident.

The intercom buzzed and North dealt with it as if he was in his own office. He flicked the switch off. As if the others had not heard he said aloud, 'He's just gone into the dining room.' He turned to Irina and touched her arm. 'Are you ready, Madame Janesky? You can first take a look through the door and if not satisfied with that then we can take a convenient table which has been reserved for the occasion. 'Shall we go?'

They all left the office but North's men and Jacko and Paula stayed in the vestibule while North guided Irina forward to the double glass doors of the dining room. The glass was netted but there was no problem drawing one of the nets back slightly. The nervous manager, preferring that none of this was happening, stood anxiously to one side.

Irina Janesky peered through. She showed no sign of nerves and, as before, no emotion. And as before, she was dressed soberly but elegantly — an upright, self-assured lady peering through the net curtain at a man who might be her husband. Jacko and Paula exchanged glances; nothing had changed, her nerve was still unbelievably strong.

Irina let the curtain go and leaned against the wall. Everybody waited for there was nothing to learn in her lack of reaction. 'He is certainly like my late husband,' she said at last. 'I can't be

69

absolutely sure. I shall have to get nearer.'

'Okay.' North hid his disappointment. 'Mr Jackson, Miss Ashton and myself will go in with you.' He turned to Jacko and Paula. 'You two form a shield when entering the room and take the seats with your back to Mirek to block his view of Madame Janesky. Just make it difficult for him to see her.'

Jacko whispered in Paula's ear, 'You watch her hands and I'll watch her face.'

It was difficult to appear normal while crossing the floor. The manager had done very well in selecting a corner table and they had but a little distance to go yet they all felt as if all eyes were on them.

The dining room was about a fifth full with more people leaving than arriving. Mirek had turned out to be a man of habit and his entry each morning had been within a ten-minute boundary. North already knew that Mirek was not always alone but this morning he was. There had never been a woman with him. North and Irina sat with their backs to the wall facing the room while Jacko and Paula sat opposite, partially blocking their view. It was an ideal situation for Irina had only to move her head slightly to see Mirek quite clearly. He was sideways to them with a view at an angle to them.

North ordered four continental breakfasts and left it to Irina Janesky to tackle the problem as she thought fit. They might have been a family — parents and adult children.

Irina's pose did not falter. She glanced up

frequently to view the man across the room, gaze firm under long lashes. She did not flinch or show any sign and her performance was a repeat of the one in France. Jacko simply did not understand how she could be so ice cool, bearing in mind her object, but there was no doubt she was trying to assess Mirek and although Jacko could not see it because he was facing the wrong way, she became adroit at taking a good look whenever Mirek turned his head. Her performance was extraordinary but hardly normal.

They went through the motion of eating croissants and drinking coffee and North tried desperately hard to get some talk going before they drew too much attention to themselves. And then they noticed a certain relaxation in Irina Janesky. She was eating and drinking normally and it seemed that she had made up her mind. Her glances across the room were less frequent. North thought it might be a good time to leave and was about to broach it to her when Mirek rose and strode across the room.

It was difficult then to act normally. Mirek, coming up from behind, had not yet reached Jacko's peripheral vision but Jacko knew exactly what was happening and was trying to keep his cup steady in his hands. What he could see was Irina lifting her head opposite to be quite sure that she got a full view of Mirek as he went past. Everyone except Irina was holding their breath.

Mirek's direction was towards the doors so his approach was oblique but he could not miss them. As he came into Jacko's sight Jacko could now see that Mirek was looking straight ahead, apparently not even noticing the group at the corner table. But Irina was intent on following him all the way and she made no attempt to hide the fact that she was studying him in some detail. Yet it seemed not to attract or concern him. And then he suddenly turned and for a dreadful moment Jacko thought he was coming over to them.

Everyone at the table froze, even the assured Irina, but Mirek simply returned to his table and picked up the newspaper he had left behind; then it was the performance as before. He reached the doors without an obvious glance at them. There was certainly nothing fixed about his behaviour; he appeared quite relaxed all the way.

Jacko turned to Paula who was sitting with her eyes closed, fingers gripping the edge of the table.

North said, 'That was close. You took an awful risk, Madame Janesky, he might have had a very good view of you.'

'It would not have mattered. That man is not Vadim.'

The following silence was painful, disappointment obvious.

'Are you absolutely sure?' North pressed.

'Of course I'm sure.' She pushed her coffee away. 'There are strong likenesses but it is not Vadim.'

'He would have changed slightly over the last few years,' North persisted.

'Of course he would. I made allowances for that. The likeness is strong,' she repeated. 'But there are differences I could pick out.' She turned to North with a bitter smile. 'It was not something I wanted to do and perhaps it is not the answer you wanted, but I have done my best.' She gazed at the table for a few moments and then said, 'You must understand, too, that I would have known Vadim at once, without hesitation. I can't help you any more.'

Hiding his feelings North said, 'I'll have you run back to the Ritz from where, presumably you will make your arrangements for your return to France. Of course, if you decide to stay in London for a few days it would be as our guest.'

'No. I'll go straight back.' She pushed back her chair and North was on his feet at once to help her. At that moment he was hiding his feelings as well as Irina Janesky had done. Jacko felt for him; it still left the problem of who had murdered Jones.

They returned to the manager's office where North instructed one of his men to take Madame Janesky back to the Ritz. She shook hands with everyone with as little warmth as she had shown throughout but was extremely polite. And then she did a surprising thing. She turned to Paula and kissed her lightly on each cheek and shook Jacko's hand a second time, holding it with both of hers. She said with more feeling than she had so far shown, 'Look after yourselves, you two. You are nice together, so look out for each other too.'

Jacko and Paula stayed in the manager's office while North escorted Irina to a car. North returned a few minutes later and his first words were, 'We've disrupted the routine of this hotel long enough. I've thanked the manager profusely; he was extremely helpful. I think we should leave him to it, don't you?'

North was quiet all the way back to his office, sitting morosely in the car as if the other two were not there. It was not until they entered his office and closed the door behind them that he showed any signs of the effect of the charade at the hotel. He flopped into his chair and spread his arms in total disbelief. 'Well, just what the hell did you make of that performance?'

'You mean Irina Janesky's?'

'Of course I mean Irina bloody Janesky's.' He glowered at them as if it was all their fault.

'You didn't believe her?' Jacko ventured.

'She was lying through her teeth.'

Paula, who was not at all sure why they had returned here with North, stared at him and understood his frustration. 'How can you be so sure?'

'Her reaction was totally abnormal.'

'There was no reaction.'

'Precisely. She recognised him.'

'So why didn't she say so?' asked Jacko.

'That's a damned good question. Did any of you notice anything about her that I might have missed?'

'At one stage she was digging her nails into the table; I thought she might snap one. That was all I saw. Jacko was watching her face.'

Jacko nodded. 'She was one cool lady. I didn't spot a twitch on her. Her gaze hardened at one stage but even that could have been the light. It was total control. I've no way of telling whether or not she recognised him. If she did it was an incredible performance. We are not talking of someone who was presumed dead here but of someone who was publicly executed. The mere suggestion that he might still be alive would floor most people. But then, she's not your average housewife, is she?'

'And a motive for not wanting to recognise him?'

'The one I gave before,' said Paula. 'She has a very rich husband who has his own private jet and she refused to take expenses from us, not because she had any feeling for us but because she has so much money it meant nothing to her. I'm damned sure she did not have anything approaching that sort of lifestyle when she was married to Bykov. She would not want to lose that.'

North was calming down. 'That's the obvious motive. There's something else. More important. So what is it?'

That challenge drew a complete silence and North eventually broke it himself by saying, 'She thought a lot of you two. She had an appreciation at least. And she was concerned about you. Why?'

Jacko had been asking himself the same question and now it turned out so had Paula.

'It was the only warmth she showed all the time we were with her.' Paula glanced from one to the other. 'It worries me. Not that she showed concern but that she is actually capable of showing concern and that she can suffer emotion. But for that one lapse she had bottled herself up tight.'

'So you agree with me? She was lying? Putting on a superb act which could have been far from easy.'

'I didn't suggest that at all,' Paula replied. 'I like

75

her in an indefinable way. Whether or not Mirek is Bykov it must have been a terrible experience for her to go through. Few people could do what she did with dignity and she never lost that.'

North gazed at Paula and it seemed that her appraisal had gone straight over his head. He leaned back in his chair, ran his fingers through his thick, dark hair and said almost to himself, 'I wonder if she knew he was still alive before you approached her.'

Jacko and Paula were stunned by the suggestion. North was not willing to admit to being wrong but then Jacko, having worked with him before, realised this was the sort of situation North would have bounced off Bulman and they were no replacement for the ex-Scotland Yard detective. So instead of coming up with a counter suggestion, Jacko said flatly, 'Well, that's it then. We've done our job. This is where we sign off and put in a claims form.'

North seemed not to have heard but when Jacko rose and helped Paula to her feet, he said flatly, 'Sit down.'

Jacko stayed upright. 'Look, we're tired and missed a night's sleep. You can conjecture as much as you bloody well like but it won't get you anywhere. Our job is over.' There were advantages in being outside the organisation and one of them was to be able to speak to North like that.

North descended from whichever cloud he'd been lodged. He sat forward, arms on the desk. 'I'm sorry. It didn't work out the way I thought it would. Perhaps I was looking for a quick solution to young Jonesy's murder. Had I taken him more seriously it probably would not have happened. I still need you two.'

'Why? I think Jacko's right. There is nothing more we can do.'

'You did extremely well, Paula. Very well indeed just to get her over. But I'm far from satisfied. None of this feels right. Let me tell you something . . . '

'Do we get a drink while we listen?'

'Christ, Jacko you sound just like Bulman.' He poured them drinks and then said, 'When I put a surveillance team on Mirek they picked up something they were probably lucky to spot as it was not part of their function. All Mirek's movements were legit; to this meeting or that, lunches with businessmen our surveillance cameras were later able to identify as bone fide. But the first day they picked up someone else who was following Mirek. Just one man. And as you know one man can't get away with it for long. We use twenty-three people on a serious surveillance job these days.'

'An innocent man would not know whether he was being followed or not,' said Jacko.

'Right. An innocent man. You think Mirek fits into that category?'

Jacko did not reply.

'Quite,' continued North. 'Now the question is was he following him or protecting him?' He gazed from one to the other, now sure of their attention. 'The fact is he obviously twigged that he was not alone in following Mirek and as we were using some very experienced people I would suggest that makes him a professional. He dropped out

77

of the scene before anyone really realised what had happened. He went to ground. Because he knew he had been spotted or because he knew Mirek was in no physical danger and his presence was not needed?' When he received no reply North showed irritation. 'Well come on. What does that suggest to you?'

Jacko said bluntly, 'Will you stop treating us like members of your staff? We don't give a toss what it suggests. It's none of our business. Thrash it out with your own people.'

'Do you agree with him?' North turned to Paula.

'Yes I do. I don't know what we are doing here. Our job is done.'

North shook his head in disbelief. 'Am I really speaking to two ex-SAS people? Your records tell us that you know all about living with and surviving danger yet you react to this as if you've learned nothing.' North thumped the desk. 'Mirek has seen you for God's sake. You're an open target just as Jonesy was.'

'He's seen Ryan too, according to you. Is he on the danger list?'

'I've packed him and his family off an holiday.'

'And you? Aren't you on the danger list?'

'Naturally, Jacko. But I'm further up the tree and an establishment man. That doesn't make me any less a target, they just have to give more thought to it if they are not to bring the weight of the whole organisation down on them. You two are freelance.'

'Expendable.'

'If you like.'

Paula uncrossed her legs and leaned towards the desk. 'But this is all on the assumption that Mirek is Bykov who is running around covering his tracks to the extent of murder. You could be horribly wrong.'

'Of course. But are you willing to take that risk? I have to make up my mind and take a stand, right or wrong. If I'm right then it's not just a matter of identity is it? What's the bugger doing here at all? What's his game after all this time and how did he manage it?'

North pushed his chair back and they thought he was going to rise but instead he just gazed at them, a limp figure, his good-looking features drawn and tired. They had all missed some sleep but North was being troubled by his conscience over Jones and was not finding it easy to live with. 'I want you to poke around for me. We've already done some but a follow-up might be useful. Mirek told us that he went to a club called the Blue Palm on the day of the murder. We've checked and the police have checked and he did. For how long depends on who you speak to. It might be useful to find out if he goes regularly or if he really knows anyone there.'

'You want me to take Paula to a strip club?'

'Work it out for yourselves. But there's another matter. I want you to keep an eye on a Department of Trade and Industry official called Jeremy Clarke. Mirek had breakfast with him at the hotel that morning. There's probably nothing in it but I can't, at this stage anyway, put a team on Clarke. There'd be hell to pay if he found out. But you two could nose around, find out what you can. I can start by giving you his address.'

'Just the two of us?' asked Jacko.

'Just find out what you can.'

Jacko and Paula exchanged glances and suspicion was etched on both their faces. Paula smiled sweetly. 'Shouldn't the police be doing this? It is, after all, a murder enquiry. In fact, you've been talking all along as if the police are doing very little. Have you nobbled them?'

'You know we don't do things like that,' North replied in all seriousness. 'Not these days. We cooperate. But we are dealing with a high-powered civil servant here; we have to operate very much within the guidelines.'

'I think Paula and I need to talk this over privately.'

North rose immediately. 'Of course you do. How long do you think you need? I can't leave the office for long.'

'We'll do it,' said Paula without reference to Jacko.

'That was a quick decision. What provoked it?' North sat down again.

'If you are willing to leave us two alone in your office you must be desperate.'

North smiled. 'You wouldn't have found anything worthwhile. Besides I trust you two or you would not be here at all.' He tapped some buttons on his computer and ran off Clarke's address for them.

'We want arms,' said Jacko. 'Browning nine mm for me.'

'And for me,' said Paula. 'With spare clips.'

North knew that Jacko had a pistol of his own and he had made it clear that he wanted official issue although that could be circumvented. 'What on earth do you need weapons for? This is a civil servant we are talking about. You're in no danger from him.'

'Probably not,' Jacko said dryly. 'But we're a little bit nervous of the guy you really want us to flush out and who might surface if we are seen to follow Clarke. You know, the bloke your team spotted on the first day.'

★ ★ ★

Irina Janesky flew back to Paris that same morning. North had arranged an escort for her to London Airport but she said nothing on the way down sitting very rigid and seemingly under some strain. The executive jet had to wait in the queue and it was some time before she actually took off and the escort returned to London only after the plane had left the ground. A little over an hour later Irina Janesky fell into the arms of her waiting husband and broke down in a flood of tears while he tried to console her.

Jurich Janesky was plump, bald, wealthy and caring in all things regarding Irina. He had known Irina before she married Vadim Bykov. He had traded with the Soviet block and still traded with the new Russia. A naturalised Frenchman when Vadim Bykov had been put on public trial, Jurich had flown to Moscow to comfort Irina and he tried to comfort her now as he walked her over to the waiting car. Anticipating a reaction whatever her conclusions, he had driven to the airport himself so that no one else would know of her experience.

For some time he consoled her in the car but even when her tears stopped she remained shivering in his arms. He understood her feelings only too well. Vadim Bykov had been nothing but trouble almost from the day he had married Irina. A proven traitor, Janesky had always suspected that Bykov had also been a corrupt official although, even now, he had said nothing to Irina and, in any event, could not prove what was only a suspicion.

As he held her he marvelled at her self-discipline. To hold herself in for two days as she had, had been a magnificent achievement. Only someone as strong could have done it in the way that she had. Now the reaction had set in and her feelings and despair poured out. After a while she quietened down and he thought she might have fallen asleep in his arms.

'That was a disgraceful exhibition,' she said after a while. 'I'm so sorry to have broken down like that.'

'Don't be silly, my darling. No one else but you could have held it in for so long and without help.' He lifted his head from hers. 'Are you able to talk about it?'

Irina pushed herself upright and dried her eyes. 'No, I don't want to talk about it.'

He said nothing for a while, just watching her in the comparative gloom of the car and saw the toll just two days had made. 'I have to know,' he said anxiously. 'Was it him?'

6

Rudolf Chaznov had lean, hard lines that had a scaring effect on most of those he met. His pale grey eyes could be described as dead in that they only ever showed an expression of unfeeling. It was doubtful if Chaznov had ever felt sorry for or had found sympathy for, anyone. He was the type of man customers in a bar would move away from. He did not court trouble but when he found it, or had been commissioned to deal with it, he knew exactly how to handle it. Women were scared of him which had been unfortunate for some of them.

It had been difficult for Jan Mirek to arrange a meeting with him. Mirek was well aware of being followed although it was Chaznov who had first warned him by leaving a message at the hotel. For day-to-day meetings it did not matter. He met people, he talked to them, wined and dined with them and always came back to his hotel for the night. But being under surveillance curtailed other actions he needed to take, and other people he needed to see. He knew that a surveillance could not last for ever but if it went on too long he would have to complain to the police.

Mirek badly needed to meet with Chaznov but the man was too outstanding to do so under police or security eyes. They had digital phone contact which helped but they really needed to get together without anyone knowing. The safest place was in a crowd and the biggest crowds were at football matches. And then Mirek saw the difficulty of holding a serious conversation among so many and realised they really needed to be alone.

He did not want to alert the surveillance team that he was aware of them and finally concluded that the easiest way was the direct approach. Chaznov would have to call at the hotel, ask for one of the guests on the same floor and then come to Mirek's room if there was nobody watching the corridor. To find the names of other guests was not difficult and cost relatively little.

Chaznov called on the evening of the day that Irina Janesky flew back to France. The agreed tap on the door was answered at once by Mirek. He let Chaznov in immediately asking him if anyone had been in the corridor. He was quite sure that a check would be made on Chaznov the moment he moved to the lifts.

Chaznov showed his contempt at the question. He considered people like Mirek to be amateurs which might turn out to be a serious mistake. He sat on the bed as Mirek offered him a drink. 'I don't drink,' said Chaznov. 'Which you well know. You have the jitters.'

Mirek sank onto a chair. 'Really?' They were speaking in Russian, but quietly, voices held low. 'Then you have this team on your back day after day and see if you get the jitters. You're stupid enough to try to wipe them all out.'

Chaznov's eyes narrowed. He would cheerfully have killed Mirek for that but knew that he must not and that Mirek knew it. 'It's easy to be brave knowing I have to protect you. But I won't take any more insults. Why did you want me here?'

Mirek reached for his drink. Then he looked across at Chaznov and said wearily, 'Why on earth did you have to kill that man? He was only a youngster for God's sake.'

Chaznov did not really understand the question. 'I'm here to protect you. He was blatantly harassing you. He followed you all the way from the hotel. What was I supposed to do?'

'Ignore him. He was quite harmless. You've caused complications we could do without. The police have swarmed all over me because they think that I killed him. And I can see their point of view. My wings have been clipped at a crucial moment.' And then, in exasperation, 'You've drawn attention to me for God's sake.'

'If they thought it was you they would have pulled you in. They are not likely to follow you again, are they?'

'You damned fool. That's exactly what has happened but in numbers.'

Chaznov stood up, a tall menacing figure who made Mirek's flesh crawl. 'I meant harassing you as that man was doing.'

'Sit down, for God's sake,' Mirek did not lack courage but knew he was no physical match for Chaznov. 'You are not in Russia now. You can't go around killing people. You've caused all sorts of complications.'

'The police don't know I exist.'

'Don't be so arrogant or so damned sure.'

'And if they did I can take care of them. They

are a soft touch over here.'

Mirek gazed at Chaznov for a while. Eventually he said, 'I don't seem to be getting through to you at all. By killing someone you've put a tight rope round me. You are supposed to guard me. Instead you've exposed me to a crime I did not commit nor would have agreed to. I was forced to enter a club I did not like in order to create a flimsy alibi for something I did not do. I should report you.'

'I did what I thought was best for you.' Chaznov was more conciliatory. 'He might have been armed. Anyway, who was he? And why was he following you?'

'We'll never know now, will we?' Mirek added thoughtfully, 'He was so unprofessional that it is difficult to place him. He might have been a crank.' He did not tell Chaznov that he had seen Jones at breakfast with another man; Chaznov would have taken that as justification. 'You have probably put us in a position where we might have to kill again just to keep ahead. You've blown it.'

'Then I'll need extra help. I'll ask for back-up.'

Mirek considered it. Had Chaznov had more help perhaps the killing might not have happened. He would be happier without any kind of protection but he knew that would not happen; his protection contained many angles not all for his benefit. 'Anyway, keep away from me until this dies down.' He privately conceded that as killings went Chaznov had been a highly capable executioner. He had chosen exactly the right moment and had operated with incredible speed, not even pausing in his stride and was gone before anyone really knew

86

what had happened. It had been very professional and Chaznov knew it which was why he was so aggrieved.

Mirek stood up slowly. 'I'll ring you at the usual times. And don't ring me unless it's absolutely necessary. You've no way of knowing who I might have with me at the time. I'm quite certain the police will be back. I'll just have to sweat it out.'

★ ★ ★

Jacko and Paula went to the Blue Palm that evening. It was an abortive trip. The police had already obtained what little information there was about Mirek's visit. Using copies of the snaps North's surveillance team had taken Jacko felt like a policeman himself and was probably taken for one as he chatted up the bar and service staff.

It was not really a strip club but a show of exotic dancing of some skill. After a while he and Paula managed to find a table and they had some drinks at exorbitant prices. They were tired and were ready to go to their respective homes.

'I don't know why he sent us here,' said Paula, sweeping her hair back. 'It's a waste of time.'

Jacko nodded. 'But we're doing it aren't we? I know how his crafty mind works. It's the house he is really interested in.'

'The address of the DTI man? I don't know why he gave us that either.'

'He wants us to break in. He won't do it and the police can't do it which leaves mugs like us.'

'If he wants to know what Jeremy Clarke was

doing with Jan Mirek he has only to ask him.'

'He won't do that. He'll take the view that Mirek won't know who is following him and will assume that it's the police. But he may not get the answers he wants and hopes that maybe we will. If we're caught it can go down to a common burglary.' He added, 'We'll have a look at Clarke's place tomorrow. There's nothing to be gained here and I think North knew it. He just wanted us to get to know each other over a drink.'

'And have we?' Paula was holding her glass by its rim, rotating it gently, her gaze challenging.

He saw the devilment in her eyes and said, 'Are you trying to seduce me?'

'I used to be good at it once as part of the job. Now I've been tumbled before I've really started.' She offered a wicked smile. 'Just shows how much I'm out of practice.'

'You don't need practice, Paula.' To kill the line of conversation he added, 'I think we should turn in. We'll need to be alert tomorrow morning when we go to Clarke's place.'

'I'm not breaking in anywhere. North can use his own people and take the can. Leave me out, Jacko.'

Jacko understood her feeling. 'You won't have to break in. I will. You keep a lookout.'

'Don't you think you are being rather silly?'

'No more than usual. I'm not being made to do it. North has no hold on me and as he will tell you, I just can't help myself.'

'I think you should try. It's one thing going to

Paris to persuade Irina Janesky to return to London to identify someone. We did not compromise ourselves . . . but breaking and entering?'

'We compromised ourselves the moment we agreed to work for North. If it's too difficult I won't do it.'

* * *

Detective Chief Superintendent Matthew Simes kept an appointment with Derek North that same evening. The Security Service premises were not unknown to Simes and he was happier on the outside of them taking in a view of the Thames. But the two men were fairly comfortable in each other's company although Simes did not trust North, or perhaps it was truer to say the Security Service of which North was part.

It had been agreed between them that Simes would interview Jeremy Clarke of the DTI rather than give a whiff of suspicion that the Security Service was in any way involved. It suited both men.

'I saw him at the DTI,' Simes explained. 'He was most helpful as far as it went.' Simes tried to get comfortable in a chair which was not designed for his size. 'He's higher up the tree than I realised. Own office, good view, knows his job and what's going on in the world in terms of trade and industry. He destroyed the civil service image by having most things at his fingertips. Would have made a good businessman in my opinion but I suppose he has security where he is and a thundering good salary.'

'And I suppose he bears out what Mirek told us?'

'Well, there was not much to tell. He vaguely recalls Ryan and Jones in the hotel dining room; thinks he said 'good morning' to them as he and Mirek passed their table. And that's it.'

'So what were they meeting for?'

Simes eyed the other chair and wondered whether he should move to it. 'Mirek is buying in, Clarke supplies him with the names of businesses and contacts in this country who are selling and looking for openings. Usual thing.'

'At breakfast?'

'Oh, yes. Working breakfasts have been around for years, apparently, except in here of course.' Simes beamed.

North smiled back. 'Have you any details of Clarke that might be useful to us?'

Simes was surprised. 'I thought you had a file on everyone including me.'

'Especially you, Matthew. We know he lives in Northwood, is divorced, she was unfaithful not he, and has access to a nine-year-old daughter and is highly thought of by the DTI. But I was thinking more of small things, like how many burglaries has he had and is his house alarmed, that sort of thing.'

The two men stared at each other, neither giving way. 'I hope you are not thinking what I think you are thinking.'

'How can I possibly know what you are thinking?'

'Then you shouldn't be in the bloody job.

Don't do it, Derek. You've caused us problems in the past.'

'Okay,' North said to Simes. 'I can promise you that the Service has no intention of breaking in. It's just information that might be useful some time and knowing you, you would already have done your homework on his background before seeing him.'

'Why don't I believe you?'

'Because you're a very experienced copper and you don't believe anyone.'

Simes laughed. 'He's been done over three times in recent years. There have been quite a few jobs done down there. It's near to London and there are still a number of wealthy people around the area. Clarke was advised to get alarms but only went so far as to have security lights put on front and back. As they only work at night when he's more likely to be there it's no wonder that he's been done during the day. I understand that there is a chance of property development and he could make a sizeable sum of money by selling at the right time. Meanwhile he hangs on and doesn't want to spend money on it.'

'So he's a mean bugger with an eye for a quick profit and has little in the house he personally values. Insured up to the hilt no doubt.'

'You know there was a time when swearing wasn't allowed in here. Everything is going downhill. There's more to this than a murder isn't there? I fully understand your interest because young Jones was your man. But it doesn't end there, does it?'

North gave it brief consideration. Simes was due for promotion to Commander and could easily go beyond that. 'We think Mirek has come back from the dead.'

* * *

Jacko and Paula took separate taxis after they left the Blue Palm. Jacko had arranged to pick Paula up the next morning around ten. When he arrived at his house and entered his den to check on phone and fax messages he found a fax giving some detail of Jeremy Clarke's house. He knew it was from North who would deny it but it was useful. He went to bed and slept deeply. The following morning he rose, showered, looked out of the window to see a couple of joggers, shivered and went into the kitchen to cook himself a solid breakfast.

He called for Paula at nine-forty-five and was surprised to find she was already waiting for him. She skipped down the steps of her apartment house, stopped at the bottom, pointed to the car and said, 'Are we going in this? You must be kidding.'

The red Ferrari was already drawing attention, even from people in a hurry. 'It's my second one,' said Jacko engagingly as he opened the nearside door for her. 'The first one was blown up. The guy who blew it up said he was sorry and bought me this.'

As Jacko climbed in beside her Paula thought he was joking and then realised he was not. 'That must be a first,' she commented. 'What happened?'

He switched on and the roar of the engine scared the foraging pigeons. 'I'll tell you one day. It's a long story. Sad. I got to like the guy.' He noted her jeans and polo-necked pullover under her jacket. He pulled out and after a couple of blocks joined the traffic stream.

It was warm in the car. Paula snuggled down and said, 'I must say that the idea of going to a burglary in a red Ferrari must be novel.'

'Nah!' exclaimed Jacko. 'Who the hell would suspect us? Burglaries are done from stolen run-of-the-mill bangers. This is class. Everyone will remember the car. Only a nutter would use it on a job.'

Paula laughed. She was seeing another side of Jacko; the action side and guessed he must have been fun to work with and very, very reliable. She then voiced her second surprise. 'Why are you dressed as if you're going to a city meeting? How can you burgle in an expensive suit?'

'No problem,' he retorted. 'I'm wearing part of my alibi.'

She noticed the ease with which he coped with traffic and got through it where he could so effortlessly. He did not get stressed out when he got caught in a jam and could sit back and wait, relaxed and ready while others around him lost patience. Jacko was at home behind the wheel of a car and at one with it.

'I'm still not happy about this,' Paula said. 'I don't mind observation jobs or the one we did in Paris, but this is against the law.'

Jacko did not take his eyes off the road; he never did whilst driving. 'I'm not going to force you or even try to persuade you. If you want to opt out

93

when we get there that's okay. I understand. Are you armed?'

Paula was fascinated by the way Jacko was handling the traffic and amazed at the way some cars gave way to them in some sort of mark of respect. 'No. We're still waiting for North to provide aren't we?'

'Yes. I just wondered why you'll accept arms, possession of which is most definitely against the law, but draw the line at a bit of investigative breaking and entering. It's a paradox.' He suddenly braked as a car swerved in front of him.

Paula turned towards him. Her fair hair was tied in a ponytail at the back and it somehow made her look a little younger and more vulnerable. She knew she could not draw his attention but was equally sure that he was well aware of her watching him. 'So now you're a philosopher. I don't know why. One feels right and the other does not. Besides, the gun will be to protect me if necessary; I don't intend to use it otherwise. If I ever get it.'

He was still concentrating on the road when he asked, 'If I really needed you inside the house would you join me?'

'That depends on a lot of things. I wouldn't leave you in the lurch if you were in a jam and I thought I could help. It's a silly question.'

'Okay. Open the facia and you'll find a bleeper. I already have one. I take it you won't be against giving me a ping if someone is coming while I'm in the house.'

'No problem,' Paula slipped the bleeper in a front pocket of her jeans. It was only then that

Jacko realised she was not carrying a bag or purse which left him wondering where she would have put a pistol.

They drove into Northwood and Jacko did a brief tour, turning off the main road and driving down the High Street, surprisingly quiet, before he circled round a couple of times as Paula realised that he was observing the possible routes out; to London, to Watford, Rickmansworth and north into Buckinghamshire, to Amersham and Chesham.

The house was on a fairly busy road. They were old houses laid very well back from the road with high hedges hiding them from the world and each other as they continued down the respective drives. At one time they would have been highly fashionable but time had not improved them and they were not old enough to be protected properties. They were large though, with big gardens at the rear.

Jacko was able to park right outside Jeremy Clarke's house because it was a no parking zone.

'What about traffic wardens? And wheel clamping?' Paula asked sensibly.

'The first sign of either, drive round the block until they've gone. I'll be as quick as I can.' Jacko switched off the engine and left the keys in the ignition. He took a billboard and pen from the dashboard and put on some plain glass spectacles. He turned and gave Paula a wink.

As he was about to climb out Paula said, 'You knew damned well that I wouldn't come in, didn't you? You sod. You just wanted me to make sure the car would be all right.'

Jacko grinned. As he opened the door the cold air rushed in. 'If you do get caught then there's a map in the dash which you can pour over so that you can make out you're lost. You might even find a helpful warden.'

'You louse. I hope you get caught.'

Jacko climbed out and closed the door. Billboard in hand he peered at the gate to make sure he had the right address, opened the small gate and stepped on to the uneven drive. He walked up to the front door as if he owned the place. When he turned to look back he could not see the Ferrari at all and the houses on either side were virtually obscured by the tall hedges.

There was a vague look of neglect about the house. The paint on the door was not chipped but dowdy. The lace curtains in the bay windows could do with a wash. The high hedges, although most useful from his point of view, made the whole place gloomy because they were so near. Jacko raised his billboard with its clipped folded form from the Consumers Association — pages of questions that would take ages to answer. Poised, he rang the bell. Even the chimes sounded dated. He stood there wondering whether there was a daily help; an important piece of missing information.

Jacko rang once more and waited some time before producing a bunch of keys he had obtained from an old lag long since retired. He was about to try a key when the Ferrari roared like thunder and he heard it leave. It was no time to distrust Paula. The fourth key sprung the lock and he pushed the door open all the way while still standing in the porch.

Satisfied nobody was there, Jacko entered the wide hall, closed the door behind him and took stock. The carpeting was good but old and as he progressed into the house that was his general impression; a good many things could be improved or replaced. It had a run-down feel and look about it and the colours were dark and gloomy.

Jacko decided to start from the top and work his way down but first he entered all the downstairs rooms just to make sure they were all empty. He climbed the narrow stairs and faced several rooms on the landing. As he went from room to room trying to get an overall picture of a high-ranking civil servant, Jeremy Clarke's physical image, as given to him by the very experienced North, did not equate with what he was seeing. By all accounts Clarke was a snappy dresser, a fine example of his profession. Nothing here reflected that image. Practically everything Jacko saw was dowdy with the possible exception of the bedroom Clarke apparently used.

The bed was made up, with an old brocaded cover, but there was nothing special about its furnishings. Clarke had been married. Nothing Jacko saw reflected a woman's touch. Had his wife lived here? According to North's information Clarke had lived here for years. He went to a rear window and peered out by lifting just the corner of one of the curtains. It was not the best time of year to view a garden. Some people ignored their house interiors and put all their energy into their gardens and vice versa but it seemed to Jacko that the same neglect applied outside and in.

North's memo had informed Jacko of the possibility of a property development but the neglect he was seeing was of years. Did Clarke really live here? Or was it a convenient smoke screen? Another woman? Jacko shrugged; there was a lot of it about.

Jacko went through the old-fashioned wardrobes and briefly examined the clothes; there were not too many of those but what there was was of better quality than the furnishings. There was nothing more to be learned upstairs so he went down.

He found the study. There was no improvement here. Cheap, lightweight desk, a filing cabinet, four tubular chairs and two rugs, one under the desk. There were drapes as well as net curtains at the windows and he could smell their mustiness. All desk and cabinet drawers were locked. He could have forced them but at this stage wanted nobody to know anyone had been there.

The only thing Jacko felt he had achieved was a complete contradiction between the man and his dwelling; the one smart and efficient, the other shabby and barely utilitarian. In some way or another Jeremy Clarke seemed to be living a lie. Unless this was not his real home. Could he have another tucked away somewhere?

As he went from room to room Jacko realised that whatever their quality they had a certain neatness. Nothing was left lying around, certainly nothing indicative of his work. And that was an impression he carried until he entered what was obviously a child's playroom. It appeared unused. Jacko knew that Clarke had a daughter of ten but she lived with her mother so the room must reflect earlier days.

In a cupboard he found boxes of toys, mainly dolls and a large doll's house. There was a huge teddy bear with one eye half out. Jacko pushed it back in and patted it on the head. There was a miniature kitchen, tiny pots and pans. He stopped for a while wondering why he was poking around a little girl's toys; toys with which she had not played for some time. They had all been packed away too neatly to have recently been used. And then he saw something that certainly did not belong to a little girl or to any child. His first reaction was to recoil and he backed well away. When he was satisfied that he had attracted no movement he drew closer.

It was no more than four to five cm long and had six splayed metal legs, three each side. He recognised the dark green, infrared-proof paint, and guessed that the front panels were sensors. He pulled it out from the rest of the toys very carefully. It was no more than five grammes in weight and he had to assume that it was disarmed. The last time he had heard of this kind of little monster it was referred to as Ghengis or Attila. He realised he was sweating and hoped he had triggered nothing. He laid it on the floor and pulled out a miniature camera just as his bleeper went.

7

Jacko heard the bleeper and cursed the timing. He crossed to the playroom door and closed it, carefully isolated the six-legged object and knelt to take some camera shots from various angles. He put the camera away, returned the strange-looking object to the box of toys and put it back in the cupboard. Beyond the door he could hear someone moving about.

He crossed to the windows which faced the back garden and found them to be locked. He could open them but not without some noise. He went to the door. His bleeper vibrated but there was nothing he could do. He pulled the playroom door ajar and gazed through the crack down the passage.

An attractive woman in her mid-thirties suddenly came into view from one of the rooms and then turned off into the study. She closed the door and Jacko decided to take his chance. He stepped from the playroom, closed the door quietly behind him and hurried down the passage to the front door, praying that the woman would not come out. He reached the front door, opened it and was through in a second. He closed it behind him and hastened down the drive, still with billboard in hand.

He did not see the Ferrari until he was beyond the gate and then he kept his nerve and walked slowly towards it. The nearside door opened as he approached as Paula picked him up in the rear-view mirror. She was about to pull away when he stopped her. 'I'll drive. I want to know where that woman is going to next.'

Paula climbed out and they changed places but as she settled in she said, 'She'll recognise the car. How could she mistake it? I kept my head down but glimpsed her looking at it as she went past. You cut it bloody fine.'

'I couldn't help it. Thanks for the warning. Where did she park her car?'

'She was on foot. She might have parked round the corner or had come by train; the services are good. Oh, and you were right about traffic wardens; I had to move off almost as soon as you went in.'

Jacko switched on but still sat there reluctant to give up the woman so easily. 'Could you drive back to town if I try to follow her on foot?'

'Of course I can but you're being carried away. You don't know when she's coming out or if she's coming out at all. And it's too risky on your own.'

Still he sat there. And then he said, 'I think I'll go back in.'

'For God's sake, Jacko.' Paula was suddenly very angry. 'You're mad. You can't keep pulling the billboard trick unless you're thinking of breaking in and that's madder still. I won't back you, Jacko. You'll be on your own.'

Surprised at her anger Jacko was still feeling he was letting something slip away. 'I didn't even get a good look at her except to see that she was well dressed. If only I could get a shot of her.'

'I got a good look at her and can give North a good description. Leave it at that before you blow the whole thing. I understand what's in your mind but it's cut and run time. Let's go.' Paula gave him a long, hard stare. 'You were lucky to get out without her seeing you. Leave it at that.'

He finally gave in and pulled out using his rear-view mirror to the last hoping that the woman would reappear.

Paula made a call to North on the car phone and as he could not see them until early afternoon they agreed to break the journey back and have lunch in Harrow. They found a good restaurant and relaxed in its warmth. Jacko ordered wine for Paula but would not drink himself; as with his concentration at the wheel he took his driving seriously. They ate well and were much more relaxed when Paula eventually asked, 'Did you find anything?'

Jacko smiled disarmingly. 'Well, you held that question in. I found the shell of an anti-personnel mine in a kid's toy box. It is an 'insectoid' mine. It's small, light and works on heat sensors.'

'I've heard of them but never seen one. Creepy-crawlies that seek you out and from which there is no escape. Nasty little devils some are trying to ban.'

'Clinton has already issued a unilateral ban on anti-personnel mines and is raising it at the United Nations to get worldwide coverage. He'll be lucky and must know it. Lip service does not constitute a ban.'

'That's a pretty cynical remark, Jacko.'

He poured her the last of the wine. 'It's a

cynical business. You'll never ban where there is demand, whatever international agreements. Mines kill twenty-five thousand people a year, mainly women and children. There are sixty-four war zones around the globe and Britain sells about five billions' worth of military equipment. We're one of the biggest manufacturers of mines in the world. Already people in America and here want to exclude the 'smart' mines.'

' 'Smart' mines? You're talking of those that self-destruct after a certain period of time?'

'Of course. Anyway, Russia and China oppose any ban and will veto. But what the hell is one doing in a child's toy box?'

'I thought you'd know the answer to that. It's like hiding jewels in a loaf of bread; who'd look there? Or in a kid's play box?'

'I did.'

'Ah, but we all know you are brilliant, Jacko. A right clever dick. Who makes these things?'

'The Creeping Terror? That's what some call it. It was developed at the Massachusetts Institute of Technology. Whether others have cottoned on, I don't know.'

Paula dabbed her lips with the table napkin. 'That was lovely.' She gazed quizzically at him. 'You're well versed about mines.' It was a challenge.

'Ever since a mate of mine was blown up by one in South Armagh, I've followed their deadly progress. They are becoming very futuristic and devilish. I go along with global ban. But it ain't going to happen. There's too much money

103

involved, balance of payments and all that. How did Clarke get one?'

They were back in the car before Paula answered. 'It was disarmed or we wouldn't be talking about it.'

'No, not disarmed. It was empty of explosive, and it only needs a few grammes, and operating mechanism. It was just a shell.'

'A traveller's sample?'

'No. A photograph would do for that. A travelling sample would need to work to get someone to believe in it. Strange.'

'But he is in the DTI. He must run into all sorts of industrial situations and arms must be among them. There must be times when he collaborates with the MoD.'

When they got back to town and met up with North Jacko passed the film over but North was already well versed about the mine. But he did become more interested in Jeremy Clarke.

'It could be a harmless souvenir from some international jaunt. On the other hand . . . I wonder if we're following the right man?' asked North. 'I think we'd better keep an eye on him but we'll have to be very careful. And you don't know who the woman is?'

'No.' Paula had already given a description which North had taped.

'Can we find out if he has another pad?' asked Jacko. 'I'm sure that place is not being lived in or if it is then it's a sort of transit camp. Overnighters, short stays.'

North was pensive. 'Can you ask around the

neighbours? Find out what they know. There's usually a nosy one.'

'The houses are pretty shut off one from the other but we can try. Have you found out anything more about Mirek?'

'Polish Police and Intelligence confirm that he's bona fide. But he could be leading someone else's life and that someone could be dead. For instance his wife died four years ago so she can't vouch for him. I'm beginning to think we haven't touched the surface here.'

North rose. 'I'm grateful to you both.' And then to Jacko, 'Whatever possessed you to look in a kid's play box?'

'The same reason as the guy who put it there.'

North was not sure that he had worked that out but said, 'Basement. Your arms are waiting for you.'

'Do we need to sign?' asked Jacko shrewdly.

'No. But you can use the range if you want to try them out.'

Jacko and Paula exchanged cynical glances. No signature, no trace back. North was covering his back.

★ ★ ★

Having bottled herself up in front of Jacko and Paula, Irina Janesky was having trouble with her nerves. She had not gone to pieces but was increasingly agitated, snapping at her husband Jurich for no good reason. She was lucky he was so understanding.

Irina had told Jurich what she had told North in London, that Jan Mirek bore a remarkable likeness to Vadim Bykov but that was all. Vadim remained dead. But it had been a nasty experience and she had been badly shaken.

Like North, Jurich Janesky did not wholly believe her. He did not think that she was necessarily lying, but that she did not want it to be true and had shut out the possibility. The implications of it being true could be disastrous. But he knew he must give her time before they could talk sensibly about it. And it was not easy for him to sit back and wait.

So when, the day after she arrived back in Paris, she suggested that she should go away for a few days, he understood and thought it would probably be for the best. He was too busy to suggest that he went with her and she realised that. Besides, for her to go alone might be the perfect solution and would give her time to straighten her mind. He felt deeply for her and wanted to do the right thing.

'Where do you want to go?' he asked reasonably.

'The villa in Cannes would be ideal and warmer.'

'Good. I'll phone George.'

'There's no need. I'll do it. It will give me something to do.'

He put an arm round her shoulders. 'Are you sure you'll be all right? I could kill the British for bringing this up.'

Irina pecked him on the cheek. 'No, my darling, they were quite right, however distasteful it was. It's shaken me, that's all. A few days in Cannes will be ideal. I'll pack a few things.'

She went upstairs while he sat in front of the log fire and reflected on his luck in marrying her. He was troubled now because she was troubled and who wouldn't be after the shock she had suffered. When she came down with just one suitcase he was surprised that she had not got the maid to bring it down and realised just once more that life in Russia had been far from the luxury she now enjoyed. He wondered at times whether she had married him for his money but it did not matter to him as long as she was with him.

He rose as she entered the room and crossed to the telephone on its period card table. 'I'll make arrangements for the plane.'

'Don't be silly, darling. I don't need the plane. I'll take the scheduled flight down. There are plenty of them. It will do me good to be among other passengers. I won't feel so shut off.'

'Okay.' He put the phone down. He often used scheduled flights himself. 'Is there anything I can do? Book a flight for you?'

She crossed the room and led him to the long settee in front of the fire. They sat down. 'Stop worrying,' she said. 'I'll book a flight after you've gone tomorrow. There are plenty of seats this time of the year. I want to see you off as usual. And I won't be gone long.'

The fact that he felt she needed a break and his love for her obscured the usually sound reasoning of an astute mind. He wanted to please her and knew she was suffering.

She did see him off the next morning. He drove into Paris as usual in a chauffeur-driven car and when he had gone she caught a plane to London she had booked the previous evening.

★ ★ ★

Jacko used a forged police warrant card made out in the name of Detective Sergeant Harris. It was one he had obtained from a nephew of the late Balls-Up Balfour, a brilliant forger who inevitably tripped up on distribution somewhere along the line. He had not used it since working with George Bulman, an ex-Detective Chief Superintendent at Scotland Yard who himself was not averse to using an illegal warrant card.

There was no time to make one for Paula so she tagged along as his assistant, DC Yates. They returned to Northwood the following morning but not in the Ferrari. Jacko hired a Ford for the day. This time they parked round the corner but still had some distance to walk. It was dry and crisp and both wore topcoats against the icy breeze. They called on the two houses immediately either side of Clarke's house and were lucky enough to find someone in each.

The pretext they used was of an anonymous call informing that an intruder had been seen at Clarke's place which they had found to be secure and empty but which they had to follow up; after all, the place had been burgled three times previously.

They got nowhere. Nobody had seen anything or

heard anything. They had heard about the previous burglaries but they were some time ago and if the owner was too mean to install an alarm then he was courting trouble around here. This was no war against the police, the occupants were as helpful as they could be. They simply meant what they said. The houses were too well secluded for them to have noticed anything. One woman did not know the name of the owner of Clarke's house. She had never met him nor, apparently, wanted to.

They went to the houses either side of the ones they visited and got no further at all. If Clarke had wanted to hide himself he had chosen a good spot and near to London.

Jacko and Paula gazed across the wide, busy road to the other side where there were similar houses and a modern block of flats. 'What do you think?' asked Jacko.

'Well, we've come this far. It would be silly not to try.'

They chose their moment to cross the road and Jacko grabbed Paula by the arm as they jogged across. They started with the house directly opposite Clarke's but it was the one next door which proved to be fruitful.

A middle-aged man came to the door on crutches. Before they could say anything he said, 'I've been watching you,' he stated. 'You the police?'

Jacko produced his warrant card and introduced Paula. He trotted out his excuses for being there, apologised for inconveniences caused but he had no need to worry; he had found a groupie who was largely confined to the house and had mounted binoculars in an upstairs bedroom to help him pass away the time.

They followed him upstairs, a painful and slow process for him, and into a bedroom that faced the street. The binoculars were on a tripod and were poking through net curtains.

'Did you see anyone go in there recently?' Jacko indicated Clarke's house.

Sid Lewis hobbled over on his crutches. Once a tall man, now rather stooped, he still had a full head of hair, but grey now. He was thin, the toll of arthritic pain chiselled into his face. He appeared to be in his early fifties and could not see where life was leading him. A pleasant man, not naturally nosy but he had to find ways of passing the time and looking out of his bedroom window was one of them.

'A couple of hours ago,' he replied. 'A smart woman went in with a man. So if you've been there and there was no reply she doesn't want to speak to you.'

'You mean she's still there?'

'Well, I haven't seen her come out.' He hooked himself on to a high stool in front of the binoculars. 'I've seen her a few times, sometimes with a man but not always the same man; young, old and middle-aged and some look like foreigners.' He smiled almost bashfully. 'Thought she might be on the game but if she's with a man it is she who comes out more often than not, and the guy stays put, so I might be wrong. Anyway days, weeks go past without anyone calling or if they do it's when I'm not around.'

Paula was playing her part of subordinate and was keeping quiet. Jacko asked, 'Do you see anything of the owner?'

'I wouldn't really know who the owner is. As you can see we're separated by a wide, busy road and traffic. Plenty of houses but no communal spirit. The place does not lend itself to mixing. I would say that most own their houses and have been in them for years so are past the first flush of youth. Largely keep themselves to themselves. The women meet at the tea shop in the high street for daily gossip.'

'What about burglars?'

'We get more than our fair share. They come down from London. This was a once wealthy area and there's still plenty of money about.'

'But you haven't seen one today?'

'No. But I'm not looking all the time.' He offered a knowing grin. 'I saw you two yesterday, though.' He looked at Jacko. 'I didn't see you go in but I saw you leave.'

'Well done.' Jacko leaned across to peer through the glasses. 'You can't actually see the front door from here.'

'I don't need to. The gate is enough. You couldn't have got anywhere with your call yesterday or you wouldn't be here.'

'I must have spoken to the woman you're talking about.' Jacko took a chance. 'She's not the owner and knew nothing about a report on prowlers. So we've returned today. Could be a hoax call. Do you know anything about the woman?'

'Only that she's the most frequent visitor. Would

111

you like me to take some snaps of her? It would be no problem. I can send them to your station.'

As Jacko hesitated Sid Lewis added, 'I've a high-class camera with a zoom. I can take the binoculars off and mount it on the same tripod. Nice steady shots.'

'That's very kind of you. When would they be ready?'

'The day I take them. I develop my own. Today if I see her come out. Give me your number and I'll ring you when they're ready.'

While Jacko hesitated Paula said, 'We'll be in the Midlands for the next couple of days, Sarge, to identify those two guys.' She wrote on a page from her notebook. 'My personal number. If I'm not there leave a message on the machine and we'll collect as soon as we can. It will save time all round and we had better not let our cameramen know we are using friendly labour.' Paula gave Sid a wink and a smile.

'Right, I'll do it.'

One thing was puzzling Jacko. 'This is a big house. Do you live here alone?'

'I was born here. And I shall die here if they let me. It might be big but I love it. The kids — well two of them are already married — want me to sell up and leave but I'm staying put as long as I can manage.'

Sid peered through the glasses. 'Hold on, the bloke is coming out.' He pulled back so that Jacko could see.

Jacko had to adjust the focus before he could get a good view and then it was only brief before the man turned away. There was nothing he could do about the man. 'How long does the woman usually stay?'

'Varies. Once or twice I haven't seen her leave. I'll try to get a really good shot of her for you.'

'That's very kind of you. We appreciate your cooperation, Mr Lewis.' Jacko said to Paula, 'We'd better go.' And then to Sid, 'Thanks Mr Lewis. You've been very helpful. We'll be in touch as soon as we hear from you. Meanwhile keep your eyes open for us.'

'You bet. If it means catching burglars, I'm your man.'

Jacko and Paula hurried downstairs and once outside Jacko said in an urgent whisper, 'This time we do bloody well follow her.'

They left the house and crossed the busy road obliquely not even glancing at Clarke's house. Sid Lewis had proved to be a useful ally and might become more useful yet. They returned to the car and Jacko eased his way to the corner, bided his time and then crossed the main road to the intersection opposite. There he did an illegal U-turn and edged the car to the corner from which they had an angle view of the house. If the woman left they were now able to go either way along the main street. The only question was whether the woman would come out at all and if she did where was her car? They just had to hope that she had not come by train.

The woman opened the gate just a few minutes later and walked towards them on the opposite side of the street.

'She dresses well,' observed Paula.

Jacko replied, 'She doesn't belong to the house; she'd never live anywhere so dowdy.'

The smart woman did not go by train but climbed into a Mercedes parked quite close to where Jacko had originally left the Ford. The woman pulled out as Jacko switched on. She approached the intersection opposite to them and turned towards London. Jacko slipped behind her a few cars behind.

'It's usually the other way round with me,' he said to pass the time. 'I'm the one who is followed.'

'I hope you're good at it,' Paula said pointedly. 'Our friend seems as capable as you in traffic.'

Jacko did not bite. He was in his single-minded mode and simply followed, closing up when there was the slightest risk of losing her and falling back again later.

Some time later the Mercedes pulled into a reserved parking slot outside a luxury block of flats in one of those long streets between North and South Kensington. Paula made a note of the address as Jacko drove slowly past. There was nowhere to park and double parking would have caused traffic jams so which flat she lived in if she lived there at all would have to wait. But it was progress.

They returned to Jacko's house in Notting Hill, had a scratch meal which they prepared together, played some music and decided to call it a day.

'Let's hope Sid Lewis does his stuff.'

'Let's see if he already has. He might have caught

the woman as she left. He was already mounting the camera.' Paula used her phone to ring through to pick up messages on her machine. She turned to Jacko with a smile. 'Our Sid's a man of his word. He's taken the snaps and has developed them. They were drying at the time of his call.'

Jacko peered up from his armchair. 'That was quick, wasn't it?'

'It took us a long time to get back in the traffic. What do you think?'

'You want to go back now?' Jacko was weary.

'I'll do the driving if you're not up to it. It would be useful to have them.'

Jacko rose. 'I'll drive. Come on then. Let's go out to dinner together when we get back. And I think we should give Sid something out of expenses for his trouble.'

Paula glanced back as she went to the door; 'You can be caring at times, Jacko. You're full of surprises.'

It was even slower going back and at times painfully slow, having run into the early peak traffic. By the time they did reach Northwood they thought it was not such a good idea. But they were there now. There was now more space where they had parked before and they entered the main road on foot. They crossed over and on their peripheral vision saw no sign of lights from Clarke's house. There were some lights on at Sid Lewis's though so they went down the narrow path and rang the front door bell.

When there was no reply Jacko rang again, and after a fair interval, again, having made allowances for the speed Sid Lewis could manage. Paula stepped back down the path. 'The upstairs lights are still on. Do you think he might have fallen down or something?'

Jacko nodded. 'The stairs were difficult for him. I'm going in.'

He sprung the old-fashioned lock with little trouble, slightly amused at Sid's criticism of Clarke's house having no alarm when he did not have one himself, nor even a security light.

They closed the front door behind them. The only light on downstairs was from the kitchen and Sid was not there. They climbed the stairs, calling as they went.

They found Sid lying prone by the upturned tripod and camera, his head smashed in and his wish to die in the house granted in the most violent form.

8

Paula, standing just behind Jacko drew in her breath. 'Oh, God!'

Jacko stood absolutely still. 'Don't step into the blood,' he warned unnecessarily. He took in the scene. The tripod with the camera still attached had crashed to the floor. It appeared as if it might have fallen by Sid crashing into it as he fell. One side of Sid's head was crushed in, the blood having poured out and the grey hair matted. 'Poor old Sid,' he muttered to himself. 'As if he hadn't enough problems.' He gazed around. 'I don't see any murder weapon, do you?'

'You don't think he just fell?' asked Paula, still standing behind him.

'Take a better look.' He moved carefully aside. 'There's no blood on the camera or tripod except where they are actually touching the pool of blood. If the camera had been brought down with tremendous force it might have done it but there is no sign of that happening. God knows what he was hit with but it's not here.'

Sid's crutches were against the window wall and were too lightweight to have caused such a dreadful wound. The stool had fallen in the opposite direction to the tripod and appeared to be quite clean. Jacko felt Paula's hand on his shoulder.

'Hadn't we better ring for an ambulance?'

'It won't do him much good. Stay where you are.' Jacko carefully moved round so that he was nearer to Sid's head and the ghastly wound. He glanced up at Paula, saw she was deeply affected and then crouched down to stretch out a hand to feel Sid's carotid artery. He stood up. 'Just to make sure,' he said. He stepped back and moved cautiously towards the camera. Again he crouched down. The blood was at the lower end of the tripod and the camera, which he could now see was dented, was clean. Kneeling he leaned forward and managed to fiddle with the film catch and awkwardly released it. The camera was empty. He closed the catch and stood up.

'Was that what they were after?' Paula had barely changed position since entering the room. She was pale but in control.

Jacko shook his head. 'There's something wrong about all this. This isn't a pro job, it's too messy. Too many chances have been taken. He's been hit by some heavy weapon with manic force; he could have fallen anywhere, and the blood could have gushed out anywhere. The murder weapon will be covered in blood and the murderer might well be. It doesn't make sense, Paula.'

Paula moved at last and stepped carefully to one side of the ghastly sight of the battered Sid. Having got over the shock she could now see faint bloodstains on the carpet leading away from the body. 'What exactly are you trying to say, Jacko?'

Jacko stepped away from the windows. 'Well, we know the woman didn't do it because we followed her. The blood is still congealing so it happened not long before we arrived. The man had already left the house although he could have come back. No, this is an amateur job.'

'Burglary then? Sid tried to put up a fight.'

Jacko shook his head. 'A very expensive camera is still here and could easily have been taken. The binoculars are on that chair by the window. It doesn't look as if Sid's pockets have been disturbed and I'm willing to bet that if he had money on him it's still there.' He glanced across at Paula. 'I don't intend to look. This is a police job, not one for North who would have to report it to the police anyway. We've stumbled on something else.'

'What about the missing film?'

Jacko stepped round the body to join her. He took her arm and realised just how tense she was. 'Is it missing? Or waiting to be found? Sid had a darkroom somewhere. Let's look.'

Paula was surprised to see his hand creep round to the back of his waistband and emerge with the Browning. 'Are you expecting trouble?' she asked.

'I don't know. But I want to be prepared for it. I just don't like the feel of this and Sid was trying to help us.'

Paula decided that one gun should be enough and left hers in her bag.

Darkrooms are often in attics or basements. They found an attic and a pole to release the catch. When the lid came down there were tuck-away metal stairs attached to it. A strip light came on in the attic and Jacko pushed the lid back straight away.

'It's not up there,' he said. 'The light comes on automatically which wouldn't do a darkroom any

119

good. And I don't think Sid could have managed to get up there. Let's look for a basement.'

They found one via a door under the stairs which was not at first apparent. The door was locked.

'I bet the key is in Sid's pocket. It's too risky to look.' Jacko produced his bunch of keys.

Paula said, 'Aren't we asking for trouble? Supposing someone comes. We are not in a very strong position.'

Jacko was fiddling with the lock. He turned briefly to Paula. 'Our bloody prints are all over the place. There's no way we can wipe them clean. And mine are on military records; I wasn't called 'Glasshouse' for nothing. So what's an extra risk or two?'

'I never knew you were,' Paula replied in surprise.

Jacko selected another key. 'Well, that's one up to Derek North. I expected him to tell you. He really has wiped the slate clean. But I doubt if my prints have been removed from file.' The lock finally sprung and he gazed down into darkness. There was a switch just inside the door and he guessed that Sid would have had to have used it in order to cope with the narrow stone steps leading down. 'Stay there,' he said. 'I'll call if it's all clear.'

Jacko switched on the light and a forty-watt bulb gave uncertain illumination to the basement steps. He went down using the wall as support and bannisters came into play halfway down. It smelled stale but seemed to be dry. He reached the bottom and saw the heavy curtains hiding the rear of the basement. He stepped forward and pushed the curtain aside.

The developing materials were laid out on a bench at one end of which was an old-fashioned sink. Prints were strung up on a line along the wall. He gazed around for a switch. It was difficult to see in the dark and he did not want to pull the curtains right back for fear of destroying anything. He finally found a switch by touch at the far end of the bench. A red light came on above the developing trays and behind the hanging prints. He peered up at prints now dry and he called up the stairs for Paula to come down.

When she joined him he said, 'There's our woman. The reel wasn't nicked at all. The murder couldn't have been for these.' He began to unpeg several prints, made sure they were dry and pocketed them. Between them they went through other prints but there were none that appeared to be relevant. The man Jacko had seen was not amongst them suggesting that he had not returned to Clarke's house that day.

'Let's go back up.'

Paula went first and at the top Jacko insisted on locking the door again which took him a little time.

'What happens now?' asked Paula.

'I'll ring the police anonymously. It wouldn't be fair to leave Sid lying around to be discovered sometime. Still no sign of the murder weapon but it's no longer our problem. We'd better get back to North and hope we are not seen leaving the house.'

'At least it's dark outside.'

'Yeah. But it's never dark enough for people who want to see.'

They stood on the top step and Jacko locked the front door. They were at least shadowed. As they crossed the road towards their car Jacko observed, 'There was no sign of a forced entry.'

'You haven't left any either.'

'I still don't think it was a professional job.' When they reached the other side he said, 'Why didn't I find a basement in Clarke's house? I'll have to go back in.'

They climbed into the Ford. 'You're pushing your luck,' said Paula, relieved now that they had left the house. She strapped up while Jacko used his digital to report the murder.

'I hope they get the bastard,' Jacko said with feeling after the call. 'Poor old Sid. He didn't have much to live for but what he had he seemed to enjoy. His only link with life seemed to be through those bloody binoculars and now that little pleasure has been taken away.' Jacko steered back towards London.

By now Paula had learned that there was not much chance of serious dialogue while Jacko was driving so she phoned North and told him they were on their way in with some news and then she huddled up and let Jacko get them back as fast as traffic would allow.

★ ★ ★

North looked at the prints. 'Nice looking,' he commented. 'And they're good shots. You say you reported the death to the police?'

'The murder. Of course. Via 999.'

'And you don't think it was tied in with your visit.'

'No. But Paula does not necessarily agree.'

'I think Jacko's probably right,' relented Paula.

'Any evidence of your visit?' North seemed to be very relaxed about the whole thing.

'Our prints are all over the place. We had no idea we were walking into a murder.'

'Well we'll see what happens. I can express an interest in the case without involving you. That way, if you later get caught up in police enquiries it will be easier for me to deal with it. You've done well.'

Jacko said, 'I'll try to break into Clarke's place again tomorrow and we can follow up the mystery woman.'

'I hope you are bearing in mind that if you go back to Northwood, the police will be swarming over the murder house. Be very careful.'

'It's not the police I'm worried about.'

'Meanwhile I'll make some of my own enquiries about the woman.'

Jacko hesitated then said, 'I don't suppose you can get a couple of men into Sid's house to take over where he left off? The camera and binoculars are still there.'

North gave it serious thought. 'It's dodgy,' he said at last. 'They won't let us use the murder room anyway until they've finished with it. And they'll certainly need to pass the binoculars and camera on to forensic. I'll sound it out.'

★ ★ ★

Anne Corrie climbed out of bed and stretched her long supple body. Jeremy Clarke was still asleep so she had a shower and afterwards sat before the triple mirrors of her dressing table to make up. 'Time to get up,' she called out and then watched him rouse himself through the mirror.

When they were both dressed Clarke went down to the lobby to collect his newspaper from the desk and returned upstairs. Anne Corrie had made coffee and toast as she did most mornings. They sat at the kitchen table, amicably quiet as Clarke rustled through the paper until he said, 'Shit!' with such feeling that Anne sat up sharply and put her coffee down.

'Have England lost at cricket again, my darling?' As she saw his expression she realised that his reaction was far from a game of cricket.

'A man has been murdered near the Northwood house.' He was still reading the news item.

Anne was fully attentive then. She sat up straight in a striking pose. 'It's a long road,' she pointed out.

'Number Seventeen,' he answered. He looked across at her then. 'That's close to the house isn't it?'

'Yes. Across the road.' She had noted the run of numbers when she had started calling there. 'Murders do happen.' But this one was too close to home.

Clarke passed the paper across, his features strained. He pointed to the report and waited quietly while she read it. 'Well?' he queried when she had finished.

Anne passed the paper back. 'Well what? It's nothing to do with us.'

'Are you sure?'

'Of course I'm sure. It's a coincidence. And a pity because it means the police will be swarming all over the place for the next few days.'

Clarke folded the newspaper thoughtfully and laid it on the table. 'There was a man in the hotel dining room the other day while I was having breakfast with Mirek. That same day he was murdered on the steps of the National Gallery. Now this old guy has apparently been murdered near to the house. I don't like this sort of coincidence.'

'Neither do I, darling. But that's all they are.'

He did not answer but sat brooding for some time. He had strongly resented the police questioning about Jones just because he had briefly been in the same room as him. It would not look good if the police started calling on all the houses near the murder house in Northwood. After a while he said, 'I wonder if we should keep away from Northwood for a time?'

Anne slowly poured herself more coffee. 'Want a cup?'

He pushed his cup across thinking how calm she kept; he had noticed it before in crisis. But there was crisis and crisis. These were two murders and he did not want publicity of any kind; the department were sensitive after some of the recent scandals.

'Have you noticed anything strange down there recently? Nobody keeping an eye on the place or anything like that?'

She did not want to be too quick with her reply so she gave it some thought. 'No. I'm sure I would have noticed.' She paused then added, 'I've often thought the place should be alarmed. Dammit, it's been burgled three times.'

'That was some time ago. The last time they did that I had already cleaned out anything worth a nickel, so they trashed the place instead. Now it's not even worth trashing. What could there be to hide?'

'What indeed?' The question was quietly challenging.

'You know what I mean. What you see is what you get. I'm far from being the only one along there who is holding out for the development plans to go through. And when they do we're sitting on a fortune.'

'Do you need the extra money?'

He looked surprised. 'I always need the extra money. So do you.' He finished his coffee. 'It might just look strange to some if I suddenly put in an expensive alarm system. A few people well know that I've let the place run down. It's land the developers want, not the bloody house; that will go under the bulldozers.'

'What about security of a different kind? A professional guard to live in. Someone who can deal with intruders. Someone who will scare the living daylights out of them?'

He picked up his cup and saucer, took them over to the dishwasher and then leaned against the machine to gaze down at Anne. 'Use a security firm, you mean?'

'No, I don't mean, Jeremy. That would appear odd as if we have something very special to protect. And we don't want to give that impression do we? I think you know what I mean.'

* * *

Irina Janesky booked into the Savoy Hotel because it would be the last place her husband would try to look for her if he thought she might have come to London. She had nothing against the hotel, it was superb, but irrationally she disliked it because an acquaintance whom she detested used it. As her loving husband would put it, it was the logic of a woman. So neither of them ever booked there until now.

Once settled in she sent for the Yellow Page directory and looked up private investigators. She selected what appeared to be the biggest, rang I.D. Soames, private investigators, and made an appointment for that afternoon.

The offices were off Oxford Street, the size seemed to meet the advertising claims and they were well furnished, clean and well decorated. The staff were friendly and there was an air of purpose about the place. She was shown into an office to meet a Mr Vince Andrews and wasted no time in coming to the point.

Irina laid the photograph of Mirek on the desk, told Andrews where he was at present staying and asked that he be followed wherever he went and she needed a daily report. If possible she wanted the names of the people he met. There was no woman involved as far as she knew. She merely wanted to know his movements.

Vince Andrews was a shrewd, experienced ex-Drug Squad officer. In his early fifties he had plumped a little but there was little he did not know about surveillance. He peered across the desk at a potential client who was obviously not English, nor was the man he was to keep tabs on, but she reeked of money and her address was the Savoy. He would do his best and she put down a substantial deposit. She never even asked the terms.

Meanwhile Derek North had realised he was getting nowhere with the surveillance of Mirek. Using a full team was a costly business and he suspected that Mirek knew he was being watched. If he did then surveillance would get nowhere for Mirek would behave correctly as up to now he had. On the other hand Mirek might have nothing to hide at all. But North clung to his belief that something was afoot that he wanted to know about. He knew he was influenced by the death of young Jones but was too experienced to let it govern natural instincts.

Mirek was an enigma in a variety of ways but North concluded that a different approach was needed. Let Mirek have his head. North was actually more interested in the man the surveillance team had picked out the first day of watching Mirek. That man had disappeared. And that was intriguing in itself. North decided to cut Mirek loose and hope that the other man reappeared at some stage; he would run a spot check. Meanwhile he would put Jacko and Paula on keeping an eye on the woman they had followed. He put out some enquiries.

★ ★ ★

Mirek was increasingly frustrated by the restriction of his movements due to the surveillance of him which the vastly experienced Rudolf Chaznov had noticed so quickly, and, as quickly removed his presence from the scene. It was a pity he had not acted in the same way over the man he had so unnecessarily killed and who was now responsible for the hold-up.

Mirek was himself well versed in spotting observers. The only reason he had not bothered was because he had had Chaznov on his tail. From the day Chaznov had detached himself because of the weight of the surveillance he had taken over the job himself and just accepted that he was being followed. From the start he had assumed it was the police who were following him because of the murder and was beginning to have doubts when he suddenly became aware that he was no longer being followed at all.

At first he could not believe it. He ran through all the routine checks, in and out of restaurants, in and out of taxis, underground trains and so on. He spent much more time than he really had to spare to make sure that he was no longer being followed. To deal with professionals demanded a professional approach. But at the end of an exhausting exercise he was satisfied that he had been cut loose. Which did not mean that they had finished with him.

When he went back to his hotel that evening he decided to tell Chaznov. He still needed someone to keep an eye on him. Too much had been happening these last few days, too many surprises, too many shocks. He had always considered himself strong enough to cope with them but matters had been confusing, all arising from Chaznov's trigger-happy reaction. And now he had been advised that Chaznov's plea for more help had been granted; more men had been assigned to keep an eye on him, to ensure that he came to no harm; he did not know how many and they all reported to Chaznov. There were those abroad who believed that Chaznov had taken the right action that murderous day.

★ ★ ★

'Anne Corrie,' announced North. 'Ex-beauty queen, model, one-time small-time journalist, political researcher. Humble background, toiler, worked her way to the top of her particular tree taking in elocution lessons along the way. Nothing there that can fault her; she worked hard for what she got and she did not like her roots. A hectoring father and a harridan of a mother, the former now dead.'

'Where did you get all that guff?' asked Jacko, impressed.

'The Force is with us.' North enjoyed putting one across on Jacko because it was not easy. 'She has a record.' He smiled. 'Only a tiny one but it put her on the sheet. She was believed to be part of a share bond scam. Three people went to prison, a much younger Anne Corrie was considered an innocent party and was released. What does that tell us about her?'

'That she doesn't mind how she makes her money,' Paula responded dryly.

'Tut tut, Paula. She was found not guilty. That's a cynical view coming from you.'

'Yeah! I just hate women.'

Jacko said, 'It's a fair chance she's on some sort of scam now. She's certainly hiding something in that house that I missed. But what is the connection with all this and Mirek?'

North glanced away from the computer. 'Perhaps none. The common denominator is Jeremy Clarke. He owns the house which she visits and he has had at least one meeting with Mirek. Maybe there are several things wrapped in here.' He gazed from one to the other and became very formal which they both interpreted as bad news. 'I've taken the surveillance team off Mirek. As I said I want you two to watch Anne Corrie and see where that leads. It might go back to Mirek. Let's see.'

'Just one thing,' said Jacko. 'What's the number of her pad and who owns it?'

'Number twenty-two and she does. Which does not mean she pays the bills.'

'Okay, but I still want to go back to Northwood.'

'Well then, just make sure Anne Corrie is tucked up in bed in London and then visit. You can sleep later.' He pushed two prints across the desk. 'That's Jeremy Clarke. You might even bump into him but as yet I can't see in what direction.'

'So you take a whole team off Mirek and expect us two to do the job on the woman.'

'I don't think she's anything like as astute on surveillance matters as Mirek. With your experience coupled with Paula's in Northern Ireland I think you can manage it. Just do what you can.'

★ ★ ★

Rudolf Chaznov was glad to be back on the task of watching Mirek's back. That was his job and he was one-tracked. He now had two compatriots working with him but still preferred to do most work himself. He wanted to be busy. He did not particularly like Mirek; he did not have to. Mirek had a way of speaking down to him, of being superior, and it was difficult for Chaznov to swallow. And the criticism over killing Jones still irritated. But he did recognise from his superiors that Mirek was a very important figure who must be kept safe and that he would do.

It had been agreed with Mirek that at first he would put in a good deal of legwork to enable Chaznov more easily to make sure he was free of a tail. On his first day back on the job he could confirm that the surveillance team had gone. No one was that good that he could not detect them at some stage. He followed Mirek around at a very safe distance and was helped by having an itinerary of his expected movements. The police had taken away the team but one man remained.

Chaznov picked him out quite late because the man was good at his job but once spotted he had no doubts. Mirek was being followed by a single, middle-aged man. Chaznov crossed the street, tucked himself behind the man who was following and wholly concentrating on Mirek, and slipped his hand into the double pocket of his topcoat to loosen his gun. Warnings by Mirek did not register. Chaznov was instinctively doing what he did best. The street was fairly crowded but he could bide his time. History was repeating itself. He kept a hand on the butt of the gun and released the safety catch.

9

Mirek believed it was time for him to use a cab. Chaznov must by now have done his homework and it was time to carry on where they had left off before the murder. He was still worried about Chaznov's attitude to the killing; it was impossible to get through to him. Chaznov was brilliant at what he did but that was the end of it. Chaznov had no capability beyond his own often deadly profession. Boundaries seemed to mean nothing to him; there were merely people who spoke different languages in different countries but until recently he had spent his life in Russia. He could adapt his craft to the needs of the moment because he was so good at what he did, but he could not adapt to a change of environment. There was no change of environment to him. Transport was little different. There were more cars on the streets and it was not so cold but the public transport system was not up to much and the underground stations were pit holes compared with the magnificence of Moscow stations.

Mirek was well aware that Chaznov did not rate the British police after being with the old KGB for so long. The police here were pussy cats. They had no idea it was he who had killed the Englishman. What also worried Mirek was that the masters in Moscow mainly thought the same. They had a contempt of the system here and believed, probably quite rightly, that it worked in their favour. They were ruthless enough to get away with almost anything. It was an attitude born of ignorance and cold-blooded mercilessness that carried them through. Meanwhile he was concerned because Chaznov was not being discouraged in his narrow outlook.

Mirek was highly critical of Chaznov's methods but it was that same expertise that he wanted to harness for his own reasons and it was difficult to know how to broach it. Chaznov could solve a major problem but there were pitfalls that needed to be thought through. And he was not sure that Chaznov would accept orders from him even if accompanied by a substantial payment in sterling.

Because Mirek had got used to casting a watchful eye over the last few days he had not entirely stopped simply because Chaznov was back. Which was why he also spotted the lone tail Chaznov had seen. And then, a little distance back he noticed Chaznov cross the street and fall in behind the man. Mirek had a rush of blood to the head as he thought, my God he's going to do it again.

Mirek almost panicked, then finally kept his head and kept walking more slowly, any thought of catching a cab gone. He took stock. The street was quite busy, but the weather toned down the numbers. He realised he would have to keep to the more busy streets until he had decided what to do just to make things more awkward for Chaznov. Chaznov needed a shock to break some of his overconfidence but it was easier said than done.

Mirek's final destination was a well-known

restaurant behind the Strand and near to Covent Garden. He had arranged a meeting with a British industrialist who was looking for ways of increasing export and who knew the regulations on prohibited goods back to front. If he was not careful he would be late. In the end he decided that the only thing he could do was to go back and warn Chaznov to leave the man alone; that everything was under control. He stopped suddenly, spun round and jogged back knocking the man behind him against the wall, apologising and then hurrying on while Chaznov could only gape and watch.

When Mirek reached the bewildered Chaznov, he said quickly, 'I know he's there. Leave him alone. I want him to see where I am going. Now point a direction out to me quick as if I'm asking the way.'

Chaznov belatedly caught on and pointed back to where Mirek had come. He was thrown off balance and annoyed that Mirek had anticipated him.

★ ★ ★

Jacko and Paula left the premises and stood outside for a while gazing obliquely across the Thames towards the sister unit of the SIS. It was rather late for a meal but not too late.

'I know a place in Soho where we can get a decent meal almost any time. Let's collect the car.'

Paula stayed where she was. 'Have you ever tried asking a girl first? I may not want to eat with you.'

'Don't be daft, of course you do. Don't fight it, Paula.'

'I still want to be asked. Anyway, I'm not dressed for dinner.'

'You are for this place.'

'That's great, you're planning on taking me to a dive. No thanks. Just drive me home and we'll meet in the morning.'

Jacko had been taking her comments with a high degree of humour, but now saw that she was serious. He realised he was taking her for granted. 'Paula, I'm not asking you for a bloody date. We're on a case. We need to discuss it. I thought that having a meal while we did it was not a bad idea. Don't go girlish on me.'

'You can pick me up at seven-thirty in the morning. We'll discuss things then if there's anything to discuss.' She turned on her heel and walked towards the end of the street where she would look for a cab. 'Good night, Jacko,' she called back over her shoulder. 'The little girl needs her sleep.'

He did not attempt to follow or call out; he knew that he had mishandled her and anything more he tried to say would probably make it worse. He cursed himself for being so insensitive. It had been a long day; he put it down to that.

★ ★ ★

Mirek was only marginally late for lunch but apologised to his companion, blamed the weather, had a good meal and completed some delicate business. He was in the restaurant for about two hours. After shaking hands with his contact he went outside to find a cab and spotted Chaznov at the corner of the street. Had it been teeming down Chaznov would still have been there. There was no sign of the other man and that slightly worried Mirek. Chaznov was not beyond asserting himself and going his own way; his kind of protection was total.

Mirek considered asking Chaznov what had happened to the man but that would add to the resentment in Chaznov. It was difficult. Chaznov would expect to give any such detail in his later report. It did not stop Mirek wondering.

★ ★ ★

Irina Janesky was in her room the following morning when Vince Andrews of I.D. Soames detective agency rang her.

'Mrs Janesky, I'm sorry to call you so early. There has been a development; can I pick you up at your hotel in half an hour? It is important.'

Andrews was as good as his word. Almost exactly half an hour later he arrived at the Savoy where she was waiting downstairs for him.

'I have a cab waiting outside,' he explained.

'But where are we going to? This is very mysterious.'

'We're going to the Charing Cross Hospital. It's no distance at all.'

They went out, she stood by the cab and said,

'Before I go anywhere I want some explanation. What is going on?'

Andrews held the door open for her. 'It will be easier to talk in the taxi. It concerns the job we took on for you. I just feel a lot of explanation can be saved by simply seeing what I have to show you.'

She gazed at Andrews, realised it might be quicker to do what he wanted and climbed in. Andrews climbed in beside her and called out to the cabbie, 'Charing Cross Hospital,' just to reassure her that they really were going there.

When they were settled back and on their way Andrews explained. 'After you left us we put a man on straight away, although effectively his duties started this morning. There were, of course, back-up reliefs so that the same man was not always following the man Mirek.'

'That is no more than I would expect.'

'Of course. But our man was found in one of the alleys behind Covent Garden. He had been dumped in a doorway by some waste bins and must have been passed by quite a few people who probably thought he was drunk until someone realised he was badly injured.'

'I'm sorry. Are you saying that his injuries are connected with what he was doing?'

'He was badly beaten up, Mrs Janesky. I think you should know just how badly so that we can decide where we go from here.'

Irina Janesky was silent. She had no wish to see an injured man; she had employed the company not the man. She felt she was being handed a responsibility that was not hers. At the same time she was aware of a deep creeping fear. She could not simply leave the cab without knowing the worst.

Seeing her agonising Andrews said, 'I really am sorry to put you through this. I'm only too aware that you are a new client and we value your custom but we have a problem and this is one way of deciding what happens next.'

They were at the hospital almost before they realised it and pulled into the concourse. Andrews paid off the cabbie and they went inside.

Jon Boyle was in a private side ward and in bad shape. There was not a great deal of him to see. His head was swathed in bandages with a hole for one eye which could be seen as a swollen purple slit, and another for a badly lacerated mouth from which a tube emerged. She shuddered at the sight of him, realising that if what little of him she could see was so bad what horrors did the bandages hide. One arm was suspended on pulleys. A huge basket of fruit was on a side table but they would long be rotten before Boyle ever got near them, if ever he did.

'He was in intensive care for a while,' Andrews explained. 'He's still in a very serious condition and the doctors will not commit themselves as to whether he will ever again be fully functional.'

'What exactly is the point you are trying to make, Mr Andrews? He looks as if he's been in a car crash.'

'That's what it looks like. In fact he was savagely beaten up and dumped.'

'Can you be sure? Why couldn't it have been an accident?'

'Because the doctors say so, Mrs Janesky. It appeared to be pistol whipping. He was beaten up while following your man Mirek. Until he can speak, if ever he does, we can't know precisely what happened, but that's a confirmed medical opinion in a top London Hospital. The hospital authorities are demanding that they call in the police; they have a legal obligation to report such incidents. Fortunately he was carrying the agency ID and they contacted us first. I've managed to stall them but for how long I don't know. I wanted to have a word with you first.'

Irina composed herself as she was so adept at doing. But she was inwardly weeping for this man who had been so brutally attacked. One thing she was sure about; she did not want the police involved for all sorts of reasons. 'I don't know what to say,' she said at last. 'I'm so sorry.' Her words conveyed more emotion than her features which were set in a pose Jacko and Paula would have recognised. 'I will of course pay for all medical treatment.'

'That helps with the bills if he's to have private treatment although we do have a limited insurance cover. But I think you understand that much more than that is involved. I don't see how we can continue to serve you if the job is as risky as this turned out to be.'

Irina tried to keep her gaze away from the figure in the bed. They were silent as a nurse came to adjust a drip and then slipped away again. She said, 'I understand what I am seeing but cannot see how you can be so sure that this happened as a result of him following the man Mirek. He might just as well have been mugged.'

Shrewdly Andrews answered, 'I leave that to your own judgment, Mrs Janesky. But I think you know the answer. Only you know why you wanted Mirek followed.'

'Mirek hasn't the strength to do this. He does not appear to be a physical man.' She indicated the bandaged Boyle. 'This is a big man and if he's an ex-policeman, trained to combat physical attack — '

Andrews gave a look of disbelief. 'He may have had help. We're going round in circles, Mrs Janesky. Why did you want him followed?'

'I am not prepared to answer that.'

'I think there is quite a lot you are not telling me which I need to know.'

'If I had the answers you want I would not have needed to employ you in the first place.'

'Then I have no option but to withdraw our labour. I will have to give your name to the police. In a case like this I won't be able to get away with client confidentiality.'

'I don't want the police to know.'

'Neither do I but it won't be in my hands.'

Irina sank onto a nearby chair. She realised that Andrews was in a fix, that, in the circumstances he had been very reasonable. An honest man who would do the right thing. But for whom? 'Is there any way at all that we can avoid the police or avoid my involvement?'

Andrews looked down at her and recognised her

misery. Then he took another look at Jon Boyle who had been a good friend and whose wife and family he knew. Boyle deserved every help he could get and if that needed the police then that was what he would get. 'There's no way that I can see. I'm sorry. This is largely routine, it's really out of my hands.'

Irina realised too late that she should have used a false name but that created all sorts of difficulties and she had not expected this sort of problem. With hindsight she realised she should have. 'Supposing I offer a substantial sum for this man's family? I've already agreed to underwrite his medical care.'

'I'm not trying to screw you for money.'

'I'm fully aware of that. You give me a figure you think his family might accept as fair.'

Andrews was thoughtful. 'I'll still have to report to the police. And they'll ask some very awkward questions about the delay.' And then, 'Just to keep your name out of it?'

'Yes. I can promise you that my name will do nothing to help the police find out who did this. Mirek did not do it; had you seen him in the flesh you would realise that. I have absolutely no idea who might have helped him if indeed the crime is linked to him. Give me a figure for this man's family and I'll make out a cheque on a London bank now.'

Andrews managed a thin smile. He inclined his head. 'Okay.' He moved away from the bed. 'My concern is for Jon here and his family and it seems also to be yours.' He straightened up and said wearily, 'You seem to be a caring person,

Mrs Janesky. And shrewd. Had you suggested recompensing me your feet would not have touched the ground.'

She did not fully understand the last expression but fully understood the next as he added, 'If I find out that this could have been avoided because of information you should have given us then it won't be just the police who will come looking for you.'

★ ★ ★

Much earlier that same morning Jacko and Paula had met and then separated to keep an eye on the apartments to which they had followed Anne Corrie. It could not be done inside the block and it was bitterly cold in the positions they had taken up, each with a view of the entrance doors. They communicated by radios supplied by North.

An early start had been necessary if they were to be certain of catching sight of Anne Corrie. Their greeting had been brief and formal, due partly to the weather but Paula was still carrying a grudge which Jacko refused to understand.

There were few problems about observation. Paula got herself onto a bus queue but never got on a bus and Jacko always managed to find a doorway to partly shelter from an icy wind. It was a routine with which both were familiar, the hardship of waiting and watching in freezing weather with no timescale on events and often hours of wasted time. But it had been some time since either had worked in this field although experience in dangerous situations dies hard.

The street became increasingly busy as traffic and people built up. Jacko could just make out the bus queue Paula was using as cover and was glad that she was wearing fur boots. He was having trouble resisting stamping his own feet.

They were waiting for Anne Corrie to appear and there was fair activity from the apartments entrance, but it was Jeremy Clarke who came out and turned in Jacko's direction. Jacko was taken by surprise and his immediate reaction was to follow. He spoke into his radio; 'Jeremy Clarke is coming my way. I'm going to follow. You stay put and see if Anne Corrie comes out. If she does, let her go; we're pretty sure where she's going. And stay there. I'll be back.' He switched off before Paula could argue; this was not what they had arranged.

Jacko slipped in behind Clarke but was separated by quite a few people. It was an art form he enjoyed, seeing bits and pieces of a prey through odd gaps created by the movement of others and reflections from whatever source. And it was doing something positive.

Clarke reached the corner. With briefcase in hand it might seem that he was going to his office as he did most mornings. He stood on the corner and Jacko drew back to edge against a wall. A taxi drew in and from the way Clarke reacted it was clear that he had been expecting it although he had given no signal. So it was prearranged. Jacko moved forward quickly as Clarke climbed in.

Jacko knew the odds of finding another cab at peak hour were remote so he ran the last few yards and caught sight of a figure already in the cab. It was Jan Mirek. The cab was already pulling away as he caught sight of the man and then it was gone and he was not so sure. Another cab cruised by slowly and Jacko gave a signal then saw that the flag was down and again he saw a figure in the back. He did not recognise the man but he heeded the feeling that crept over him and the deep warning it carried.

As the cab went past the inspection was mutual, the man in the back leaning forward to get a good look at Jacko. Very briefly their gazes locked, neither giving ground until the cab moved off. When it had gone Jacko was tense. His body was rigid for a while and then he slowly uncoiled, feeling the muscles ease and realising that in spite of the cold he was sweating.

He stood back against the wall knowing that he had seen something important. It would be pointless to try for a cab; the other two were already lost in the traffic. He thought it strange at first that he was lining the two cabs up together but then accepting that he was not. The information he wanted was in the first cab; the danger to him lay in the second. It might explain a lot.

He walked back slowly towards the entrance and checked on his radio with Paula before reaching it. 'I lost him but I'll tell you about it later. What about Anne Corrie?'

'If you hadn't pitched up in the next ten minutes I was going to push off. I'm frozen. She's gone. Left shortly after Clarke, who I saw incidentally but couldn't say so before I was so rudely cut off.'

'I'll see you at the entrance.'

They met outside the raised entrance to the apartments. 'So they're living together,' said Jacko. 'And I think I've seen the man who was so briefly seen by North's team and then disappeared. Not a nice sight.'

'Did he see you?'

'Oh, yes. We won't forget one another.'

'Be careful, Jacko. If Mirek did not kill Jones, he might be the one. Someone did it. It seems that Mirek has a minder. An extremely ruthless one. So what is it about Mirek that needs minding so much?'

He put his arm round her shoulder. 'Will you have dinner with me tonight?'

'You should wait until I've thawed out before asking that. Now what?'

'Now we have a look round Anne Corrie's flat. It might turn out to be Jeremy Clarke's who is obviously not so bloody innocent as North seems to think. You chat up the porter while I slip up the stairs.'

'And then I wait for you in the freezing cold again. I'll come with you.'

They went in arm in arm and chatting animatedly as they crossed the foyer towards the lift. The porter looked up from sorting the mail and Paula gave him a captivating 'good morning'.

'They really did train you in Fourteen Int,' he remarked as they entered the lift.

They stood apart as the lift went up. 'That wasn't training. That was covering your inadequacy. The porter was not really satisfied. He'll be wondering now why he let us go.'

'Well at least he doesn't know which flat we're going to.' And then, 'Why are you being so bitchy? Do you resent me being in control?' Jacko was watching the numbers pass on the indicator; he had pressed for the top floor. He had no idea on which floor Anne Corrie lived but knew the number; they would work their way down the stairs.

'Is that what you are? I don't recall North nominating you.'

The lift stopped and they got out. It was immediately clear from the run of numbers on the board opposite the lift that the flat was below this level. As they went down the stairs Jacko said, 'Is this all because you think I took you for granted? Jesus, Paula, you've suffered worse.' And then with a bitter edge to his voice, 'If you want to take over that's okay by me. You can start by springing the door locks. And you're not using my keys.'

When Paula did not answer Jacko added, 'Maybe we're incompatible. In which case we had better tell North. I thought we were bloody professionals; we don't have to like each other to do the job.'

They reached the next landing down, checked the run of numbers and then went down another flight to find the apartment they wanted.

'Well?' asked Jacko as they stood outside the door which was at the end of the corridor and in view of the lift.

'You do it, boss,' said Paula and stood aside.

It took him time to open the door. There were two modern sophisticated locks. While he worked

148

away the lift was occasionally used and as soon as it whirred they would dash round the corner which led to another apartment, come back and start again.

As Paula watched Jacko work she said, 'I'm sorry. It's really not like me at all to be so touchy. Perhaps I like you too much and am worried for you.'

Jacko sprung the first lock as she spoke. He was on his knees with the locks at eye level. He gazed up at her from fur boots to woollen bobble hat and liked what he saw, although only her face was visible from the padding. 'You're right,' he said. 'I did take you for granted. It won't happen again. And don't worry about me, Paula.' He smiled boyishly. 'After all I've got you to protect me.' He turned back to the lock and sprung it in half the time it had taken him to do the first. They went in and closed the door behind them.

It was not a luxury apartment but no more than a grade down. It was the complete antithesis of the house in Northwood. Everything in it was good quality and seemingly fairly new. It was spotlessly clean and somehow neither Jacko or Paula believed that Anne Corrie would do it herself, which meant a service contract, raising the question of which days the cleaner came.

They searched systematically and with care. There was no pretence about Clarke living here. His framed photograph was in the lounge and another of he and Anne Corrie together at some ski resort was on a modern Japanese upright piano. There was a small study and the desk drawers were unlocked and contained nothing of importance. There were some receipted bills all in Anne Corrie's name and Paula noticed that they had all been paid very promptly. There were no final notices anywhere. At one corner of the desk was a small fax machine.

They made a note of the ex-directory telephone number which had been scribbled on one of the telephone dials. That apart it would seem that the couple had nothing to hide; it was all so innocent but it was home. Bookcases contained a mixture of modern fact and fiction and there was a large newspaper rack. A music centre contained a catholic choice of CDs and tapes from pop to jazz to classics. Music lovers but which of them played the piano?

Almost in disgust Jacko exclaimed, 'This is too bloody good to be true.' He moved over to the TV which had a small cabinet close by full of videos. Examining the spines revealed the same wide taste that they had in music. He said to himself but loud enough for Paula to hear, 'I wonder if what we see is what we get?'

'How do you mean?'

'There are various film and events titles on these videos; supposing it's a cover for something entirely different? Let's take a couple back with us.'

'No.' Paula almost snapped and tidied them up in the cabinet. 'If you are right they would notice and then know there had been a break-in. It's too risky. I think this place is no more than their love nest. There is nothing here to see except their association. The real work is done in Northwood.'

Jacko stood in the middle of the lounge and gazed round. There was no lived-in feel about the place yet he felt Paula was right. There was no reason why Anne Corrie and Jeremy Clarke should not live together except that she had a record, no matter how small; it was the nature of it that caught the attention. Was she still working an old scam? Clarke was in a very useful position for all sorts of information.

'Maybe he doesn't know she uses the Northwood place for whatever reason.'

Paula raised a disbelieving brow, clearly not impressed by that theory and moved over to the windows. With the tip of one finger she pulled back the net just a fraction so that she could look down into the street. She stiffened at once. 'She didn't go to Northwood. She's on her bloody way up. You'll never relock the door in time.'

10

They had tidied as they went and both took a last, desperate look round before heading for the door. As soon as they left the flat Jacko dived across to ring for the lift. He waited until he heard it whirring, swore with relief then said urgently, 'When it arrives jam the bloody doors open with anything you've got. If she uses the stairs we've had it.' He went to work on the locks hoping they would not take so long to lock as to open.

Meanwhile the lift arrived and Paula stepped into the gap to keep the doors open. A woman's voice carried up the shaft and she guessed it was Anne Corrie talking to the porter. She turned to see how Jacko was getting on but he had his back turned and was being outwardly calm about the whole thing.

The lift doors were giving pressure on Paula's back and arms but she could maintain that for some time. The real problem was if Anne Corrie decided to take to the stairs. She heard one of the locks click and as Jacko was still there guessed he had managed only one. It would be useless to try to hurry him but time was running out as the voice below became more irritated. She gazed across at Jacko silently imploring him to hurry and knowing that he could not.

There was a silence from below and then the sound Paula dreaded. She listened intently: there were faint footsteps on the stairs. Paula whispered urgently to Jacko, 'She's on her way up. Leave it.'

Jacko must have heard but chose to ignore her. He continued at the lock while the footsteps became more audible. It was impossible to judge just how near Anne Corrie was but to Paula she was far too near. The only favourable thing was that she was slowing down as she climbed.

At last Jacko stood up, wiped the sweat away from his face as he ran towards Paula. He took the pressure of the lift doors, bundled her in and waited for the doors to close.

Lift doors do not close quickly but never had they been so slow as now while Jacko and Paula willed them to speed up. The sound of Anne Corrie's heavy breathing was quite clear as the doors began to close. Jacko and Paula were opposite sides of the lift and it was Paula who saw a leg appear and then the rest of the body which was being squeezed to a sliver before the doors finally met. Jacko quickly pressed the button for the ground floor.

They leaned back in relief as they slowly decended. 'Did she see you?' Jacko asked.

'I don't think so. I saw a bit of her body but not her face. There was very little gap at the time. Thank God the doors are solid and not grids.'

'Amen to that.' Jacko grinned and Paula responded but they were the reactions to a very close thing. 'It might set her thinking, just the same. There was only one other apartment on that floor as far as I could see.'

As the lift came to a halt they linked arms again and steeled themselves for the second act with the porter. They crossed the hall, chatting amiably and halfway across the porter was about to leave his position behind the counter when Paula delivered, 'The lift doors are playing up. They were sticking but they seem to be all right now.' By the time she had finished they had reached the main doors and were gone before the porter decided what to do.

'We'd better report to North,' said Jacko. 'He should keep an eye on this bloke Clarke which might lead to a back door way to see something of what Mirek is up to.'

The car was in an underground parking lot some distance away and they were walking briskly when Jacko said, 'We have a tail.'

'So you noticed to. He must have been waiting outside the flats so how did he know we were going in?'

'At a guess? Mirek's mobile minder saw me keeping an eye on Clarke. I'm in the street where Clarke lives and he puts two and two together. Smart guy. He radios for back-up. Simple.'

'He's not the man you saw in the taxi?'

'No. But he's from the same part of the world.'

They had been walking separately but he now grabbed Paula's arm. 'It's open warfare now, isn't it? They know about us.'

'But they won't know that we broke in will they?'

'Not unless they examine the locks very closely. But if there is nothing to hide there they may not bother. That puts breaking back into Northwood in a different light. We're in a straitjacket, Paula. We've been on the sidelines and now we're the main players. No wonder North armed us.'

Paula tugged at his arm and offered a smile. 'Never mind, Jacko. You've got me.' But behind her flippancy she was concerned. They had lost all their advantages. 'Come on,' she continued, 'Let's lose fatso.'

★ ★ ★

Irina Janesky considered her options. She was very upset about the private detective finishing up in hospital in such a state. She had been as good as her word and had made financial arrangements about the man's medical care and also about his family. The transactions called for a good deal of money, amounts she could not have dreamed about while in Russia. But Jurich had been generous from the start and had insisted he open up a substantial account for her.

Irina had terrible misgivings about Jurich. Soon he would find out she was not in Cannes and then he would be worried sick and start to look for her. She wanted this matter resolved before he found her. That same evening she went to the hotel where Mirek was staying, took a table in the bar and sat facing the entrance. She ordered a vodka on ice and waited as the place gradually crowded up.

As she sat sipping her drink she realised she was taking a long shot but Mirek was staying here so it was not beyond the bounds of possibility that he would have a drink in the bar. And she was right. Mirek did enter some time later with another man who might have been mid-European and they sat at the bar talking and drinking. As their backs were turned to her she could not see what they were drinking so she changed her position to view them better.

The bar was about a third full so table space was still available but some preferred sitting at the bar. Irina ordered another drink and cursed the angle of her observation; the change of position had not helped much. She had missed dinner and imagined that most of those in the bar were enjoying after-dinner drinks. She ordered some bar snacks. They had no sooner arrived than Mirek and his colleague showed signs of leaving, finishing their drinks and easing off their stools. Without hesitation Irina left the table and hurried to the exit.

She waited outside the doors with her back to them. Yet she timed her move to perfection. As Mirek and his friend came out, still talking, she suddenly turned and bumped straight into Mirek. Instinctively he grasped her by the arms to steady her and said in English, 'I beg your pardon, madam.'

Their eyes met and there was not a flicker between them. Just for a moment they formed a tableau, no movement, no speech. And then Mirek pushed her gently away and walked on. Irina stood where she was, rooted in shock and thinking this man's eyes are dark grey, Vadim Bykov's were brown. It was the other man who turned back to her and asked if she was all right and it pulled her out of her trance. She nodded her head, pulled herself together and strode back into the bar.

She took the seat she had vacated and started to chew the bar snacks which were still there. She then swallowed her drink in one slow movement and put down the glass with an unsteady hand. She was now not sure that it had been a good idea to come. She sat for some time while she tried to straighten her mind and analyse what she had seen and to look back nine years. She could not have been closer to him which was what she had wanted but she was not sure that it had solved anything. There were differences but none that could not have been arranged and it was this that confused her. He had reacted as any man might have done in the circumstances but still she was not satisfied.

Irina reflected that her marriage to Bykov had never been really successful after the first two years. And after that they often slept under separate roofs and eventually drifted apart to a degree when they hardly saw each other. Bykov was up to his neck in politics and certainly knew how to make progress. It was in his nature to make contact with the British or others she did not know about. He could not help himself, always had to prove how clever he was. And he was clever to have survived betrayal for so long. Like so many of his kind he became overconfident and those searching for the leaks had narrowed the field. But he had carried an awful lot of knowledge and knew a great many important people in many countries. Without a doubt the KGB, even during their last days, would have tortured him for that information before killing him. His execution was well recorded and she had been offered a copy of an official video showing it taking place. Irina had declined; the offer was simply to remind her not to step out of line.

Irina called for one more drink, sipped it slowly and tried to shake the shock from her system so that she could think more clearly. Why was this happening? She was happy with Jurich, had made many friends in Paris, and now she was more confused than ever. She had flown to London to settle the problem and had finished up totally bemused but insistent little messages were prodding away at her subconscious. There was a hard core gnawing away inside her which she tried to but could not ignore. Eventually she left the bar and asked the concierge to find her a taxi. When she was in the back of the cab she called out to the driver, 'Do you know where I can get a gun?'

The cabbie braked so hard it flung her forward. He pulled into the side. 'What did you say?' He pulled the screen back.

'Can you tell me where I can find a gun?'

'No, I can't. I don't want any guns in my cab. You want to drive on?'

'I am not asking you to supply one but to tell me where I can get one. I will pay very well for the information.'

The cabbie gave it some thought. 'You don't intend to kill anyone do you?'

'I want it for my protection. And urgently. Someone is trying to kill me.' She realised the strong possibility of the truth of that before the doubt reasserted.

'If someone is trying to kill you you should go to the police.'

'You must take my word that the police could not help me with this. It would be impossible to explain to them. Just point me in the right direction.'

'How much money are you talking about?'

'Whatever you think the information is worth. In cash.'

The driver sat thinking with his arms over the steering wheel. It had been a long tiring day. He blew out his cheeks. 'Well, I can't personally help you but I might know a man who can.'

★ ★ ★

North listened to what they had to report and said nothing for some time. Jacko and Paula were sitting opposite him and he thought they looked tired. They needed help he was reluctant to give; at this stage anyway. It was not that he did not want to help them but as things stood they were still working as outsiders, a situation which suited him greatly just now.

After a while North admitted, 'It does make another break-in to Northwood more difficult. Do you think you can handle it?' It was North's way of asking them to go ahead.

'How far did you get with asking the police to use Sid Lewis's place as an OP?' asked Jacko.

'I haven't asked them. I don't want to declare an interest. Not at the moment, anyway.'

'So, what happens when they find our prints all over the place?'

'There are probably thousands of prints in the house. Hasn't he got grown-up children and grandchildren? You were careful how you handled the gear near to him, the tripod and binoculars and stuff; that's where they'll concentrate. I've told you that I'll cover for you if anything arises that threatens you.'

'At which time you will be involved,' said Paula sweetly. 'Do you think I can have more money up front? I haven't Jacko's resources and I would like to spend some while I can.'

'Come, Paula, it isn't that bad.'

'So why arm us?'

'Because you know how to use them. More importantly, you know when not to use them. Just a precaution, no more. Look, I'll make some more discreet enquiries about Jeremy Clarke. There's no reason why he should not be seeing Mirek given the fact that it's part of his job to encourage sales abroad and it seems that Mirek is the kind of astute businessman that his country needs right now.'

'Wouldn't it be interesting to find out which British businessmen Clarke is contacting? And is he drawing them and Mirek together for commercial deals? And what would those deals be?'

North sighed wearily. 'Don't try to do my job for me, Jacko. It's all under control. But I don't want Clarke to get wind of it.'

'Well, he must have now, mustn't he? Mirek's gorilla saw me and another followed Paula and me and Mirek must have been warned and in turn would have warned Clarke. It's all out in the open.'

'If it was all out in the open it would be over and we'd know exactly where we stood. Have you seen any sign of Mirek doing a runner? He still has deals to complete. He feels safe in spite of what he sees going on. He probably thinks he has police surveillance following the murder which I am increasingly sure he did not commit. If he doesn't feel safe but is still operating then there must be an enormous force of persuasion behind him. Perhaps he's expendable.'

Jacko and Paula exchanged weary glances. 'We're going out for a meal,' announced Paula to show that she had forgiven Jacko. As she rose she added, 'It would be nice to know just exactly what deals Mirek and Clarke are pulling.'

North shrugged. 'I can only say that his department are content with what he's doing.'

'The part they know about,' Jacko rose to join Paula. 'We'll let you know what we decide to do about Northwood. We might need something more than pistols. Listening gear would be helpful.' They reached the door and Jacko turned round and said, 'It's bloody funny, isn't it? This was all about checking on a bloke who seemed to have returned from the dead. Is that still on the agenda or are we doing something else?'

North leaned back in his chair and clasped his hands behind his head. 'Oh, it's still all about is he or isn't he? I think that holds the clue to the whole thing. Answer that and you've answered most of the rest.'

When they had gone North rang Detective Chief Superintendent Matthew Simes and invited him over. Half an hour later they were drinking in North's office where Simes found a larger chair

161

had been installed for him and a drink already poured out.

'I'd have come over to the Yard,' said North, 'but thought you might like the change.'

'Bullshit,' said Simes without rancour. 'Have you anything to tell me?'

'About young Jonesy's murder?'

'No. Whether Villa are going to knock the shit out of Arsenal on Saturday. I hope this isn't a wasted journey; my blokes are trying to solve a murder.'

'Do you think Mirek did it?'

'No.' Simes tasted his whisky. 'Why do you always give me the cheap stuff? If I was Bulman you'd bring out the single malt.'

'You were friends, you two? Served together?'

'No, I don't think Mirek did it,' Simes repeated, ignoring North's unwanted question. 'But it would be no surprise to me to find he is involved in it. I think it was a very professional job. I still want to know of your interest in Mirek.'

North shrugged. 'I told you before. We thought he was someone else but as that man was shot dead he can't be, can he?'

'But you're still interested in him or you wouldn't have asked me over. Are you having him followed?'

'I can promise you that no one in the Security Service is following him. And my interest is that one of my men has been killed.'

'Why is it that I don't believe you?'

'Because there was a time when we might have spoken to you with forked tongue.' North tapped his chest. 'Those days are long gone. It's on public record that we now cooperate. My officers are not following Mirek. I just hoped that you had turned something up that might help us place him. What about Jeremy Clarke?'

'He's doing what he's supposed to be doing for Queen and country. Getting some business in and making the right introductions. If you want to go beyond that and without some evidence, it's really a job for Special Branch if you think something funny is going on. Do you?'

'I'd forget the whole bloody thing if it wasn't for Jonesy's murder. That pops up every time I weaken. I was hoping that you might have produced some witnesses.'

'We're dealing with a guy who knows how to avoid witnesses. I think he's too good for one of our lags. I think he's foreign labour which brings us back to Mirek. Is that what you wanted to hear? If it is, with all due respect you can come over to my place next time because I haven't the time. We could have done that over the phone.' Simes stood up, a powerful, forbidding figure. 'You were hoping for something else weren't you? There's something else you think I know. Well, if there is you'd better damn' well tell me.'

★ ★ ★

Using a digital telephone was safe but as Mirek had found out before with someone like Chaznov he really needed to see him face to face with the hope of picking up some sort of reaction. They couldn't keep meeting in his hotel room, Chaznov

163

was not a man who could be missed in the lobby. So he used the digital to arrange a meeting and used the taxi ploy as he had done with Clarke but now in reverse.

With no commercial dinner lined up for the evening he ate in the hotel and afterwards went to his room to get his topcoat. He then stood on top of the hotel steps under a cupped awning which protected him from the icy rain. Cabs came and went and then one came in and flashed its lights and Mirek went to meet it. He pulled open the door and climbed in next to Chaznov who sat well back in the shadows and would be difficult to see from the street.

They sat in each corner as if to get as far away from each other as possible. They spoke in Russian. Mirek said, 'Did you tell the driver to flash his lights or is he one of yours?'

Chaznov often believed Mirek asked stupid questions. They rankled each other and it was as well that although they worked together they were separated in so doing. He decided not to answer and that way believed he could avoid being rude, not understanding that a snub was worse. These two men would never get on but they needed each other, now as never before.

Chaznov brought Mirek up to date in detail about the man he had seen chasing after Clarke's taxi and later the same man and a young woman leaving the apartment block where Clarke lived with his lover.

Mirek found it much more disturbing news than

164

a police surveillance. 'Where did they go?' he asked quite reasonably.

For once Chaznov did not like his own reply. 'He lost them.'

Mirek would normally have been delighted at failure from Chaznov's department but this was too serious. 'He lost them,' he echoed. 'Or did they lose him?'

'What difference does it make? He lost the trail.'

'If you don't know the difference what are you doing in the job?' Before Chaznov could show his anger Mirek continued, 'If they lost him they knew he was there, wouldn't you say? Do you think they are the police? Security?' He hoped not the latter because that put an entirely different complexion on the reasons for following. In prospect it meant much more menace and would not be directly about the murder.

'I don't know. I have not seen the woman and I didn't recognise the man. I don't think the man is police.'

'You must have a reason.'

Chaznov was struggling during this meeting and was not used to it. But he knew the answer was important. 'He . . . ' he struggled for a description, 'was different. Maybe a hard man.'

'Not the sort you would find easy to kill on the streets?' Mirek could not resist the jibe; it was unique in his experience to get the redoubtable Chaznov on the run.

Chaznov changed position. 'If that was what was needed to protect you then that is what I would do.

No matter how difficult.' He turned more fully so that he was facing Mirek. 'You had better bear in mind that I discovered your man Clarke has a tail who has a woman accomplice, that his apartment has probably been turned over and all you can do is to nit-pick.'

'And you had better bear in mind that all this is a result of you being stupidly over-zealous. Without the killing none of this would be happening. Is there any way you can pick up the trail of this man for whom you seem to show a reluctant respect? And to find out just who the hell he is working for? It could be the opposition.'

'I don't think so. I'm sure we'll meet again. I'll keep you informed.'

The taxi did one more circuit and then pulled up outside the hotel. Mirek climbed out to leave Chaznov burning with resentment and would not be happy until he was once more on top of his job.

Across the street Irina stood behind a row of cars, the rain cascading off their tops like a floodlight wash. She was well covered against the weather and a hood protected her head. The interior light of the cab came on as Mirek climbed out and dashed up the steps for the protection of the canopy. Before the cab door closed she saw a man lean forward to pull it and she caught a glimpse of Chaznov before the interior light went out. Irina did not recognise Chaznov but she did the type and she shuddered. She had seen so many like him when in Moscow and particularly at the time when her husband Vadim Bykov had been arrested. The old KGB no longer existed in the way it had but its old members did. They were still around doing what they did best. She shuddered again and felt for the piece of paper in her raincoat pocket which contained the name and address of a possible gun supplier.

Sight of Chaznov frightened her a good deal more than that of Mirek. None of what she had seen made sense. It was like putting the clock right back but how could it be happening? She was afraid and for the first time, doubtful about what she was doing. She had seen one man in the cab but how many more were there? Where they went deep trouble went with them.

Irina strengthened her resolve because she was a very strong lady. She subjugated the warnings which were now screaming in her head but she tried to shut them out as she searched for a cab to take her to the now crumpled address in her pocket. She was scared of what she was doing but could not control her own actions, which increasingly she saw as self-destructive.

11

Van Creterre arrived at London Heathrow the following morning from Brussels, took up modest accommodation in Bloomsbury he had already arranged and unpacked his single case, went to a nearby restaurant and had lunch after which he arranged a car hire and then caught a Metropolitan train to Northwood.

Van Creterre knew London well and had been to the house in Northwood before. He was well used to driving in Britain but the train services to Northwood were good and he wanted no fuss or parking tickets while over here. He was a stocky man who showed little sign of humour, dressed well, too well for the hotel in which he stayed but was not a man to make compromises about clothes. His hair was thin on top and he wore rimless glasses, the expression in the eyes behind them uncompromising. He was an arms expert.

★ ★ ★

Nick Harley also flew into Heathrow that day. But he was a little later and had come further, from Massachusetts. He was taller and burlier than the Belgian who had arrived earlier. He appeared to be fit for a man in his fifties and indeed worked out regularly. Unlike Van Creterre he did have a sense of humour but it was rather on the sick and

168

sadistic side. In his rough cast way he was quite good looking. Once through customs he called a cab and went to the Savoy Hotel where Irina Janesky was still staying and was at this moment sitting in her room examining a well-used Colt semi-automatic pistol with a silencer attachment.

Harley ate in the Savoy and then he too went to Northwood taking a train as Van Creterre had done, but to his distaste. Harley had money and liked to benefit from it. He would only compromise if it enabled him to make more. He was an arms expert.

★ ★ ★

Fahid Omar Jahilla left his well secluded house in Surrey during the early morning of the same day. He was an Iraqi subject and close to the seat of power although his name was nowhere to be seen in the hierarchy of Iraq. He was a very wealthy man but led a low profile life and much of his time was spent outside Britain. He had a weakness for women but could buy them in surreptitiously without causing a stir. When doing business he could be single-minded to the exclusion of all else.

The reason Jahilla did not arouse attention was because he carried an Egyptian passport which had been carefully doctored to carry his photograph and details. He was well known in the City of London and an anglophile. No one it seemed, had a bad word to say about him.

Because Northwood was an awkward journey from his part of Surrey he decided to drive to it instead of having to change trains. Normally he would take the Bentley but today he drove a Ford with power steering and automatic gears because he had no wish to draw attention. He realised he was stepping out of character and hoped nothing would be go wrong, but great things were expected of him in Baghdad. He was an arms expert.

★ ★ ★

Jeremy Clarke had given notice at the DTI that he would be away during the afternoon and had made arrangements to meet two British exporters who he believed he could help and thus help the country. He had no need to leave this information as he was largely answerable only to himself and it was perhaps a sign of his growing insecurity that he did. By now he had been warned that Anne Corrie's apartment had probably been searched. The search did not concern him, there was nothing sinister to find, but the reason for it was worrying. He considered pulling out but soon realised that there were too many powerful forces that could prevent him, even terminally. The prize was high so he decided to soldier on and call for some help. There would always be risk when the stakes were high, he recognised that, but he was not sure what was actually happening.

★ ★ ★

Meanwhile Jacko and Paula were making plans to break in to Northwood and to search for the same sort of cellar Sid Lewis's house had under the stairs but which was not at all evident in Jeremy Clarke's house. The best North had been willing to come up with in audio surveillance were a couple of directional mikes which could pick up conversation from the vibrations on windows. Jacko had wanted much more than that, but acknowledged that some of the more sophisticated gear was heavy and bulky to carry around; as it was the batteries for the equipment he had were heavy enough. Jacko and Paula really needed a team to help out but North had refused that and they both knew why.

They had gone to Jacko's house to talk it over and for the first time Jacko was having real qualms, not about himself but Paula. It was easy to forget when working together, that Paula was a woman. She neither asked for nor expected any special privileges because of her sex but Jacko had an old-fashioned streak which, when the chips were down, wanted to protect women especially in very dangerous situations. He showed none of this to her, the opposite in fact, but he was not happy about her safety. It hadn't helped that before they had gone out to dinner the previous evening she had insisted on changing first so they had gone to her place and she had dressed in something stunning which made her both lovely and vulnerable. Up to that point they had been wearing working clothes that suited the rough and tumble of the job and he had not seen her dressed like that before. It was difficult to equate with the Browning she carried in her bag and which she undoubtedly knew how to use. Now they were dressed for work again but he could not erase the much softer image he had seen the previous night. He did not convey his thoughts and if he did she gave no sign of noticing. As the visits seemed to take place during the day it seemed to be logical to break in at night.

Paula said, 'Are you happy about this?'

'No. They know we're on the scene and that will make it difficult.'

'That's an understatement. They'll be waiting for us.'

'Possibly. If we find it too dodgy we won't go in. Is that okay?'

'It's a bit negative. I think we should make North give us help.'

'We can't make North do anything. We can opt out if you're too worried.'

'I'm not worried.' Paula swung her legs over the arm of her chair. 'Yes I am. And scared too. I'd have been happier if we hadn't been seen.' After some thought she added, 'You think Clarke and Mirek are on some sort of fiddle, don't you? It could be kosher.'

'And Jonesy could have shot himself through the heart.'

'So why isn't North taking an official line?'

'I don't know what's in his mind but can guess. Over recent years there have been so many scandals regarding public figures, from women, to corruption, failing to declare business interests, suspected insider trading, the SIS disgracefully willing to let industrialists they have used, and who have helped them, go to jail rather than reveal their interest and so on. With an election imminent everyone is waiting for the next bomb to go off. They are all walking tightropes.'

Jacko threw a packet of crisps over to Paula and opened one himself. 'North is as straight as intelligence men go but in fact there is no such thing. Personal feelings will always be sacrificed for the sake of national security and people along with them. Which is why he's using us; he can publicly deny that the Security Service are involved.'

'So why are we stupid enough to help him?'

Jacko studied a large crisp before answering. 'Because we are stupid enough to like what we do. We can't help ourselves but there is the added motive of actually caring. We know something dodgy is going on and it's probably much bigger than we think. It's impossible for us to walk away from. We have to know, damn it.' He thoughtfully crunched away at the crisps then examined the inside of the packet. 'If we opted out we'd spend the rest of our lives wondering what we missed, and if something bad happened we'd blame ourselves because that's the way we are and are cursed by it.'

'That was quite a speech, Jacko. I thought you were all muscle and no brain.'

'You're not wrong, Paula, or I wouldn't be here discussing it. I know my reasons but what of you? I've never heard you mention a husband or boyfriend,' he paused, 'or even a girlfriend.'

Paula appeared amused. 'I'm straight in case you are wondering. I've never come out because I've never been in. I've never had a husband but I have been close. And currently I have no boyfriend. I think they find me difficult to live with.'

'Amen to that. I've had the same problem.'

'So you think we do the dirty work and if we come up with something really positive North will take over officially and get all the credit.'

Jacko crumpled the crisp packet. He gave a self-satisfied grin and uncharacteristically loftily pronounced, 'Aye, it has ever been thus.'

Paula threw a cushion at him; they were getting to know each other but this only worried Jacko more. 'Why don't you opt out, Paula? There's a lot of trouble ahead.'

Paula still had her legs over the arm of the chair but now swung herself upright. 'That's sweet, Jacko. You really care.'

'Stop taking the piss. He had no right to involve you.'

'I've played my part. Besides I promised North I would protect you. Neither one of us can do it alone.'

Jacko nodded slowly. He glanced up and threw the empty crisp packet at the waste-paper basket and missed; he got up and put it in. 'Okay. But I'd think no worse of you if you did opt out. I've had some experience in these situations.' Before she could say anything he stood over her and jabbed a finger, 'And don't say so have you because this is different from Northern Ireland.'

'Thanks, Jacko. I really am touched by your concern.' She held out a hand for him to pull her to her feet. 'But my experience did not stop with Northern Ireland.'

They were standing close together then and

suddenly and naturally embraced. They held each other quite tightly and did not move for some time. They did not kiss but when they gently pulled apart it seemed that they were both slightly bewildered at what they had done. Jacko bent forward and kissed Paula on the forehead before saying, 'I don't want anything to happen to you.'

'Nor do I, Jacko.' Paula lightly patted his face.

'I've seen Bulman caught up in these situations. I've known him to resign from them. He's a man who tells North exactly what he thinks. But the strange thing is he is always there at the end. He just had to have the answers and most times he found them. Not the last time, though. I think that's why he took a holiday, reckoned his batteries needed recharging.'

Paula went into the hall for her coat and when she returned she said, 'I never met him. I have heard whispers about him, though. Is he your guru?'

Jacko laughed. 'We're as different as chalk and cheese. He couldn't hit a wall at five paces. He's as devious as North and often better at it. But where it really matters he's as straight as they come. And he's always there for you.'

'He obviously means a lot to you.'

Jacko crossed over and lightly placed an arm round her shoulders. 'I wish he was here now. I could use his advice.' He helped her on with her coat.

Paula asked, 'What's the ETA?'

'I'll pick you up about ten. It's no use going too early. I'll bring a couple of hoods with me unless you have one. You'll be wearing heavy clothing anyway because of the cold and there will probably be some hanging about. With gloves and being well covered the heat sensors on the security lights will probably fail to pick us up as long as we keep our faces turned away. The danger will be stray cats and dogs. Come on, I'll run you back.'

When they were in his car Paula asked, 'Do you think this man Mirek is Vadim Bykov?'

'That's what everybody is trying to find out. I really don't know.'

'But how could he be?'

Jacko smiled to himself in the darkness of the car. 'Easily,' he replied without giving an explanation. 'But that doesn't mean to say that he is. I'd give a lot to know what Irina Janesky is thinking. I wonder if she's sure one way or the other?'

'And if she's not how can she live without knowing under a cloud of possible bigamy?'

'She's a strong woman. She'd do something about it. Leave nothing to chance whether or not she's sure. She won't want her life messed up again, not with what she's got.' Suddenly he braked and cursed. 'I'm talking too much. I must concentrate.'

★ ★ ★

The news that North had been waiting for came through just as he was leaving the office that evening. Had it not been for a mistake at passport control at Heathrow airport he would have known much sooner. To trace her through the hotels had

176

taken longer. But now he knew. Irina Janesky was staying at the Savoy Hotel. Why not the Ritz which she had shown she preferred?

North went back to his desk to decide what to do. To have her followed was an obvious choice but while she might not detect a tail the man North had no doubt she had come to see or at least view again, might well do. He believed she was here to fully make up her mind and decided to give her a loose rein and to see what happened. He could make sure he was advised should she leave the Savoy. He smiled to himself feeling vindicated for believing she would return.

★ ★ ★

Jacko called for Paula at ten p.m. as arranged but once there considered it too early. He reasoned that they would reach Northwood before eleven if they left then and that it might be still too active traffic-wise. So he went in and had a coffee and gave her a woollen hood with two holes for the eyes and which came well down the neck. The battery and the directional mike were in the boot of the car.

By the time they left they were both hyped up into a silence that went with covert operations. Neither knew what to expect but realised that this trip would be very different from the last. They also had to bear in mind that there might well be a police presence outside Sid Lewis's place across from Clarke's house. One police officer outside the premises was enough to make things awkward.

Jacko had tried to get North to contact the police to see if they had left someone on duty. But North did not want to show an interest which might make the police wonder why he wanted to know and which might get back to Detective Chief Superintendent Simes. North's only advice was if in doubt abort.

Jacko kept well within the speed limit on the way to Northwood. The rain had stopped but it was freezing up and the streets were becoming icy. They did not talk on the way. Jacko knew that he could not park outside the house as he had done with the Ferrari just in case there was a policeman at Sid Lewis's.

In the event he parked in a small side street near the railway station and where other cars were parked. It left them some distance to walk and the battery was heavy. Before off-loading Jacko did a quick recce to find if there was a back way in via the long garden at the rear of the house. There was but it was too difficult to try and meant entering the property behind Clarke's, access to which was in a parallel street. Getting the equipment over walls and beyond other people's property would be extremely difficult. It would have to be via the front gate and open to view.

After the recce they returned to the car to discuss strategy. It was decided that Paula would walk past Sid Lewis's house and try to spot a police presence. Jacko offered to drive her to the corner but she shook her head and left the car to walk briskly up to the junction. It was now past midnight, traffic was light, pedestrians scarce, and the street lights cast orange balloons on each side of the street.

Paula crossed the road as soon as she reached the junction. She walked with head down as would be expected in this weather and kept a steady pace. As she neared Sid Lewis's house the temptation was to slow down but she kept going, scanned Clarke's house across the street to see that it was in darkness and continued on. When she reached Sid Lewis's house she peered up the narrow stretch of drive and took in what she could. She continued on, crossed the street further up and turned right at the next junction. When she was round the corner she quickened her pace noticeably and turned right again at the bottom onto a street which would lead her straight back to where they had parked.

To the waiting Jacko she was ages. When she eventually climbed in beside him he said, 'Do you want the heater on for a bit, you look frozen.'

Paula beat her gloved hands. 'No. We might attract attention with the engine running. There was no one there; not that I could see. The police tape is across the driveway and I think I saw it across the front door. They've sealed up. Unless they were skiving there was no one on duty but if the security lights do go on at Clarke's they'll create an oasis of light which could not be missed by anyone around.'

Jacko gave it some thought. 'They are too high up the building to tape off the sensor. I just think the back way is too far and too awkward. It would be all right without the gear.'

'Do we really need the gear? I mean the house is in darkness. If anyone is there they are asleep. If we expected to pick up conversation we should

179

have come much earlier.'

Jacko nodded slowly. 'Our main aim is still the same: to find a cellar like the one at Sid Lewis's. There seem to be too many visitors to do that by day. But the gear will pick up movement as well as dialogue.'

'At this time of night I don't think it matters. And we can't lug it inside the house; we'll hear any movement ourselves.'

Jacko sat back. 'This makes me look like a charlie. We should have done a separate recce by night but I didn't want to expose ourselves given the number of bods around. Okay. We'll do it your way.'

Paula touched his arm. 'There's nothing wrong with a little improvisation. How many capers go exactly to plan? North hasn't helped by leaving it all to us. It's now or never.'

They climbed out. Jacko locked the car. There was a faint glow of lights from the station but the street lights seemed subdued in the heavy weather. The street was empty as they crossed it and the lights fell behind them as they rounded a corner to find the row of houses that backed on to Clarke's. They walked along the deserted street counting the houses as they went. With one exception they were all in darkness except for the odd night light casting reflections on bedroom windows.

'I reckon this is it,' Jacko stated. The row was very similar to the street which ran parallel to it where Clarke's house was.

Paula agreed that they were outside the house which backed on to Clarke's. She noticed Jacko's hand creep round to his hip where he kept his Browning under his top coat. He now removed the gun and placed it in his topcoat pocket. Paula already had easy access to hers. 'Let's hope to God we don't need them,' said Jacko. 'We'll have the whole bloody neighbourhood down on us.'

They put on their hoods, opened the gate of the house and walked down its gritty drive. They followed the path along the front of the house to a small garage with a narrow gap between it and the house. They went through the gap, heard a dog bark inside the house, kept still. Someone called out to the dog but the dog was not fooled so Jacko and Paula hastened down the garden away from the acute smell and hearing of the astute animal. There was no action from the house and they put distance between it and themselves.

It was so dark that they stumbled along, crossed some sort of flower bed and almost crashed into a small greenhouse at the bottom of the garden, but were saved by a slight reflection on the glass. They reached a sturdily built fence. Jacko cupped his hands for Paula to step into so she could rise and peer over.

A decorative bar ran the length of the fence and enabled her to straddle it and to peer down. She lowered herself down on the other side without making a sound.

'Okay.' Her voice softly trailed over the fence and Jacko just heard it.

Jacko had to jump for the top and made more noise than he wanted but Paula was in no position to help him until he was lowering himself down

181

the other side. They waited by the fence for a minute or two but nothing stirred and the only sound was of a car moving down the wet street beyond Clarke's house. By now their night sight was fairly well adjusted.

They could see the dim shape of Clarke's house in the distance against a vaguely lighter sky. The rain was still holding off although there was a threat of it in the air as they began the long walk up the garden.

The gardens were disproportionately long to the width. The fences on both sides were in good condition and fronted by rows of Leylandii in need of trimming but the dark shadows cast by them added to the general gloom and helped their cover. They kept to the centre hoping to avoid garden beds but the garden had been so neglected that it was full of pitfalls and at times they had to pick their way carefully. As they drew nearer the house they kept their heads lowered and at times clung to each other for balance. Whispered expletives were virtually inaudible.

When they were near enough Jacko whispered, 'Wait here. I'll just make sure we've got the right place.' He went forward on his own and was soon lost against the backcloth of the house. Paula squatted while she waited. This would be a good test to see if they were adequately clothed to fool the lights. None came on, Jacko had disappeared completely and she could hear no movement at all. He was so long she began to worry. Then he suddenly rose in front of her so unexpectedly that she reached for her gun. 'Give me a bloody signal next time,' she said in relief.

'It's the right house,' he said, his head close to hers. 'I think the back might be easier to break into than the front. And fewer eyes to see. Ready?'

Paula nodded in the dark. 'This time I'm with you all the way. Let's do it.'

She had no sooner spoken than there was the sound of racing cars and a police siren wailed in the street. The cars were travelling at speed and then there was the squealing of brakes as they slowed by the house, blue flashers finding the gaps between the buildings and creating a pulsating halo eerily silhouetting the building. Jacko and Paula froze and slowly sank to the ground. A light came on in a front room of the house next to Clarke's but they could only see its reflection from the street. Should they stay or run back. 'Wait,' said Jacko tersely. 'Wait.'

12

It was difficult for them to know exactly what was going on. Car doors slammed, voices were raised, but it was all happening in front of the houses. More house lights came on along the street but nothing happened in Clarke's; it remained in darkness.

Jacko and Paula were still crouched low and with the damp and the cold cramp was setting in where Jacko had once received shrapnel in the leg. He bore the pain and remained still puzzled why nothing had happened in Clarke's house when the whole neighbourhood had been aroused by the racket.

After a while it began to quieten down at the front. The sirens had stopped and the blue flashers went off one at a time but there was still the sound of voices and briefly, the sound of struggling. A voice called out, 'It's all over. Sorry to wake you.' Presumably a policeman reassuring anyone who was brave enough to face the biting cold by leaning out of a window.

The cars drove off one at a time and the house lights went out more rapidly as things returned to normal. 'A car thief or joy rider,' said Jacko. 'It's sod's law that they caught him here.'

Paula said, 'There can't be anyone in the house. It was the only place to show no sign.'

'I don't believe it,' Jacko responded. 'With the

way things have been going they are bound to have someone there unless they've stopped using it.'

'Low profile then. Didn't want to show a presence.'

'That's more like it. But if anyone's there they'll be awake. We'll have to leave it a little longer.'

They waited another half hour by which time the whole street had returned to a silent darkness. And then they went forward towards the house. They moved in short stages with Jacko trying to locate the security light so that they might move wide of it.

Just before locating the house Jacko found the light. He grabbed Paula's arm and said, 'It's right over our heads and our gear hasn't saved us. It must be a bloody good light.'

She gazed up and saw the tiny blinking red light, looking enormous in the dark. 'So why isn't it working?' she asked, mouth close to his ear.

'It's working all right. It's bloody well switched off but the sensor is still operating.'

'What are you telling me?'

'That they have night callers and don't want anyone to know. They're satisfied with internal security and that must mean someone is there. Don't make a sound, Paula. Let's try the back door.'

'How do you know a signal is not being emitted inside the house?'

'I don't. But they'd have done something by now.'

Bolts are only as strong as the people who force open a door. But opening them by brute force creates noise and that they dared not do. The back door was both locked and bolted so Jacko went round the windows one by one to find each one secure. It seemed that the back of the house was more secure than the front.

'I'm losing my touch,' said Jacko after a while. 'I've been away from it for too long. Should have brought a glass cutter and suction pad. We'll have to go round the front and I'll do the front door like I did before.'

'You couldn't have broken the glass, it would have declared a break-in. Come on.'

They crept round the front and were grateful for the high hedges and the overall seclusion. In the acute silence it was difficult to believe that there had been pandemonium in the street a short time ago. Jacko risked using a pencil torch while Paula stood behind him to block off the view from the street.

When the tumblers sprang he switched off the torch and waited a short while before slowly opening the door. It was as dark as pitch inside the hall and once they were both in he used his torch again, shielding it with his hand.

Knowing the layout from his first visit he went straight to the base of the stairs. Where Sid Lewis's house had a door underneath the stairs here there was a blank wall. While Paula held the torch he ran his hands over the surface from top to bottom. He tapped lightly and then more heavily. 'It's bricked up,' he whispered. 'Solid.' He felt round the edges. 'No hinges. It really is solid.'

Jacko leaned against the wall and Paula switched

off the pencil torch. The only semblance of light came from a small fanlight at the top of the front door.

'Maybe there never was a basement?' Paula suggested.

Jacko shook his head slowly; he did not agree with the idea. What did the callers call for? It could be just a meeting place but he believed it was more than that in spite of the fact that he had found nothing. He moved to his right and propelled Paula towards the front door. The study door, where he had seen Anne Corrie enter, was halfway down the narrow hall and when they reached it he tapped Paula on the shoulder and carefully opened the door. Once inside he closed the door and stood with his back to it, Paula at his side.

'I need to have a really good look round,' he said. 'Have you anything to pad the strip under the door?' While he groped his way to the windows Paula removed a scarf and packed it along the base of the door. Jacko reached the windows. The curtains were already drawn and were thick, if shabby, velvet. He ran his fingers down the drapes where they met to make sure there were no cracks. 'Okay,' he whispered across the room. 'Switch on.'

For a study the room was almost bare. The desk was serviceable but plastic with light alloy legs. The chair behind it was tubular. There was another chair at the front of the desk and two more along the wall. Apart from a standing metal filing cabinet there was nothing else apart from a shabby rug under the desk and another, larger rug between the desk and the door. The floorboards were in good condition but had not been polished for some time. And yet this uninviting room was the one Anne Corrie had gone into.

Jacko quietly moved towards the desk. The drawers were now unlocked and contained nothing but the mundane. The filing cabinet, also unlocked, was full of suspended files on runners, all of which were empty. While Jacko was doing his check Paula remained by the door keyed up for any movement inside the house. Jacko returned to the window and they faced each other across the room, padded and hooded figures too far separated to communicate sensibly. Yet still Jacko did not move, convinced that the answer had to be somewhere here if there was anything to find at all. There had to be; the house was being used for something.

Jacko pointed to the desk and they both moved towards it. At a signal they each took one end and tried to move it away from the rug. It would not budge. It was obviously fixed to the floor through the rug. They tried again with no result. Jacko knelt down, lifted the edges of the rug and could see nothing untoward, but it would only lift as far as the legs.

They stared at each other across the desk. Jacko sat sideways on it wondering what next to do when he felt a slight movement under him. At first he thought it was tiredness causing an illusion. He pushed at the desk and again there was the slight movement. He stood up to stare at the desk and then gave Paula a signal. She removed the front

188

chair while he pulled back the desk chair leaving the desk as an island. And then he pushed while Paula pulled and with surprising ease the desk slid back. Clearly it was on runners of some kind. When it had gone as far as it would go they tried to lift it again, but again it would not budge.

'Shit!' But Paula barely heard Jacko's expletive.

'Try hinging it back,' Paula suggested.

Jacko was slow to react but once he caught her meaning he lifted his end to discover that the desk needed one more push to disengage from the catch that was holding it and it began to lift back, the carpet coming up with it. He swung it right over while Paula caught the other side and slowly helped it to the ground so that it lay on its front section. There was no trapdoor underneath because the desk was secured to the trapdoor. Below them yawned a hole about two feet square with concrete steps going down into the darkening cellar.

His heavy clothing impeded him as Jacko descended the steps into the basement. At the bottom he found a light switch and fluorescent light flooded the cellar. He signalled for Paula to stay on guard where she was until he indicated an all clear.

He turned round slowly and saw the only part of the house that had been properly cared for. It was like a large reception room with comfortable chairs, some too big to have got through the hole above, suggesting that there was or had been another way in, a table with magazines and newspapers and at one end of the room two drinks trollies with an impressive selection of liquor and cut glass.

The walls were not rough cast like Sid Lewis's but plastered and painted and the whole effect was well-to-do. The only jarring note was the concrete floor.

Yet it was the glass-fronted display cabinets that covered most of the wall space on either side of the room that attracted Jacko's attention. On one side it appeared that he had walked into an optician's. An array of sunglasses and clear glass spectacles was on display covering part of one wall and on the opposite wall a variety of guns.

The glasses intrigued him. And he knew what they were although he would deny as much to North as he was not supposed to know. They were code named CVS 3500 and were an American development. The sunglasses could constantly alter tint according to the light and could filter out UV rays to protect the eyes. That in itself was far from new but the refinement of efficiency was. The bridge contained a miniature camera and microphone, the wire running down from the back of the earpiece to a battery worn at the back which could instantly transmit pictures and sound to monitors within their substantial orbit. The last Jacko had heard about them from their UK importers was that they cost £3,000 a time. Their value in surveillance and in difficult situations was enormous.

On the opposite wall were more common and better known small arms mounted behind glass including the Barrett Light Fifty M82A1 sniping rifle at present being used by the IRA to pick off the security forces. It fired a .50 round and its muzzle velocity was so high that it could penetrate armour plating and concrete. It could kill up to a mile. But it was not new as were the glasses which were being refined all the time. There was an array of other arms well known to him but when he had finished identifying them he was left with the strong feeling that he had not seen the most important. Apart from the glasses he was seeing dangerous weapons, still very much in demand but largely old hat. Where was the rest? The empty mine casing in the child's play box came to mind. This was a show room. Where were the others?

He walked over to the opening and saw Paula gazing down, her eyes anxious in the sockets of her hood. He signalled her down and she climbed awkwardly, impeded by her clothing and with gun in one hand.

Paula took it all in but raised no queries from which Jacko assumed that she knew as much about what she saw as he did.

'The real stuff is missing,' he said still keeping his voice low.

'The real stuff?'

'The walking bomb I told you about for a start. There would be a huge demand for that. But I bet it doesn't end there. Apart from the standard equipment, these people are operating with virtually unobtainable gear. The glasses indicate that but the glasses don't kill so they're on display. They must be here somewhere. Let's find what little trick they've been up to this time.'

They prodded and probed at the display cases, tried to move them this way and that but they were solidly mounted into their wall recesses. They searched the place for hidden cavities and switches but found nothing. They would have given up much sooner than they did had it not been for the difficulty they had found in finding the secret of the desk.

Frustrated, Jacko said, 'There must be a list of clients somewhere too. They can't operate from memory. There have to be some financial records somewhere.'

Paula simply gave a nod. She felt that wherever records might be they were not here. She was hot under the bulky clothing and wanted to tear her hood off. But at least they had learned that Jeremy Clarke was up to his neck in an arms racket. She lowered herself onto one of the comfortable chairs and gazed up at the puzzled Jacko.

With the hoods on communication was difficult unless they were close together so a good deal of sign language was going on between them. Jacko was gazing at the cabinets as if he knew the secret was there but like a good code needed some breaking. The answer was probably simple, as the desk had been. He prowled slowly round the cellar and then stopped suddenly. Paula froze in her chair at the same time.

Jacko indicated that he had heard a sound from above and Paula nodded an agreement. They did not want to be trapped in the cellar so Jacko climbed the steps first and stood at the top with gun in hand to protect Paula as she climbed up after him after putting out the cellar light. They stood either side of the study door and waited.

Nothing happened. Jacko gazed back at the desk lying on its front and the gaping hole beneath. He signalled Paula to stay and crossed over to the desk to raise it carefully and then to push it back on its runners. He tidied the edges of the carpet and rejoined Paula at the door.

Paula indicated that she had heard nothing more and then they both heard a slight shuffle outside. Jacko signalled her to switch off the light and to pick up her scarf. The total darkness which followed was impenetrable. They waited and a short while later the door handle began to turn; they could not see it but could hear the faint movement. A wedge of sludgy light crept through as the door began to open.

And then the light came on and the door was pushed back hard against the wall just missing Jacko; someone hurled himself into the room towards the desk. Jacko and Paula were blinded by the light but saw the figure fly past them and turned their guns towards it. A man was rolling and firing at them with a silenced gun. They fanned out the moment they saw him crouching by the desk but the shots were uncomfortably close as Jacko closed in. He stood over the man and to one side of him, his Browning aimed straight at his head. Paula came in from the other side. There was no sign of fear on the man's face but he recognised that his shots had missed and he was now sandwiched between two guns in the hands of two hooded figures.

'Put it on the floor,' said Jacko, 'or I'll blow your bloody head off.'

The man answered in a tongue neither understood and which they each guessed was Russian. But the gun was laid carefully on the floor and Jacko put a foot out and flicked it towards Paula who carefully picked it up and pocketed it.

'Stand up,' said Jacko, indicating with his gun. 'Slowly.'

The man rose slowly, uncowed, his expression vicious. He had made the mistake of thinking only one person was there and had paid the price but was quick to guess that the second person was a woman. He was glaring at Jacko and mouthing savagely and then swung his left arm round to hit Paula a tremendous blow to the head with something he had removed from his sleeve.

Paula went sprawling and in the split second of shock that descended on Jacko the man turned to strike at his gun hand. Jacko's reflexes, perhaps not quite as sharp as they had once been, withdrew his hand but the knife the man was now holding caught the end of the barrel and was enough to partly dislodge the gun from his hand. And then Jacko was fighting for his life as the knife came up in a swinging uppercut.

Jacko's heavy clothing impeded him but also saved his life as the knife plunged into the padding. And then the two men were fighting a terrible battle which took them crashing round the room. Jacko was slowed down by his clothing but training was impossible to forget. Both men employed every dirty trick in the book as they fought a bloody battle.

Paula, who had taken the blow from the handle

of the knife on her chin, had flown back against the wall and had crashed her head against it, falling down like a puppet, head lolling forward, legs splayed. She came round slowly, chin feeling as if it was broken and head pulsing with pain. She felt she was passing out again but could hear the tremendous struggle of the two men and the urgency to come round grew with the realisation that everything had gone wrong and she had to make the effort. It was painful just opening her eyes but what made her really stir was the sight of her own gun out of reach and of Jacko's actually lying nearer to her. She lifted her head and the pain shot right through her eyes but she managed to get a grip on herself to avoid drifting back to unconsciousness. She pulled herself to a sitting position against the wall and at once saw the disadvantage Jacko had in the bulky clothing, struggling to keep the knife away from his throat.

Paula climbed to her knees and almost passed out again. She clung to her senses while she fell sideways. She pushed herself up again and managed to clear her head as she crept forward towards the gun aware that her movements were so slow and yet she could go no faster. Her head felt as though it would burst as she clung on and edged forward. She toppled over again and then lay on her side as she stretched for the gun.

Both men must have picked up her movement. The Russian glanced over quickly towards her. Jacko used the change of concentration to make a supreme effort to avoid the knife and managed to throw the Russian off balance. Paula had tried too

195

hard and momentarily passed out again and when she came to she saw the Russian still straddling Jacko but badly balanced as he stretched to reach the gun she was after.

Everyone was straining to their limit as she made another effort to reach the gun. Her hand and the Russian's briefly touched and then separated as Jacko took further advantage of his change of effort. The Russian, realising that if Paula reached the gun he would have lost all advantage, had to adjust his priorities. He lunged sideways as Paula at last got a grip on the gun and grabbed her hand.

The man's effort gave Jacko the moment he needed and with a frantic effort he threw the Russian sideways and managed to scramble from under him. As he rolled clear he saw that his hand was streaming with blood and wondered what had happened to the knife; he must have grabbed the blade.

Meanwhile the Russian had moved his attention to Paula and was trying to break her wrist in an effort to get the gun. Jacko was on the blind side of what was happening to Paula but then saw Paula's gun a distance from where she had fallen and made a dive for it.

Jacko had to round the table to get at the gun, saw what was happening to Paula and that the Russian was about to break her wrist because she would not let go of the gun, swivelled and kicked the man in the head. He swayed sideways, eased his grip on Paula who pulled her hand away from his grip and then smashed the gun at the spot where Jacko had kicked him. The Russian rolled over on his back, his face already swollen.

'Jesus, he's a tough sod.' Jacko picked up Paula's gun, handed it to her and took his own from her. 'Let's have your scarf, love. We'll truss this bastard up.'

Jacko cut the scarf with the knife the Russian had still been loosely holding. Between them they rolled him over onto his face and Jacko tied his arms behind him and then his legs together. When that was done they sat on the chairs to recover while Jacko roughly bound his cut hand with a handkerchief. 'How's your face?' he asked.

Incongruously they were still wearing their hoods and kept them on in the event of more surprises. 'My bloody scarf helped save me,' replied an exhausted Paula. 'I'd wound it round my neck after picking it up from the door and it just took a bit of sting out of the blow. God, he's powerful.' She glanced over to where the Russian still lay unconscious but neither was betting on him staying like that; a scarf was not an ideal rope: it was too slippery. 'Now what?' Paula asked.

Jacko rose slowly. It had been a tough fight and he could still feel the effects. 'Let's see what damage his two shots made. I think they hit the wood by the door.'

Paula guessed what was in Jacko's mind but remained where she was to keep an eye on the Russian who appeared to be still unconscious, his breathing shallow and his podgy face, made worse by the swelling, now grey.

Jacko found a splintered section on the door lintel. The round had just chipped the wood, a splinter hanging out, and buried itself in the wall close to the wood. He used the Russian's knife to dig out the bullet, cut the splinter of wood off and took stock. He called out to Paula, 'Can you see it from where you are?'

'I can see where the paint is missing from the wood; just a sliver. But I can't see where the round lodged because it's in shadow.'

'Right. Let's see if I can find the second shot.'

He found it quite high up in the hall. The shot had gone through the open door on a rising trajectory from where the Russian had been rolling on the study floor. He put the hall light on; if there was another person in the house they would have been here by now. He decided to leave the bullet embedded as it was just above his reach and returned to the study.

'I think we can get away with it.' Jacko gazed round the room, straightened the chairs which had been flung around in the struggle and adjusted the rucked carpets. 'What do you think?' he asked.

Paula, gaining a hint of what was in his mind, scanned the room wearily; she was still in a lot of pain and spasmodically dizzy. 'You could be right. There's no obvious sign of a struggle.'

Jacko was ferreting inside his heavy coat and produced his mobile phone. 'The shot in the hall can only be seen by accident. It's high and the light is bad.' He pointed to the plaster and wood chips by the door. 'That's the biggest risk. No one need ever know we've been here.'

'What about him?' Paula observed dryly; she was having difficulty in hanging on. Waves of pain and nausea were sweeping over her. The Russian had still not moved.

'I'm going to take care of him now.' Jacko punched out a number and waited. He pulled back his sleeve to see the time. It was now two-fifteen.

North came on the phone and cursed when he heard Jacko's voice. 'Do you know what time it is? You've woken my wife, for God's sake.'

'We're down at Northwood. Had a spot of bother. We have a carcass that needs moving.' Jacko knew that would get North's immediate attention.

All traces of tiredness disappeared as North responded angrily, 'What the hell are you talking about? Are you saying you've killed someone?'

'We're not sure. He's alive at the moment but needs shifting quickly. Can you get a clean-up team down here straight away? We can't move him and if we could we wouldn't know where to take him.'

'Don't be ridiculous. I can't do something like that.'

'Yes you can. And unless you do it damned quick we're going to set him loose and that will be the end of your caper. Finished.'

'Are you trying to blackmail me, Jacko? Have you lost your senses?'

'Yes I am, and no I haven't. If matey disappears no one will know exactly what happened. There was a police presence in the street last night. It might be seen that he got windy and scarpered. That leaves us to fight another day and to carry on here for a while longer.'

There was a long silence from North before he

said, 'We don't do things like that. It's too risky.'

'Not as risky as the ones we took. And don't give me the innocent crap. We've tidied up. The chances are that nobody will ever know what happened here. It gives us a chance. And don't tell me you've dispensed with those comfortable little cells pugged away here and there along with the safe houses. It all depends how much you value an answer to all this. But you'll have to get your skates on.'

As he waited for a reply Jacko heard a scuffle and turned round to see the Russian struggling up against the wall and suddenly his hands appeared with the trailing remnants of the scarf. There was a murderous look in his eyes and it flashed through Jacko's mind that he might have been listening and understood English. To shoot him was the last thing he wanted, there would be too many complications, yet he had to be stopped. But first he needed an answer from North before the Russian got out of hand again. The man was struggling with something inside his jacket and for a moment Jacko thought he might have another gun. Jacko swallowed an expletive and prayed that North would answer before it was too late.

13

Paula was staggering towards the Russian, holding onto the desk with one hand and fighting off a wave of nausea. The Russian's hand emerged holding something which was smaller than a gun. Paula raised her gun and was partly blocking Jacko's view as he yelled into the phone, 'Well?'

'I'll get someone out. You stay put.'

But Jacko had already rung off before North had finished. He stuffed the mobile inside his coat and at the same time bawled out to Paula, 'Duck.'

Paula stumbled more than ducked and Jacko raised his gun and fired. The roar was like a cannon in the room. Paula dropped to her knees from shock and exhaustion and a small black box went flying through the air as the Russian clutched his arm in pain. Jacko did not stand on ceremony but hurled himself across the room and smashed the Browning down on the Russian's temple and then again as he fell.

He went to retrieve the small object the Russian had produced. It turned out to be a small digital and he breathed a sigh of relief when he saw that it was not switched on. He slipped it in his pocket.

Paula was trying to heave herself up by using the table and Jacko crossed to help. She straightened up at last and gasped, 'What the hell have you done? Everyone will have heard that shot.'

'What I've done is to save our bloody bacon. He

was just about to page for help.'

She lowered herself to the edge of the desk and gazed over towards the Russian. He was unconscious, head lolling sideways but his arm was in a strange position and then she saw the blood seeping through his sleeve. 'You bloody well shot him. I thought you were supposed to be such a crack shot.'

He was about to retort angrily and then realised that she was in a bad way and that her jaw under her hood was probably as swollen as the Russian's. Her condition was catching up on her but she was still thinking things out. There was not a lot he could do for her, she needed time.

'Paula,' he said in an effort to explain. 'All I could see of the bloody bleeper was about an inch of plastic. I had to go for the arm. And as for the sound, well we're well inside the house and it's deep sleep time. Forget it. It would have been far worse if he'd have got through for help. North's sending a team.'

'Good.' Paula seemed partly to recover at that. The bad spell slowly passed and she sat fully on the desk, a depleted, padded figure still in a good deal of pain.

Realising he might be pushing her too far he said, 'Are you strong enough to go to the kitchen? It's straight down the hall. We need some string or cord, something to make a proper job of this monkey. It's better that I stay here with him. Just in case.'

Paula said nothing but eased herself off the desk and walked unsteadily to the door where she paused while she clung to the lintel before continuing on.

Jacko felt sorry for her but it was too dangerous to leave the Russian untied; even wounded he would be a handful and Paula was in no state to guard him. He sat on the edge of the desk where she had sat and gazed down at the Russian with a reluctant respect. Only now did he realise that Paula had almost certainly saved his life. She had made a tremendous effort and was now paying the price. She was getting a reaction as they all did after a dangerous caper and this one had almost gone wrong. He would accept her rebukes and hold his tongue.

When she returned with a ball of twine she seemed to be brighter and steadier. 'I drank loads of water,' she explained. 'And sploshed it over me.' Her hood was wringing wet. She passed the twine over and said, 'There were scissors but I thought you might prefer his knife.' As he took the twine from her she said, 'I'm sorry, Jacko. What I said was out of order.'

'No, it wasn't. You saved my bacon. Let's truss this monkey up again and make a better job of it.'

They tied the Russian up; the twine would not slip as the woollen scarf had done. After the hands and ankles were tied they pulled his legs up behind him and trussed them to the cord binding his wrists.

'How long do you think they'll be?' Paula was sitting on the desk again as if wary of the chairs.

'I've no idea. He has to get a team together and then get them down here.' Jacko picked up the strips of Paula's scarf and handed them to her. 'North will have to buy you a new one; make it expensive.' He grabbed the ball of twine and asked, 'Where exactly did this come from? I'll put it back.'

'Directly under the sink by the dishwasher powder.'

He left the room and placed the twine in the only space available under the sink. And then he saw the upturned glass on the draining board and went back to ask Paula if that was where she had found it or should he put it away somewhere.

She was still sitting on the desk but had now swung round to fully face the Russian, her Browning held loosely between her hands and dangling between her legs. 'It was already on the draining board, exactly where I left it.'

'Fine. I'll check; I might have moved it.' When he reached the kitchen he found a tea towel on a rail and dried the glass before putting it back. It was small things like that which could give the game away to an observant eye. He said nothing to Paula when he returned except to say that he was going back down the cellar.

He wanted to help her to a chair but felt she might resent it and then he pulled the desk back on its runners again and went down the steps. He examined the structure of the show cases again. A good deal of money had been spent on the cellar. The cases were not just suspended on the walls but embedded into them so they were actually recessed by about five inches. He tried everything he had before and was no more successful.

The front of the cases comprised two glass doors which were locked but would open out if unlocked. He was tempted to use a picklock and did not see a problem in opening them, but like drying the glass in the kitchen, the tiniest mark could give away the fact that they had been examined and he did not want to risk scratching the polished wood around the lock. He did push at the lock though, in case there was some automatic release, and heard a faint click.

Jacko cocked his head, not quite sure where the sound had come from. He pulled at the brass handle of the cabinet door but it did not open. He pressed again. Nothing happened. Then again and he heard the click again. He grasped the brass handle and instead of pulling outward pushed sideways and the cabinet began to move with ease. He smiled to himself. Someone had been expert in the use of non-stick runners. This was a well thought out installation.

As the cabinet slid sideways the sunken runners were revealed with a blank wall behind them. The cabinet moved about three feet before stopping. At the blank end of the cavity was the side of what looked like another case and had a recess in the wood into which he slipped his fingers and pulled. Another case slipped sideways into view. And in it, on three separate shelves, were the walking heat sensor mines, known to some as 'creeping terrors'.

There were other mines too, mainly anti-personnel, designed to maim rather than kill, but much more familiar and well tried. The array of creeping terrors posed a good deal of questions, like how had they come from Massachusetts to here when there was a strong lobby to ban them?

Paula called out, 'Are you okay?'

'I've found the mines. But wait until North's men arrive. I'll be up in a minute.'

In the study Paula heard the Russian groan but he seemed to be still out, the broken bruises on his distorted face ugly and very swollen. She did not like the trussing — if he got cramp he would be in agony for he could not move — but her feeling of concern was tempered when a strong twinge of pain shot through her jaw. She wished the team would arrive.

In the cellar Jacko had found another extension on the cabinet opposite the mines where the camera-cum-microphone glasses were on display. When they had been pushed out of the way Jacko found a display of handguns. There were many varieties but it was the Belgium-made Five-seveN that caught his eye.

The Five-seveN put the .44 Magnum in full perspective. With twenty times the range and penetrating power of most military pistols there was no handgun that came near it. The first pistol to fire sub-machine gun bullets, it could kill up to a mile. And it could penetrate brick walls and even tree trunks.

Up to the time he left them and as far as he knew the position had not changed — the SAS, as a back-up to their HP-5 sub-machine guns, used Browning 9 mm firing 8-gram bullets at a speed of 350 metres per second. The gun he was now looking at had a muzzle velocity of 650 metres per second using only a 2-gram bullet. It could punch through 48 layers of laminated Kevlar armour at 200 metres. It was formidable. The SAS were after it but whether or not they had it he did not yet know. It would be a boon to anti-terrorist forces. *And to the terrorists themselves.*

Jacko knew that the makers considered the Five-seveN as too potent for normal police work and it had been designed for anti-terrorist and hostage situations. But there would be a good many illegal organisations after them, some with a bottomless purse. So where had these come from? That they were on display suggested that the selling stock was elsewhere. The elaborate design of the cellar could not be justified by the number of weapons on display, as valuable as they were.

Jacko closed the cabinets to appear as he had found them and then went up the steps, pulled the desk back, straightened the carpet and took a good look at the Russian. 'How are you feeling?' he asked Paula.

'I thought you had forgotten me. You certainly get your priorities right. Much better, thank you, Jacko. Do you think we can take off these bloody ski masks now?'

'Wait till the team have gone.'

'You mean you don't trust North's men?'

'I start with North. I trust him until we become part of a conflict of interests; at that point we are second to whatever he sees as his duty.' He lightened his tone. 'Look, if they can't see our faces they can't bloody well remember them, can they? Why put temptation in their way?'

'You're as bad as North.'

'Never. After they've been, if ever they come, I'll show you what I found. There's a pistol down there with sixty per cent less recoil than a Magnum, is much lighter and holds four times as many rounds. How have they got here?'

'How do any illicit guns get to where they shouldn't be? Happens all the time. It's one big merry-go-round. Corruption, secret deals, armed raids on armouries and military installations. You name it. But I'm teaching my grandpa to suck eggs, aren't I?'

Jacko grinned beneath his hood. 'Glad to see you're feeling better, Paula.'

They were both tired and there was nothing they could now do but wait. It had been a busy night and they had been hammered by the Russian who still seemed to be unconscious. The doorbell rang during one of the increasing lulls, making them visibly jump.

'Cover me,' said Jacko going down the hall.

Paula switched off the hall light behind him and they crept down the narrow hall, guns in hand. Jacko reached the front door and peered through the spy hole, however it was really too dark to see anything but a dark shape standing close to the door.

'Get your gun over my shoulder,' said Jacko and he opened the door very slightly.

A figure stood in front of him and Jacko could now see the bright plastic jacket of a paramedic. He looked past him to a white vehicle beyond the gate.

'I understand you have someone needing treatment?'

'Who sent you?'

'Uncle Derek. I don't want to hang about. We've got a private ambulance outside. The man turned and signalled another who came up with a stretcher.

Jacko let them in and guided them down the hall to the study. No questions were asked but the Russian had miraculously recovered and was threshing about on the floor as he realised what was about to happen to him. The two men grabbed him, one gave him a quick injection on the back of his hand and the Russian went out almost immediately.

They started to untie him and Jacko stood by with the gun. 'You sure he's out?'

'He'll be out until we get him to bed all cosy. His arm needs seeing to; did you shoot him?'

'No, he shot himself. Own goal. Lucky for us.'

The men dressed as paramedics strapped the Russian to the stretcher and carried him out. Jacko followed while Paula remained in the house. The ambulance was one of those small private jobs not much bigger than a van. The street was unbelievably quiet but police cars did patrol and they all wanted to get away as fast as possible. The Russian was loaded on, one man climbed in with him and the other joined the driver who had remained in the ambulance. Without another word the ambulance pulled out and was away.

Jacko dashed up the path, entered the house and closed the door behind him. Paula switched on the lights and they tore off their hoods almost simultaneously. They were smiling with relief. They entered the study again and Paula said, 'You'd think they called on hooded figures every day.'

'Perhaps they do. It's after four, Paula. If you're up to it I'll show you what I found and then we'll go home.' He was worried about the swelling around her jaw and the discoloration. But the main problem was gone and the relief was instant.

'Show me,' said Paula. 'And then you can take me home. I can make a bed up for you if you like; there's precious little night left.'

After he had shown her the secret cabinets their inclination was to leave immediately but they went round all the areas they had been and checked for obvious foot and hand marks; they might have brought mud in on their feet even though the ground outside was hard. They particularly checked the study for blood traces; the Russian's arm had bled but it seemed into his clothing and not the floor. Only when they were satisfied did they leave.

They went out by the front door and it was still so quiet that they decided to leave by the gate. The thought of climbing over the fences at the back again convinced them to take the risk. They stood in the porch, listening for any sound when Paula said, 'You've forgotten to lock the front door.'

'No I haven't. If we're to leave the illusion that matey did a bunk then locking the front door before he bolted would be the last thing he'd think of doing. Let them sweat it out. Unless they find the two bullet holes they can't know that anyone has been in.'

They walked to the gate, their feet crackling on the early morning frost, the sky now clear above them, paused at the gate and then walked along the deserted street. A car engine revved some distance away but it was the only sound apart from their own crisp footsteps. Paula took Jacko's arm as if they both needed support.

They reached the car at the rear and climbed into its near freezing interior. In no time at all it was fogged up from their breath. Jacko switched on the engine and then the fan, waiting for the windscreen to demist. Paula hunched up beside him.

'Not a bad night's work,' Jacko said as he pulled out. 'And the timing's right. Another hour and things will be on the move down here.' As if to bear him out a train pulled into the station as they went past it. 'In spite of your kind offer I think you'd better stay at my place,' continued Jacko. 'I've spare beds. You'll be safe.'

'Did I say I wanted to be?'

He grinned. 'Don't tempt me. I think we've spent enough energy tonight. I'll make us a nice hot drink.'

'I have no night clothes or make-up and all that stuff.'

They were already clearing the outskirts of Northwood as he replied, 'I can provide all that. Georgie's away in Cyprus and I'm not sure she's speaking to me any more; I haven't heard from her.'

Paula turned to him. 'Would that salve your conscience?'

Jacko replied seriously, 'This is not the time to discuss my personal problems. I'm an old-fashioned guy with old-fashioned loyalties.'

'And Georgie's the same?'

'Is this what they taught you in Northern Ireland? To seduce? Change the subject, Paula. But keep talking. I'm having trouble keeping awake.'

After a while they ran out of lighted streets and onto the darkened stretches to London. With hardly another vehicle on the road Jacko ran on full beam. It was not a long journey on virtually empty roads and any other time he might have enjoyed it but he was now feeling desperately tired and Paula, who had tried hard to keep him awake, had now dozed off herself, her head bent forward. He switched on the radio, something he normally hated doing when driving.

The harsh beat of music roused him and Paula too. 'I'm sorry,' she said. 'I dropped off.' And then in an effort to keep talking, 'At least North has had to come out of his hole.'

'Right. But we're no nearer knowing exactly who Mirek is and what he's actually up to. He's tied in with the arms somehow but in what capacity? What we did tonight seemed to have drifted away from his part in this. It's just possible that his contact with Clarke is legit.'

'Sure,' said Paula in disbelief.

'Tomorrow there's someone I want to phone in Switzerland. She's well up in what goes on in the gun-running business.'

'She?'

He did not answer but grinned in the darkness.

* * *

Anne Corrie called at the Northwood house at midday that same morning. When she tried to unlock the mortice she found it already unlocked and this startled her. She rang the bell to be on the safe side. She had not been keen on a stranger living in the house but recognised the need for safety. That he was a Russian did not make her happy even if he did speak reasonable English and he had one of those unpronounceable names so she had called him Boris much to his amusement.

There was no answer to the bell. There was someone calling in about an hour and it was important she was able to receive him. The Yale lock was self-locking on closing the door from outside; the handle could not be turned from the outside, so she unlocked the Yale and pushed the door open. She had no weapon and had never been in a situation where she needed one but she felt the need of one now even if she did not know how to use it.

She left the front door slightly ajar and went down the hall calling out to Boris. She searched the downstairs and then more reluctantly the upstairs. Boris's bed had been slept in, although the blankets had been thrown back as if in a hurry. She wrinkled her nose and left the room. Downstairs she went into the study and tried to place the faint but stringent smell that cloyed there. Had she been

213

familiar with guns she would have recognised it as cordite but she was sure that it had not been there before. The smell disturbed her.

She pulled the desk back and went down into the cellar. Nothing that she could see was disturbed. The cabinets were all in order as were their contents. She sat on the arm of one of the chairs and wondered what had happened to Boris. She went back to the study, the smell of cordite slightly less now the doors were open but still there to her sensitive sense of smell. Suddenly remembering she had left the front door open she went down the hall to close it and then returned to the study.

Anne Corrie sat at the desk and rang Jeremy Clarke on her mobile. The call was routed through the switchboard at the DTI and he was immediately angry. 'I told you not to ring me here.'

'It's urgent. Boris is missing.'

'Missing? What do you mean, missing?'

'What does anyone bloody well mean by missing? He's simply not here. His bed's been slept in, the mortice wasn't locked as if he left in a hurry.'

'Oh, Christ. It's difficult for me to speak here. Anything else wrong?'

'Nothing that I can see. I've been all over the place. Everything seems all right. But there is a strange smell in the study.'

'What sort of a smell?' Clarke wanted to hang up but had to know what had happened.

'It's difficult to describe. It doesn't belong here, I know every damned smell in the grubby place. It's a bit like dirty exhaust fumes but rather sharper. Pungent? Is that the word?'

How the hell would I know without experiencing it? The thought flashed through Clarke's mind but he held his tongue. He was worried and so was Anne who was not given to panic. 'Do you feel you're in . . . ' he tailed off wishing this was on his mobile which would be frowned on in the office.

'Danger?' Anne said it for him. 'I did at first but not now. The place is empty, nothing disturbed that I can see. It seems that Boris has just done a runner.'

'But that doesn't account for the strange smell?'

'No. I'm sorry but I had to ring you.'

'I understand. I'll contact the necessary people.'

As a high-ranking civil servant Clarke had important issues to handle. His work often took him out and he lunched with businessmen and overseas visitors on a fairly regular basis, but this day was an office day. He was well aware of spending too much time outside the office lately and there was a danger of drawing attention to himself. He badly wanted to contact Mirek but had to sit on his feelings until lunchtime. His frustration was reflected in the way he handled his staff and he was well aware of being awkward but was unable to control himself. He was rattled and wished that Anne had not phoned.

At lunchtime he left the premises and hurried as far away from the DTI as he could before standing in a busy street and dialling Mirek's number on his mobile. He prayed that Mirek was on standby but he could not get through. He went to his usual restaurant and sat at his usual table at the rear of the place and tried again. Mirek was switched off.

There was really nothing else he could do except to leave a message at the hotel where Mirek was still staying and he was reluctant to do that.

As he sat there, the place quickly filling up now and becoming noisier by the minute, Clarke became more flustered and worried. He could ring Anne Corrie back and ask her to contact Mirek and he was actually punching out her mobile number when he stopped dead. Mirek well knew of Anne's connection with him and of the extremely important part she played but he had always dealt directly with Clarke and seemed reluctant to use what Mirek saw as a subordinate. Clarke had always assumed that he simply did not like dealing with women.

While he floundered his favourite dish was put before him and remained untouched as he agonised over what he should do. Something was not right. He was less concerned with Anne's description of the strange smell in the study than of Boris clearing out. It was all very worrying and he did not know what to do but knew some action was required and Mirek had to be informed quickly.

Clarke eventually pecked away at his food, confused and nervous. Everything had run so smoothly until the man Jones had been killed and his interview with the police had confounded and frightened him. In fact he had handled himself very well and had thought so at the time but a series of unexplained incidents since had undermined his confidence. He needed Mirek's advice. He had always needed Mirek's advice.

Now he had an added worry. If Mirek was to see him, a near nervous wreck, it was possible that Mirek might cut his losses and Clarke had never had illusions about who controlled Mirek. Suddenly Clarke felt very small and inadequate and did not know which way to turn. It was time to return to his office but he was not sure that he had the strength to cope with that. He signed the chit for his meal but could not make out what had happened to him, what had driven him to this kind of brink. There had to be a better reason than Boris hiving off. So what was niggling him so much that at the moment he was afraid of his own shadow? His temptation was not to return to the office; self-survival demanded that he did. How had it come to this? He knew how, and had done for years.

As he walked down the restaurant he saw his reflection in the glass windows and it was like walking towards a very frightened man.

14

Jacko took Paula's breakfast into her while she was still in bed. He laid the raised tray across the bed and noticed that the swelling on her jaw was not so bad but the discoloration was something she would not want to see. After she thanked him with a sleepy smile he sat on the nearest chair, produced his digital and punched out a number.

As she chewed on a piece of toast Paula said, 'I'm impressed. Do you carry all the numbers in your head?'

'I've always been able to remember telephone numbers. This one is in Geneva.' And then into the phone, 'Billie? It's Willie Jackson. Jacko. How are things?' He held the phone away from his ear as she told him what she thought of him and asked why he was still alive.

'Aw, come on Billie, I wasn't that bad. We got out of it, didn't we? Didn't do your trade any harm, did it? Should have got you new clients; I've passed your name around to the safe and the wealthy; you must have noticed.'

Billie's tone softened a little while Paula, who could only hear Jacko, stared in wonder. She sipped her coffee eyeing Jacko curiously.

'Billie, has the Belgian Five-seveN come your way?'

'I wish it would. Why, can you get some for me?'

'I might. I've seen some locally. I'm phoning from London. I thought they were under tight control. Have you heard anything?'

'Only rumours that there are some around but where they've come from or whether anyone else is doing some illicit manufacturing I don't know. Maybe some have gone missing.'

'Would that be the answer to the Genghis and Attila too? There seem to be some of them about.'

'I don't deal in mines. Small arms only, you know that.'

'Yes, but have you heard any rumours?'

'The only thing I heard was that the US were clamping down on all information regarding them. Some sort of cover-up which might suggest that some have gone missing. But that's just a guess.'

'From a very well-informed person.'

'Still flattering, Jacko.' There was a pause before Billie added, 'In spite of the anguish, not to mention the danger you put me in, I'm glad you came through. Any chance of coming over?'

'Not immediately. Tempting, though. I've still got the bruise where you kicked me on the knee and I'm walking with a limp.'

'You will be if you try that line again. The girl fully recovered by the way, you probably heard.'

'Look, if you come up with any news on those two items can you give me a call? I can give you my mobile number. I'd only do that to someone I loved.'

'Bullshit. You haven't changed much. Still looking for something for nothing. Okay, Jacko, give me the number although I'm not likely to hear anything, I'm too small.'

When he had finished Jacko closed the phone and looked across at an amused Paula who was slowly chewing on some bacon.

'I'd only do that for someone I loved,' mimicked Paula in a small girl's voice. 'Well, well. Was she worth it?'

'She might have been. Knows small arms inside out.'

'I thought gun running was a man's province.'

'You should know better. Women don't allow men any men's province these days; they're taking over. Did you bring me my breakfast? Not a chance. But she's good at what she does,' Jacko added reflectively.

Paula swung her legs from under the tray and sat on the side of the bed. She reached for the coffee. 'We're still talking about small arms are we? Good coffee.'

'It looks as if the stuff we saw might have been stolen. Neither government would want that to become too public.'

'So they were brought from the USA and Belgium to a suburb of London.' The doubt was clear in Paula's tone.

'No problem. Happens all the time. Including huge shipments of illicit gold bars. Now you see it now you don't. The routes to here might have been anything but direct.'

'Have I got time for a shower before we see North?'

★ ★ ★

They met by using a variation of the taxi picking Mirek up at the hotel. In spite of present evidence to the contrary they still operated on the basis that someone somehow might be keeping an eye on them even if intermittently. So Mirek arranged for the taxi at the hotel, left in it about mid-morning and picked Chaznov up a couple of blocks away. They drove to the Ritz and walked along to turn off to Hyde Park.

It was still bitterly cold and Chaznov was complaining, not about the cold but the damp that came with it and ate into his bones. Mirek had no thought for the weather. They kept walking. It was too cold and the seats too damp to sit down.

The two men had sprung an uneasy alliance acknowledging that they were on the same side but that their jobs were quite different. As things were going they needed each other's support. They brought themselves up to date and Chaznov was showing Mirek an unexpected respect as if he had been warned by those who employed him to toe the line and realise the importance of Mirek. So when Mirek said to him, 'Do you ever do private jobs?' Chaznov was somewhat surprised but took the question seriously.

'While I'm assigned to an official job?'

The quaint phrasing amused Mirek who could not envisage Chaznov doing anything official. 'Yes. If you had the time. And were well paid for it.'

'Would it interfere with guarding you?'

'It could facilitate it. Make it easier for you

221

afterwards. Believe me I am well aware more than ever that I need your protection. I simply think what I have in mind would help.'

'And you would pay well?' As he spoke, Chaznov was doing no more than humouring Mirek, acting out his instructions to be helpful rather than brusque.

'The equivalent of fifty thousand sterling in any currency you like in any country in the world. My contacts are widespread.'

Chaznov now took the matter very seriously but hoped to get the offer increased. 'Explain to me what it is you want.'

★ ★ ★

It was not until Jeremy Clarke left the office for the day that he was able to raise Mirek on the phone. He related what Anne Corrie had told him and there was a long silence before Mirek said, 'We'd better get down there. Tell your girl to wait there or if she's left to get back there. I'm on my way.'

Clarke cursed once he had switched off. He wanted to get home and bury his problems in the arms of Anne. She could always make him forget his worries in many different ways. He rang her to find that she was still at the Northwood address having sensibly held on there until advised to the contrary.

It had been a long day for Anne Corrie. After speaking to Clarke on the phone she waited for further instructions and when they did not come waited in the knowledge that for one reason or another he had found it impossible to come back to her. But after she had dealt with her visitor and had shown him what was on offer it became lonely in the house and far from comfortable. She made herself a meal from what was in the refrigerator, slept a little but became increasingly agitated as the day wore on. She knew that she dare not ring Clarke again. When he finally rang she was close to the point of leaving.

Mirek was the first to arrive. He came by train because it was quicker at rush hour. Chaznov was always close by. He walked briskly from the station and rang the bell on arrival at the house.

Mirek and Anne Corrie had not actually met although they had seen each other, but they knew about each other. Mirek approved of her because he believed she provided a stability to Clarke which was essential. Mirek reflected that she might operate much of what Clarke received credit for but he did not object to this as long as everything ran smoothly.

She recognised him as soon as she answered the door, smiled politely and stood aside for him to enter. He introduced himself knowing that she recognised him and she said, 'Jeremy said you would come. I thought he might be here first.' She led the way to the frugal lounge, unaware that he had been here before and that he carried keys in spite of him ringing the bell. There was much that she did not know about Mirek and did not want to know as long as they all made good money.

Mirek did not sit down immediately but said,

'Jeremy mentioned you reported a strange smell in the study.'

Anne took him to the study and he gave the impression that he had not been in it before. Mirek sniffed but could pick up nothing but a general mustiness. While he was doing this Clarke arrived and Anne let him in and took him straight to the study where Mirek was still sniffing the air.

'Can you smell anything?' Mirek said to Clarke as a greeting.

'No,' Clarke replied, circling the room. 'Nothing specific. A bit musty, no more.'

Mirek turned to Anne. 'Can you still smell anything or has it gone?'

Aware that she could look a fool she said, 'I'm not one to panic. When I came in this morning there was a smell in here which did not belong. I don't think I can detect it now but I might have got used to it.'

'Or it might simply have evaporated.' Mirek smiled and when he did he could be charming. 'We do not doubt you Miss Corrie. You're a very level-headed woman and I'm sure that you did smell something.' He produced his phone and spoke in Russian as he said, 'Get in here straight away.'

Chaznov arrived within a minute. Mirek opened the door for him, led him straight to the study and still using Russian said, 'Can you smell anything in here?' He turned questioningly to Anne before adding in English, 'Something pungent. It was here this morning so might have gone. Try hard.'

Chaznov stood in the middle of the room and

turned slowly. He gave no impression of sniffing the air but he was in no hurry.

The others watched him and Clarke, who had always suspected that Mirek had a minder, now knew for certain that he did while Anne Corrie for the first time wondered what she was getting into. It was one thing dealing with Jeremy Clarke and she knew he cooperated with Mirek but it was becoming clear that it was Mirek who held the control. And now this big Russian had appeared on the scene and it was not difficult to understand his part. She was being given a lesson in priorities and authority and was not sure that she liked it. She could control Clarke but realised that she could never do that with the two foreigners. From being in control of her destiny she suffered a setback and felt uneasily out of her depth.

Chaznov would not be hurried. He was doing what good bodyguards should do, trying to locate danger to his charge. Nor was he trying to impress anyone. He now circled the room while the other three got out of his way; all eyes were on him but he was unaware of it. He crossed over to the door and for the first time seemed to be visibly sniffing. He stopped by the door and examined it.

Chaznov was now conveying the impression that he was not happy about something. He ran his fingers down the door lintel and over the rough edge of wood where Boris's shot had taken a sliver from the frame. And he found the bullet hole. He pulled out a flick knife and probed the hole where the bullet had been. Standing back he said slowly in his heavy English, 'The smell is cordite. Very faint, only just there. I wasn't absolutely sure until I found the bullet hole. Someone has picked the bullet out.'

The silence was instant and deep. Whatever they had expected it was not this. Shots fired and the guard missing? Nobody knew what to say. Suddenly everything was on an entirely different footing. Things were happening they did not know about. This was not police work. Intelligence then? A rival faction and there was certainly competition although up to now they did not rate it.

Leaving them in a worried state of silence Chaznov went into the hall and searched the opposite wall reasoning that if a shot hit the door frame others might have passed beyond if the door was open at the time. Taller than Jacko, Chaznov found the second bullet high up but not too high for him to dislodge it with his knife. He returned to the study with the bullet held in the palm of his hand and held it out like a sacred offering, all eyes centred on it.

'It's one of ours,' he pronounced. 'The type we use.'

Having broken the silence they all wanted to speak at once but Mirek cut through, 'Couldn't someone else have been using the same sort of ammunition?'

'Sure. Particularly if they were using one of our guns which are Russian.'

'So our man fired the shots?'

Chaznov shrugged. He did not know. 'Whoever fired missed. There are no other signs. No blood anywhere. If other shots were fired they might have

226

hit someone and stayed in them. How much blood depends on where they were hit. There's no trace of blood.'

'What about in the other rooms?' Mirek was raising all the queries.

Chaznov turned to Anne. 'Was there a cordite smell in any of the other rooms?'

'No.' She said no more, not sure whether Mirek and Chaznov knew about the basement room.

'Then it all took place here. Whoever was here must have got our man. He would not have run away.'

'So who the hell are we dealing with?' Mirek posed the question and then turned to Chaznov as if to say, 'This is your department. Search and destroy.'

Reading his thoughts Chaznov inclined his head in acknowledgement. On a signal from Mirek he said, 'If that is all you want of me I'll wait outside.'

When Chaznov had gone Clarke turned to Anne. 'What about downstairs?'

At that she accepted that Mirek must know about the arms display and slid the desk back. 'Everything seemed normal. No sign of any disturbance.'

They went down into the cellar and as Anne had said there was no sign of disturbance. Mirek would have been happier if Chaznov had a look round down here with his more professional eye but he would rather Chaznov remain in ignorance of what exactly Mirek was doing here.

They went back up and Mirek said quietly, 'We can hardly ask around. But we must find out who was here and deal with the problem.'

There was something chilling in the way he spoke, rather to himself than to the others, which disturbed Anne Corrie very much. She gazed at Clarke and saw no hope of a solution from him.

As if understanding her feelings Mirek said, 'When the stakes are so high we must expect the odd inconvenience. We will take it in our stride.'

His comment did nothing to reassure Anne Corrie, rather did it scare her. She realised it was in all the way or try to get out now.

★ ★ ★

Detective Chief Superintendent Matthew Simes made an appointment with Derek North and suggested he called at Scotland Yard. North went to the window of Simes's office and gazed down at the revolving sign outside the building.

'Want some tea or coffee?' asked Simes amiably.

'No thanks. No time. I must get back as soon as you've finished with me.' North returned to his seat aware that Simes had something up his sleeve.

'Did you hear about that murder in Northwood? Old feller called Sidney Lewis had his head bashed in. He was a peeper by all accounts. Had binoculars mounted at a front window. And a camera handy. Wondered if you'd read about it.'

'I seem to recall it. Why, have you found out who did it?'

'The locals solved it. Apparently the elder son did it in a fit of rage because the old man wouldn't sell the house and the son wanted his share now.

It's always money or sex, isn't it?'

'Nearly always. Is that what you had me over to tell me? You must be short of real news.'

'No, no.' Simes was enjoying himself. 'I wouldn't have known about it but fingerprints of a man and a woman were found all over the place. The woman they couldn't identify but they traced the man's. Willie Jackson. Ex-SAS sergeant. Bit of a wild card. I think he's done odd jobs for you.'

'Really? Who told you that?'

'Oh, we pick up these rumours.' Simes smiled broadly. 'Police work. The locals passed on the information to us and I'm passing it on to you.'

'I certainly know the name. I wonder what he's doing these days?'

'Time, if we are not kept informed.'

'Why? Do you think he's involved in the murder?'

'I shouldn't think so. They have their man. And Jackson isn't stupid enough to leave his prints around if he's out to top someone. I just wondered if he was doing something for you bearing in mind Jeremy Clarke's house is across the way. Is there anything I should know, Derek?'

'Well, I can tell you but it's really hardly worth a mention. We have an interest in Clarke as you have. Our angle is different. We are not pursuing him with regard to the murder of young Jones. That is clearly your field. But we are tightening up considerably on Government employees holding delicate positions, particularly in places like Cheltenham and where defence is concerned.'

229

Simes chipped in, 'Clarke isn't involved in defence.'

'At the DTI? Of course he is. We'll take any orders we can get within the international parameters set. It's part of his job to help companies sell abroad, to smooth things over where he can. And that brings him in touch with a lot of people.'

'Like Mirek?'

'Like Mirek. Don't think the KGB is dead; they've merely redirected their interests. Russia is desperately short of money and they want shortcuts to information, industrial and arms. We're keeping an eye on those we employ who are overspending or in debt, or are suddenly flush. Money problems play a big part. Clarke falls into that category.'

'So you send Willie Jackson down to see what he's up to and he uses Sidney Lewis's house.'

'I didn't say that. You've been a copper too long, Matthew.'

'That's a fact.' Simes managed a smile. He knew he would not get the exact truth from North but it was near enough and bore out his own reasoning. He placed his spatulate fingers on the desk and gazed down at his hands. 'Hell of a coincidence though, isn't it? Our interest in the man happening at the same time. Remarkable.'

'Not at all. We simply followed up after the Mirek business; is he or isn't he? It seemed to be an opportune moment. But as you've raised this matter, and as I've been far more open with you than my job demands, perhaps you can do me a favour in return?'

★ ★ ★

Derek North had tea brought in for Jacko and Paula and acted as mother in pouring. He passed across the biscuits. 'You two did extremely well even if you did land me in it. We have a problem on our hands with that man. We can get nothing out of him — he's so violent we've had to keep him partially sedated and if the European Court got to hear of that the country would be sent to the dogs.'

'The bloody man tried to kill us, for God's sake,' retorted an exasperated Jacko.

'That no longer matters. Villains have their rights even at your expense, it would seem. Everyone goes to the European Court these days. You ever heard of a case being thrown out? Countries, particularly this one, are guilty before being proved innocent. It's the new norm. Of course, we can't adopt that same criteria. So if we are to survive we have to keep matey under lock and key until we have a few answers. He's probably an illegal anyway. Meanwhile we've had a medic remove the bullet and dress the wound; fortunately it was not too serious. In due course we'll deport him.'

'So what are you going to do about Clarke and his girlfriend?' Paula brought things back to basics.

'Nothing. Not yet. If we pull them in it will frighten the rest and it's the rest we really want. We can get Clarke any time we like.' North realised his tea was getting cold so took a couple of sips. He put the cup down thoughtfully. 'So we know they are

231

running arms, very specialist arms which on paper it's almost impossible to get hold of although that might be a naive observation. Who's doing it and who's it going to? What precisely is Clarke's part and who else might have been corrupted, but more importantly and getting closer to the top, what part does our mysterious Mr Mirek have to play?'

Jacko was having trouble concentrating. 'Look,' he said. 'We've done our bit. It's now up to others.'

'The police are willing to let us use Sid Lewis's place for surveillance. They haven't quite finished with the place so there will be conditions but it might pay off.'

Jacko shook his head. 'We already know what it's used for; it's a sales office for gun running. What we want is a list of who's being supplied and who is actually supplying. Clarke is just a useful pawn this end, probably very useful bearing in mind the contacts he must have. But he's a link man and I believe so is Mirek but much further up the tree. This is a Russian Mafia job if ever there was one and they are using Clarke, while Mirek has other qualifications. If he is Bykov how did he stay alive and who was shot?'

'It would still be useful to know who's going in and out. The police need Sid Lewis's binoculars and camera as part of their evidence so I'll supply replacements.'

Jacko was still not happy. 'I think I should have a word with Anne Corrie; shake the tree a little and see what falls out.'

North considered it. 'If we do that we show our hand.'

'We've got to fall off the bloody fence sometime. She must know where records are kept; she, the saleswoman, must know who she's dealing with.'

'It might be easier to scare Clarke.'

The two men turned to look at Paula after her suggestion.

'Do you think he knows as much as his mistress?'

'Probably not but he'll be more easily scared and that can communicate. Frightened people are inclined to panic.'

'Not a bad idea, Paula.' Jacko nodded agreement. 'I know a couple of people who can frighten the living daylights out of him.' He turned to North. 'In for a penny . . . We'll need a safe house.'

There was a long silence. North was being forced to stick out his neck further and further if they were to get anywhere. 'I still want a surveillance on the house. But, okay, we go for Clarke. No visible signs, Jacko. I want him back at work or the whole thing collapses.'

'Have you got a place with a two-way mirror?'

North stared in disbelief. 'Do you think we run knocking shops?'

'Have you?' Jacko insisted.

North silently appealed to Paula but she was clearly with Jacko. 'I might be able to arrange it. But I don't want any villains running wild on our property. They must not know who you are working for.'

Jacko stifled a yawn. 'So who's going to tell them?'

But North was still concerned. 'Be careful. And don't forget the guy who saw you when you were chasing after Clarke near his home.'

Jacko replied very soberly. 'I'm never likely to forget him. We know what we know about them. What we don't know is what they know about us. What are we really up against? Of course I'll be careful.' He smiled across at Paula. 'And I've got a helluva good minder.'

'It's not a joke, Jacko.'

'I know. It's my way of coping.' He held out a hand to Paula. 'Come on. Let's go find our contacts and then we'll get Clarke.'

North watched them go, unhappy at what they were about to do, not on moral grounds but because whatever impression he gave to the contrary he cared about them. He was uneasy because he was sure that there was a hidden agenda he might have missed. He felt there were forces they had yet to see and it would not be safe to assume that the opposition had no knowledge of the Jacko-Paula break-in. Suddenly Jacko and Paula, for all their training and courage, seemed to him to be diminutive and he wondered what they were walking into yet had no real reason to stop them. He heard them laughing while waiting for the lift and it made him feel worse.

15

'Mirek knew of the basement.' Anne Corrie had left the accusation until they were back in the apartment in London.

'So?' Jeremy Clarke had his jacket off and was undoing his tie. He placed the tie on the rack in the built-in wardrobe with its sliding doors.

'So who exactly is running this show?' Anne was quietly fuming but outwardly cool. 'I thought you were.'

'Well I am. In this country. But the organisation stretches way beyond me. Who knows what happens in Europe. And the Middle East.'

'I thought you were damned well supposed to know.' She managed to tone down the sting. 'This Russian fellow Mirek seems to have taken over. Do you take your orders from him?'

'Don't be silly, darling. Anyway he's Polish not Russian.'

'He seems to speak Russian very well.'

'How would you know? It might have been bloody awful Russian.'

'Stop playing with me, Jeremy. I thought I was answerable to you. Running things while you were at the office. I seem to have found a new boss and one I don't particularly care for. And I don't like the thug who came in. He must be following Mirek around.'

'He's Mirek's bodyguard. I thought that was

obvious.' Clarke slipped off his trousers and put them in the press.

Anne considered this. 'If he needs one why don't you and why are you so afraid of him? I mean how did you meet?'

Clarke disappeared into the bathroom. He was not keen on answering the question. He turned on the tap and began to clean his teeth so that he did not have to answer. When he had finished he saw her in the mirror over the washbasin. She was in a slip, her long legs crossed, feet in high-heeled mules. Her expression belied her body language. She had hit a nerve and wanted to know why.

'Tell me,' she said. 'I thought he was just another overseas buyer but he's much more than that isn't he? When did you first meet?'

Clarke wiped his mouth and hung up the towel. 'I met him a few days ago. When he first came to London. He had an introduction from a contact.'

'And yet he's running the show already.'

'He's not running the show.' Suddenly Clarke flared up. 'You mention his knowledge of the basement. I took him down. He's a buyer for God's sake. He wanted to see what we had like the rest of them.'

'But unlike the rest of them he's still here and very much involved in what we are doing. It doesn't add up, Jeremy, you're hiding something and by your attitude I'd say quite a lot.'

'Don't be ridiculous. It was a good job he was there tonight. We'd never have known what happened.'

'We still don't and that worries me a great deal.

236

Come clean for God's sake.'

Clarke brushed past her and went into the bedroom. He put on his pyjamas and sat on the edge of the bed. 'I'm exhausted. Do we have to go into this now?'

'Yes we do. I want to know what I've let myself in for and to know whether or not it's worth it.'

'Your bank balance should tell you that.'

Anne had turned round to face him but still leant against the door jamb, arms crossed, expression stony. 'Money is no good to me if I'm dead.'

'Dead?' Clarke's head shot up, alarm showing as he tried to meet her gaze. 'What are you talking about?'

'There were shots fired in the house, which means someone broke in without leaving a sign and shots were fired as a result. We don't know if anyone was killed. We don't know anything at all when it comes down to it.'

'Mirek will sort that out.'

'Which brings us right back to square one. Who is he and exactly what is his part? I don't trust him and his bodyguard gives me the creeps. Stop running away from what's happening and give me some answers.'

Clarke gazed at the plush carpeting under his bare feet. 'He's both a buyer and supplier. You must know that the Russians have the biggest arms racket in the world. They've got a massive stockpile of surplus arms.'

'He was a Pole just now.'

'Don't be childish. Poles, Russians, Czechs, they're all at it.'

'So why does he need us?'

'Supplying is one thing, distribution another. There are so many international laws to get past. Transport. The whole logistics of the thing can be mind boggling but at which we British are experts and are second to none. We have an ideal sales set-up here in a quiet area no one would suspect, but our strength is in the contacts we have worldwide who are able to provide certain specialist items which are otherwise almost impossible to obtain. We've cornered certain markets. And one thing leads to another. But it's a vast and profitable field and needs a lot of people in a lot of different countries to manage it safely. It's all about contacts and Mirek is about as good as they come. He has enormous contacts abroad in places it is difficult for others to penetrate.'

Anne did not move. She gazed down thoughtfully at Clarke reflecting that he had told her very little she did not know already. He had really told her very little about Mirek. She could see the weakness in Clarke as she watched him now and had seen it before from time to time but it had not mattered as everything had progressed so smoothly.

It had started to go wrong when the man was killed in Trafalgar Square and Clarke had been interviewed by the police. She had never believed that he was capable of killing anyone and that the police enquiry was routine as he had briefly seen the murdered man. She understood all that but it was at that point his weakness began to show itself more regularly. He would never be a match for someone like Mirek. And that made her take stock of her options. She crossed to the dressing table as Clarke said, 'Satisfied?'

'Of course, darling. I just wanted clarification.' And then, turning to him with a tired smile, 'It's been a long, exhausting day.' Which offered both a peace offering and an excuse to go straight to sleep.

* * *

Jacko reasoned that the best time to pick up Jeremy Clarke was after he had left his office for the day. It was already dark at that time and people were hurrying home to escape work and the weather. He looked up a couple of old friends, one Knocker Roberts, now ageing but still formidable, who had fortunately mellowed otherwise Jacko dare not use him. Knocker had one side of his face mashed up like a Brillo pad, a permanent reminder of a very early brush with another villain who had not survived the bloody encounter.

The second man he recruited was an old colleague in the SAS who worked for a security firm. Sandy Tate was about Jacko's age, not yet in his forties, bored with his job and only too pleased to do a little on the side if there was some promise of excitement. The timescale fitted in with his job and the extra money would be useful. And, like Jacko, he could look as if he might be a policeman if required.

It took a day to find and convince them, so it was left to the following evening before they attempted the kidnap of Clarke.

They had not followed Clarke at all. They simply waited outside the DTI building hoping he would emerge with the evening exodus. Jacko knew that Clarke went home by underground and the idea was that he never got started; but the timing had to be absolutely right.

Jacko and Tate were standing either side of the main door as the crowds began to swell, arriving in a steady and increasing stream from the buildings around. Tate, who did not know what Clarke looked like, was relying on Jacko for the initial recognition. In the event Clarke was picked out quite quickly. He was one of the first to leave and was in a hurry.

Jacko closed in fast, came alongside Clarke, produced a police warrant card which had been forged for him on another case, and said, 'Mr Jeremy Clarke? I wonder if you can spare me a moment.'

Clarke, who wanted to get back to Anne Corrie and try to rebuild his bridges with her, stopped angrily. 'Just what the hell do you want, Sergeant? Do you realise how embarrassing this is?'

'It won't take a moment, sir. We can talk by our car, just over there.'

Clarke peered towards the kerb and saw a Jaguar ghosting in and stopping almost opposite them. A blue flasher, not in use, was perched at an angle on the Jaguar's roof so he supposed it was a plain squad car and the flasher had been used as an emergency to get through the traffic and to park on the double yellow lines. He stopped, unwilling to go but aware that colleagues might see what was happening. 'This isn't still about that bloody murder, surely?'

Clarke had only just realised that another man was close to him on his other side. He turned in surprise and Sandy Tate gave him a reassuring smile.

Jacko said, 'Oh no, sir. We know you are not involved in that. This is about your place in Northwood.'

'What about it?' Clarke was already in a nervous state at the mere mention of Northwood.

'Let's move over to the car, sir. We're in everybody's way.' He took Clarke lightly by the arm and guided him forward. Clarke felt like making a run for it but realised in time how that might look to any of his colleagues who were still leaving the building.

They stopped by the car and Clarke demanded haughtily, 'Well?'

'Perhaps it might be better if we get in the car, sir. That way no one can see you.'

Clarke gazed around. The place was thick with people and traffic. 'Say what you have to say here. I'm not getting into the car.' And then, 'I intend to make a complaint about this. I don't like your style.'

'You'll like it even less if you don't step into the car, sir.'

At that point, and from Jacko's tone, Clarke knew that something was wrong. He weighed up his chances and decided to make a break for it. Before he could move Tate had moved close and rammed a gun in his back.

Clarke said, 'What the hell do you think you are doing? You can't shoot me in public.'

'Why not? Mirek's man did it. Get in.' Jacko opened the rear door but retained a grip on Clarke's arm. Jacko had gambled but was working on the premise that Clarke, like himself, was not certain who had killed Jones.

It was the mere mention of Mirek's name that stunned Clarke. For a moment he was rooted. And while he was in that state Jacko pushed him forward and Tate gave the final shove that helped him into the car. Once in Clarke recovered enough to put up some kind of fight and tried to get out the other side.

Jacko had rushed round to the offside of the Jaguar and as the door opened he pulled it all the way and pushed Clarke back in. Tate, who had climbed in after Clarke having grabbed the blue flasher and tossed it on to the front seat, closed the door behind him and tapped Clark on the base of the neck with his pistol to put him out. Jacko pushed Clarke away and climbed in. 'Okay, Knocker.'

Knocker Roberts, who had the engine running, pulled out into the mainstream traffic. Jacko and Tate pushed Clarke right down on the floor between the front and rear seats. While Jacko held him Sandy Tate taped Clarke's mouth and bandaged his eyes. They then pulled Clarke's arms back and taped his wrists, keeping his head down while Knocker rode with the traffic.

'Not too bad,' Jacko exclaimed in relief.

'Better than routine security,' agreed Tate,

keeping his hand on top of Clarke's head. 'How far have we got to go?'

'North London and it will take time in this traffic. Knocker knows where to go.'

All they could do from then on was to sit back and let the very experienced Knocker get on with the driving. It was no time to be reckless.

It took them an hour in the heavy traffic during which time Clarke came to, struggled a little but found it difficult from where he had been pushed, and with his mouth taped could only make groaning sounds. Every time he tried to push himself on to the seat they pushed him down and Tate threatened to hit him again if he did not keep still. After a while he seemed to be crying. He was terrified, a condition which suited Jacko.

When they finally reached a quiet row of terraced Edwardian houses Knocker first drove slowly round while Jacko pointed out the actual house and then round the block to get the layout and to settle the parking, which would be difficult. He wanted a slot as near to the house as possible as they had to get Clarke in unobserved and the street was far from empty.

There was no vacant slot near to the house so Knocker parked as best he could, climbed out, said he would not be long and walked back towards the house they wanted.

At first Knocker thought he might have to move two cars but found a large, shabby estate car quite near to the steps leading up to the house. He chose his moment, produced the long wire to release the lock and opened the door. He had not expected an alarm due to the condition of the car. In his cynical way Knocker reflected that the owners were probably hoping the car would be stolen to claim on insurance. He connected the wires under the dash and the engine fired. He drove away to the end of the street and as he went past the Jaguar gave Jacko a signal.

Jacko climbed into the driver's seat as Tate was well able to take care of a restless Clarke and did a tight U-turn to hasten to the space Knocker had created for them. He reversed in, switched off and they waited for Knocker to return.

At this stage Clarke made an unusually spirited struggle. He did not know what was going to happen to him and assumed the worst. It was unfortunate that Tate had to tap him again knowing they could not take a struggling Clarke safely out of the car.

When a panting Knocker returned they had to wait their moment before Tate could open his nearside door and he and Jacko climbed out. Jacko went to help Tate with Clarke while Knocker locked the car and then returned to help the others.

They dragged Clarke up the steps, his legs trailing as if he was going to his execution. Halfway up the steps he started to struggle again and his legs threshed out. He was heavier than they anticipated but they eventually dragged him into the porch while Jacko fiddled with the keys North had given him. Once in they showed their relief in different ways, one of which was to drop Clarke like a heavy sack.

Jacko found the light switch. They were in a

narrow passage, the stairs halfway along. Clarke was kicking out and caught Knocker on the shin so he bent down angrily and side-handed Clarke who collapsed once again.

'Where to?' asked Tate.

'I've been told to use the upstairs,' replied Jacko. 'Our hosts don't want the downstairs messed up while they're sunning in Jamaica. But I think that might be a problem. Let's see what's downstairs.'

While the other two stayed with Clarke Jacko went round the ground floor rooms. They were all well furnished and comfortable. Wondering who North used the house for or whether it was now surplus to requirements, he returned to the others.

'There's quite a large utility room behind the kitchen. If there's a mess it will be easier to clean up.' He gave Knocker a hard look. 'But I hope there will be no mess at all.'

Knocker said quite seriously, 'That depends on how easily he bleeds.'

Clarke had come to again just sufficiently to hear the last words and he began to tremble as if he had a fever. They lifted him to his feet and with three guns pointing at his head he almost passed out again. Jacko was hoping his fear would change to terror and that he would talk quickly and save them all a lot of trouble. By the time they got him into the utility room and sat him on a kitchen chair he was too afraid to speak even after having the tape removed from his mouth.

Clarke's wrists remained taped and Knocker now taped his arms behind the chair back, still leaving his legs free. There was a big chest freezer, a washing machine and a tumble-dryer in the room plus sundry cupboards. The three men leaned against the various equipment staring down at the terrified Clarke who was positioned in the middle of the tiled floor.

Tate said of the tiling, 'This will be easy to clean up. We have water, a mop and a bucket over there. No problem. And we'll need it, the dirty bugger's wet himself. I wonder what his friends would think of him now?'

Clarke, close to despair, managed to stutter out, 'Look, what have I done to you? I'm no threat.'

'You're not now.' Jacko almost felt sorry for him until he recalled what Clarke was up to; not just the betrayal of trust and his country but the deadly game he was actually involved in, the killing machines in his basement. And where was the main stock? 'I'll tell you what we want to know and then we'll let you go. But it will have to satisfy us.'

'You'll let me go?'

'Of course.' Jacko managed to say it without complete conviction to increase Clarke's level of fear. It was a skilled game. If he overdid it Clarke might reach a stage of such despair that nothing mattered to him any more. It was all a question of balance and the three kidnappers had all been trained to resist such techniques and, therefore, how to apply them.

Clarke fell into a near paralytic silence. He found it painful to look up at these three armed men who seemed to be so casual about the whole affair. For a while they seemed to ignore him completely and conversed as if he was not there at all.

'We don't want too much blood,' said Jacko. 'It's difficult stuff to clean up even on this type of floor.' He turned to Knocker. 'And I don't want another body on my hands. It means we'll have to bury him and that takes time and risks. But I don't mind if you break a few bones.'

Knocker replied a little heatedly, 'I didn't know the bloke had a dodgy ticker. I didn't kill him, he conked out.' He looked down at Clarke with contempt. 'Have you got a heart condition before I start on you?'

When Clarke tried to answer but failed to get the words out Knocker added, 'I'll take that as a no.' He turned to Jacko. 'You want me to start now? You'd better bring that bucket over.'

Tate brought the bucket and placed it on the floor in front of Clarke. He said to Knocker, 'You want us to leave? I can't stand screaming. I'd rather you croaked him than that.'

Jacko said, 'Maybe he'll cooperate before we start on him. Can you hear all right?' He raised Clarke's head by his hair. 'Look at me.'

Clarke's eyes were bloodshot and his gaze focused on Jacko reluctantly. His fear was obvious but there was also an expression of mute pleading. He was imploring Jacko to work a miracle and let him go.

'Just what do you want?' he managed at last. 'I've done nothing to any of you?'

'Us personally? Maybe. But what about the various wars around the globe? Wars that you thrive on. The children in Africa being maimed

247

daily, legs, feet, arms, hands blown off. Mines that are difficult to find that will stay there long after the war is over, still killing, still maiming. What about your betrayal of your country?'

'I've done nothing to harm my country. On the contrary, it benefits from my work.'

'Is that what you call it? Work? Not murder?'

Clarke had been given something to reason about and was able to focus better. 'That's a naive concept. There will always be wars whatever we do.' The courage he had suddenly mustered scared him almost as much as the men around him. Clarke was suddenly afraid of his own answer. 'People have different outlooks, some idealist, some realist. It's a toss of the coin. If we are to talk morality then why have there probably been more wars over religion, the supposed vehicle of peace, than any other cause?' Clarke believed he was fighting for his life and in an oblique way he was. It had taken what little courage he had to answer at all but having done so what he said was logical to him. He knew he had to be convincing even if it drained him.

'So you accept the inevitable and make a lot of money from it?'

'Doesn't everybody? Aren't you being paid for what you are doing now? You preach but you are nothing but kidnappers and torturers.' Clarke's mind had slipped into autopilot. He was scared of his own answers in the event of annoying his captors yet they had come out almost without him thinking as if someone else was talking for him. And he found it helped him to talk even if his voice did sound shaky.

'So you've no regrets? You want no opportunity to repent?'

Knocker moved the bucket with his foot and made a racket in doing so to remind Clarke it was still there and had a purpose.

'Tell me what you want of me. Come out with it, for God's sake.'

'We want a list of all your clients who visit Northwood. Bear in mind that the house is still in your name and is being used as a sales centre for some particularly nasty weapons. Just give me a list.'

Clarke stiffened. He was now faced with another fear and his muddled mind had to try to evaluate one against the other. He was forced to compare the threat of Mirek and Chaznov against these three strangers. It would be useless to deny any knowledge; that could bring pain. These men knew what he was doing but lacked the detail and the ramifications. The comparison created a hidden steeliness about him. He had to survive and to work out which way to jump.

'Were you the one who broke in last night?' he said to Jacko.

'Broke in? Where?'

'You know where. Northwood. What happened to the man who was staying there? Perhaps the police should know.'

'Don't threaten me with the police. You dare not go within a mile of the police.' Jacko took a chance. 'Okay, the man who was guarding the place is dead. We shot him. A cleaner way of dying than you will have if you don't start answering the questions. Where's the list of clients, Clarke, and where is the main supply of arms? Northwood is only the showroom.' But Jacko was disturbed by the obvious fact that Clarke knew there had been a break-in; someone had spotted the bullet holes and that was bad news.

'I haven't got a list.'

'Then who has?'

'I don't know. I really don't. It's not my job to have a list.'

'So what is your job?'

'I just help with introductions. There are British businessmen who are interested in our products and in selling them abroad.'

'Under phoney licenses which you supply. Documents that disguise the nature of the goods?'

'It's only bending the rules a little. The country needs the money.'

'Sure. Blood money. Who knows in the department what you are doing?'

'No one.'

'And Anne Corrie? What is her part?'

'She has nothing to do with it. She is my companion.'

'So why does she visit Northwood so often? And who are the men she meets there?'

'I don't know. I'm at the office or meeting people. I think she wants the place done up so she probably has interior designers in.'

'You sure she's not on the game? Strange that they're all men and so many of them.'

'Why do you say a thing like that?' Clarke was

doing much better than at first but was rattled by the implication. 'I can't be expected to account for her movements while I'm working.'

At this point Knocker said, 'He's found some dutch courage. Let's show him we mean business.' He said to Clarke, 'Stand up.' And then pulled Clarke upright with one hand, the chair clattering behind him. 'Stand against the wall just there and don't move.'

Clarke stood facing the wall, scared again, and then the bucket was shoved hard over his head and everything went black as the lights were turned out and almost immediately he began to feel the effects of disorientation. And a disembodied voice was demanding, 'Now tell me about Bykov.'

16

Clarke believed he was floating, his legs had left the ground. He wanted to tear the bucket from his head but his hands were still tied behind his back. Different voices came to him from different directions and they were confusing him. Many hands grabbed him and one of the voices said, 'Stay on your feet. Keep still.'

Clarke believed he was on his feet but as he was lifted realised that he must have fallen. His only stability was when he put his head against the wall but with the bucket in the way it was painful and breathing was already difficult.

'Bykov,' yelled Jacko close to the bucket. 'Tell me about Bykov.'

Clarke tried to think but his whole body seemed to be doing strange things and was no longer joined to his head. Someone tapped the bucket with a metallic object and he thought his eardrums would burst; it was like church bells right inside his head.

'Bykov,' yelled Jacko again.

But Clarke did not understand the question. One of them was using a foreign language. He tried to reply and his own words reverberated inside the bucket and it sounded garbled. 'What is Bykov?' he called out but it was all so muffled.

'Mirek. Is he Bykov?'

'He's Polish,' Clarke replied still not understanding.

Standing right next to Clarke but not actually touching him for that would give Clarke a sense of reality, Jacko realised that Clarke really had no idea what he was talking about. And that was disappointing.

'Okay,' said Jacko. 'Who are your suppliers, who are your clients and where is the list of both?'

'Can I have this bucket off? I'm standing on my head. I don't know where I am.' Which were the truest words Clarke had spoken. He felt as if his mind would blow.

Jacko said, 'We'll remove the bucket if we get some answers. The moment we think you are lying the bucket goes back on and we leave you here alone until morning. By then you'll be a rambling lunatic. Do you understand?'

'Yes.'

The bucket came off and the light went on simultaneously. Clarke staggered round the room temporarily blind, and disorientated, his legs gave way and they had to help him to a chair. It was no time to let up.

'Who has the detail we want?' Jacko demanded close to Clarke's ear.

Clarke was having difficulty sitting on the chair and Sandy Tate held him steady. Clarke's lips moved but nothing came out and Jacko bawled, 'Get the bloody bucket again.'

'No. No. Please. My mouth is dry, it is difficult for me to move my tongue.' It certainly sounded like it; Clarke was almost incoherent.

'Get him some water.'

They gave him a drink but did not let him linger

253

over it and took it away before he was satisfied.

'List,' said Jacko. 'This is the last time I'll ask.'

'I don't have it. I've never had it. All I know are a few businessmen in the UK who are prepared to bend the rules. They are so few I don't need a list for them; they are in my head.'

'But you can write them down?' Jacko produced a pad. 'Call them out to me.'

When Clarke had finished he glanced over towards the bucket and swallowed with difficulty. 'If there is a list of buyers and dealers then Mirek has it.'

'Mirek seems to be all important.'

'Yes.'

'Do you think he shot the man Jones?'

'I'm sure that he did not. He would not want the attention.'

'Do you know who did?'

'No. But he has a Russian bodyguard. Maybe he did. I don't know.'

'Describe the bodyguard to me.'

Clarke's description was far from perfect but it was sufficient for Jacko to recognise the man he had seen in a taxi when he had followed Clarke from his apartment. Jacko provided a notebook and pen and told Clarke to write down his business contacts. When Clarke had finished he said to Jacko, 'Most buyers are foreigners. I don't know them.'

'But Anne Corrie should. She's the one who's been seeing them.'

'I'm sure she knows nothing. She is merely acting as a host.'

'Stop trying to protect her. She would not do

254

the same for you. Did you know she has a police record for fraud?'

'I don't believe you.'

Jacko smiled sadly. 'You don't want to believe. It was not a big deal but I promise you she has a record. Watch your back.'

Clarke seemed to see that as an end to his suffering. 'Can I go now?'

The other three all grinned widely, the plea was so plaintive, so unsure; a little boy's plea.

'What will you do if we let you go?'

'I don't know. I need time to think. Everything's a mess.'

'Will you tell Mirek about this meeting?'

Clarke had not yet dared to think about it but he tried to now and found no answer.

'Let me help you,' said Jacko. 'There aren't many alternatives but these are the obvious ones. You can go to the police and report what's happened. If you do that you incriminate yourself. You can report to Mirek; tell him what happened. If you do that what do you think he'll do?'

It did not bear thinking about. 'I don't know.'

'Yes you do. He'll protect himself. He'll kill you.'

Clarke did not attempt to argue for it made terrifying sense.

'Or you can tell Anne Corrie what has happened. What do you think she will do?'

'She'll help me. Tell me what is best to do.'

'You really think that? Anne Corrie, with the police record which she did not confide in you, will look after Anne Corrie; first and last. And if that means feeding you to the lions that's what she will do. Doesn't leave you with many options does it?'

Clarke did not reply as he thought furiously for a safety net.

Jacko anticipated him when he said, 'Or you can do a runner. But the moment you do that you'll have the police, Interpol, Mirek and the Russian Mafia after you. One of that lot will find you. It's a bleak future isn't it? And a very short one.'

'Why are you telling me all this? What the hell do you care?'

'I don't. Not what happens to you. You deserve anything you get. But there is one more alternative. You can go home and act as if nothing has happened. Just play along. Say you've been working late. You do sometimes don't you?'

Clarke nodded affirmation but said, 'I can't do it. I'd never get away with it.'

'You can if you consider the alternatives.'

Tate and Knocker had backed off to the far corner out of Clarke's sight, aware that they were on the point of achieving a result.

Clarke looked up. 'Look at me. I haven't the nerve.'

'You had the nerve to go bent and do some very specialised gun-running. That required a lot of nerve. This requires less.'

Clarke shook his head slowly, a sorry figure full of despair. 'I was forced into it. It was a long time ago but they had something on me. There was nothing else I could do.'

'And now we have something on you and there's

still nothing else you can do.' Jacko was eager to learn what they had on Clarke and who had recruited him and when. But that would distract; he felt close to success and had to persevere in the line he was taking.

Clarke remained silent so Jacko added, 'We can ruin your life or throw you a lifeline.'

'You've already ruined my life. There's no lifeline.'

'Not ultimately keeping your job, that's true. But if you help us now we can help you disappear. No court case, no false promises of remission. You must already have enough salted away to give you a fresh start somewhere else. Think about it. It's open to you. If you handle it right you might even persuade Anne Corrie to go with you. She must be sitting on a nest egg, too.'

Clarke at last conceded that it looked like his only chance. 'What do you want me to do exactly?'

'Just carry on as you've been doing. We'll pose no further threat to you so that should steady your nerves. In fact we're your ticket out in due course. We'll arrange a number where you can contact us day and night so that you can report what's going on. Nothing could be simpler. Easy.'

Clarke's voice was a little stronger as he said, 'Just who are you?'

Jacko smiled. 'I sometimes wonder. It does not matter who we are. All that matters is that we know what you're up to and you are going to help us stop it. You should be grateful; you were heading for complete disaster.' When Clarke failed to respond Jacko said, 'And you probably knew it.'

Clarke gazed down at himself. 'Look at me, I'm a wreck. I can't go home like this.'

'We'll help tidy you up. You'll be okay.' Jacko scribbled a number on his pad and tore off the sheet. He gave a signal to Knocker who released Clarke from the tape; he immediately began to rub his wrists. Being free of restraint alone gave Clarke added confidence. He took the sheet from Jacko and glanced at it to see a telephone number.

'Memorise it,' advised Jacko. 'It's a very easy number to remember. Don't carry it on you and don't let anyone else see it.'

'I'm not likely to. Will this number reach you?'

'No. It's an answering machine. All you do is to leave a telephone number and a time when it's safe to contact you and we'll ring back. Don't try to trace the number; it's untraceable. And don't be afraid to use your office number; it might be the safest. We'll make sure it will be all right for you.'

'You're the Security Service, aren't you? That's who you are.'

'If we were you'd be behind bars by now and so would your girlfriend. Stop trying to work it out. And just remember we are the best bet you have of survival.' Jacko pushed himself away from the freezer he had been leaning against and asked, 'Can you stand? Come on, let's get you cleaned up.'

★ ★ ★

'Do you think he will cope?' asked Paula who heated them both a microwave meal at Jacko's place. It was now ten at night and Jacko was showing signs of tiredness. They sat at the small kitchen table; it was more convenient and intimate than the dining room.

'I don't know,' Jacko replied. 'He's all we've got. We have to hope it works. We put the fear of God into him but once he starts thinking logically he will see that we offer the best chance of survival. The question is whether or not he trusts us enough. He knows he can't trust Mirek when his own interests are at risk and I think I've put the seed of doubt in his mind about Anne Corrie. But it's all very iffy. He's not the strongest of characters and could well panic.'

'All right. I'll go down to Northwood tomorrow to see her. Armed with what you've given me I'll at least have that advantage.'

Jacko sat back almost too tired to eat. 'I wonder if that is wise bearing in mind that they know about the shots which is a bit of a blow. They can't know exactly what happened to Boris but it's now unlikely that they think he did a runner.'

'I can use that to advantage,' said Paula. 'Don't worry.'

'She'll be a lot tougher than Clarke. Want me to come with you? After all I had two guys with me.' He smiled to himself. 'It was good seeing Sandy and Knocker again after so long. You wouldn't believe how much Knocker has mellowed; he didn't even break a finger.'

'I wouldn't know,' said Paula. 'I've never met him. And no, I don't want you with me. This will be woman to woman stuff. I have a police ID from one of North's men.'

Jacko pushed his half empty plate away. 'Thanks for the meal, Paula. You won't be going back to the flat at this time will you?'

She replied impishly, 'Why? Do you think you're fit enough to ask me to stay?'

★ ★ ★

By morning Paula had agreed to let Jacko drive her to Northwood but that she would interview alone. He drove her to Sid Lewis's place and they went in, North having arranged keys for them. Two of North's men were in the room where Lewis had mounted his binoculars and camera and where he had been killed. Not much had changed except the quality and size of the equipment: both camera and binoculars were of high professional standard.

None of them exchanged names, North had warned his men that Jacko and Paula would arrive but the greetings were short on cordiality; North's men did not appreciate outside help and resented part-timers but had to accept the position.

'Has the woman arrived?' asked Paula.

'No one has called so far. Did the guy who was murdered here say there were daily visitors?'

'No. Not daily. But when the woman did come someone else would follow.' Jacko stood clear of the window.

'So she came to receive them?'

'Presumably. Do you mind if I hang on here if my colleague decides to go across?'

'Help yourself.' The reply was noncommittal. The man, in spite of the chill in the room, had his jacket off and his tie pulled down. His colleague wore a thick polo neck. There were high stools for them to sit on while they took turns to peer through the glasses. There were two collapsable canvas chairs and a small trestle table held a supply of wrapped sandwiches and thermos flasks. Jacko and Paula were offered no refreshments.

Anne Corrie arrived just before midday. She was alone and in no hurry.

'I'll give her half an hour and then go over,' said Paula.

'Supposing she has a caller?' Jacko pointed out.

'That's her problem. You'll all be watching.'

North's men were vaguely intrigued by this exchange. Their duty was to observe and they did not like the idea of anyone on their team making a call which could upset the person they were observing.

Much to Jacko's surprise Paula gave him a peck before leaving and he realised she was nervous. The three men watched her cross the road from the window.

'Dresses nicely,' observed the man on the binoculars. 'Nice legs and walks well. I hope she bloody well knows what she's doing and doesn't cock it up for us.'

'That's my girlfriend,' said Jacko icily. 'While I'm here watch what you say.'

'I'm sorry. I didn't realise.' The reply was unconvincing and Jacko wondered why he was bothering in such a resentful atmosphere.

Meanwhile Paula had crossed the road and was

261

approaching Clarke's house knowing that the three men were watching her. She closed the small gate and went up the short uneven path and rang the bell. There was no response. As Paula had heard the chimes inside the house she guessed that Anne Corrie might be down in the basement. She rang again and held the bell push down. With the bell echoing it sounded so empty in the house. Still nothing happened and from that Paula assumed that whoever was calling was not due for a while or Anne would have been waiting. She rang a third time knowing that Anne was in there somewhere.

Paula heard no one approach and was taken by surprise when the door suddenly opened and Anne Corrie stood there, clearly not in a good mood.

'Yes?'

Paula produced her warrant card. 'Detective Sergeant Johnson. May I have a few words, please.'

'What about?' Anne Corrie was almost rude but mellowed her tone at the last moment; it was no time to antagonise the police.

'Can we go inside?'

'It's not terribly convenient. I'd like to know what you want.'

'We had a report about some shooting.'

'Shooting? What sort of shooting?'

Paula said heavily, 'I'm not prepared to discuss this on your doorstep. Either let me in or you can come down to the station and we can talk there.'

Anne Corrie knew she was handling it badly which was unusual for her but she had much on her mind. She managed an insincere smile and said, 'That sounds suspiciously like blackmail.'

'No. I'm simply giving you a choice.'

'Well, I hope it won't take long; I have someone coming.' Anne opened the door wider, Paula stepped in and was glad when the door closed behind her so that she was out of sight of North's men across the road.

'You'll have to forgive the state of the place, but it's on the market and little has been done to it.' Anne Corrie led the way to the shabby lounge and was clearly willing to stand in order to end the matter quickly but Paula chose the most comfortable looking chair and sat down.

Anne reluctantly sat on the arm of the opposite chair. 'Shots?' she queried heavily.

Paula saw Anne as a very attractive woman but her hardness came through, not only in her voice. Jacko was right — she was a tough lady whom she suspected could be very soft indeed if the rewards were big enough. She had a bare glimpse of the Clarke-Corrie relationship. 'We had a report this morning that shots were heard coming from this house in the early hours of the morning. I wondered if you knew anything about it?'

'Who in God's name told you that? Someone must have been having nightmares.'

'Obviously someone near enough to complain about it. I can't give a name. It wouldn't change anything if I did.'

Anne spread her hands in disbelief. 'What am I supposed to say to that? It's absurd.'

'So there were no shots?'

'It would come as a complete shock to me if there were. It's a crazy notion.'

'Are you saying that you would have heard them had there been?'

Anne faltered, seeing the trap. 'No. I wasn't here.'

'So how could you know?'

'Well wouldn't there be signs or something? Does someone just go into a house and fire shots? What for?'

'Was no one staying here at all then?'

After the barest hesitation Anne replied. 'The house was empty. I left it empty. What would anyone be firing at?'

'That's a good question. Perhaps someone gets in and sleeps here knowing that the house is empty. It could be very convenient for someone wanting a billet.'

'How would they get in?'

Paula shrugged and smiled. 'Well, Miss Corrie, I think you know that's a naive question. So you are saying there is absolutely no sign of disturbance or a struggle and that everything is as you left it yesterday.'

Anne Corrie had stiffened. 'How did you know my name? I don't own this house.'

'Oh, we know that a man called Jeremy Clarke owns it. I did do my homework before calling.'

'You haven't answered my question, Sergeant.'

'And you haven't answered mine, ma'am.' Paula let the little mystery hang knowing that Anne would raise it again and that she had shown the first sign of concern.

Anne stared coolly at Paula knowing that she must be careful. 'You don't look old enough to be a sergeant. They must promote them young these days.' Perhaps attack was the best policy.

'Thank you for the compliment. I obviously look younger than I am. You still haven't answered the question.'

'Signs of shots? I'm not sure what signs I'd be looking for. But I've seen no evident signs of shots, damage or of anything disturbed. It all looks as I left it. Don't you think the notion is absurd?'

'I don't know. I was not the one who reported it. But it was obviously real to someone.' As Anne was about to reply Paula added, 'The report came from more than one source.'

'There must have been an explosion somewhere, a gas mains or something.'

'There are no reports of gas mains blowing. Tell me, Miss Corrie, what is your connection with this house?'

'What the hell has that got to do with you?'

'It might help me decide the veracity of what you have told me.'

Anne rose angrily. 'How dare you! You have absolutely no right to say something like that. Which is your station? I'm going to report this.'

'You are pretty indignant for someone with form.'

Anne sank back onto the arm of the chair. She had paled a little. 'So you've dug up a paltry charge made when I was a teenager.'

'A little older than that, I think. I told you I had done my homework. Fraud wasn't it?'

'A piddling offence. God, it was years ago and I was desperate. I should never have been charged.'

'But you were and found guilty. So I ask again, what is your connection with this house and Jeremy Clarke?'

'Can you tell me what this has to do with shots?'

'Just answer the question.'

'I keep an eye on the place for him.'

'So you are employed by him?'

'No. We are partners. I help where I can and it saves him coming down here.'

Paula leaned forward. 'I'm sorry but I'm a little puzzled here. Mr Clarke is a civil servant. What sort of partnership could that be?'

'Now who's naive. I thought you were too young to be a sergeant.'

'Do you mean you are lovers?'

'You are going too far, Sergeant. None of this has anything to do with shots. I think I've spent enough time on this.'

Paula rose and gazed round the room. 'Do you mind if I look around?'

'Have you a warrant?'

'A search warrant? No. I don't want to search but merely to look around to see if I can see something you might have missed. I have still to make a report.'

To refuse her might make it look as if she had something to hide. But the bullet holes were still visible and a trained eye might pick them out as Chaznov's had done. 'Report what you like. I think I've helped enough. It was a stupid idea anyway.'

'Okay. Just a couple more questions. You said

you are expecting a visitor. Do you get many visitors?'

'Some. I told you the house is on the market. It's better that someone is here when they call wouldn't you say?'

'Doesn't an estate agent cope with all that?'

'It's still better that someone who knows the place is at hand.'

They had reached the door of the lounge and Paula stepped out into the narrow hall. Memory of Boris and the fight with Jacko were still fresh in her mind and she suffered a strange experience as they reached the study. She was gazing up at the ceiling and around the doors and Anne, who was just behind her began to get nervous.

Paula said, 'My information is that Mr Clarke is hanging on to the house waiting for a developer. There is strong talk of blocks of flats going up here in which case this place would be worth far more than market price for the house. So why is it on the market?'

'You'd have to ask him. Anyway, that's old hat. You do dig don't you, Sergeant?'

Paula did not reply but gazed straight at the spot where Boris's second bullet had gone. Behind her Anne waited anxiously but was completely surprised when Paula asked, 'Do you know a man called Bykov?'

'Bykov? No. I've never heard of him.'

Paula turned to face her. 'A man called Mirek, then?'

Anne hesitated too long. She had not expected either question. 'Not that I recall.'

'And you would recall a name like that wouldn't you?'

'I would think so.'

'Well, the next time you see Mr Mirek ask him if he knows a Mr Bykov.'

Paula went to the front door knowing she was leaving behind a very worried Anne Corrie. She opened the front door herself and once outside turned to say, 'By the way, there was at least one shot. There's a bullet hole high up opposite the door down there. That's something else to tell your Mr Mirek. Unless, of course, he already knows.'

Paula gave a stunned and very worried Anne Corrie a sweet smile and went down the path, calling out behind her. 'Don't leave town. I'll be back.'

17

They were down to using their digital telephones, the taxi meetings having worn a bit thin and a change necessary. Part of the problem was that both Mirek and Chaznov were satisfied that they were still without a tail but that one could appear at any moment to catch them out. The digital was adequate communication but far from ideal on important issues.

'This woman keeps popping up,' Chaznov reported. 'Not actually following but around the hotel. Her interest seems to be in you.'

'Describe her.' Mirek did not need a description but he did need a little time.

Chaznov gave a fairly accurate description of Irina Janesky and waited for Mirek to respond.

This was where Mirek found telephones restrictive; he needed to take time to think. He took so long that Chaznov said, 'Did you hear me?'

'Yes I heard you. Just wait for a moment.' This was ridiculous. Even though he knew they could not be overheard or bugged he really needed Chaznov to be there so that they could chew over the complications. After long deliberation he said, 'This is the favour I wanted of you. The private job.'

'You want me to deal with her?'

There were times when Mirek was not convinced that these digital telephones could not be tapped.

This was a terrible exchange to have over a phone and yet it was safer than in his own room. 'Yes,' he said at last. 'Yes.'

'You don't sound sure. I want you to have no regrets. And we have not discussed an actual fee.'

'I won't quibble about the fee. Look, that is the job I want done but put it on hold until I give you the okay. That will also give you time to plan. You can't leave this one on the steps of the National Gallery. There must be a proper disposal, never to be found again. Work it out. She must literally disappear for good. She must never be found.'

'I understand. You know she's Russian?'

'It doesn't matter. Do it when I give the signal. There might not be much notice.'

★ ★ ★

The rest of the day went all too slowly for Anne Corrie. The visitor, when he finally came, proved to be someone with grand ideas and little in the way of finances to back them up. He knew his stuff but she suspected that he was acting as an agent for someone else. She wondered how he had found about them and it struck her as dangerous. This rarely happened but it was one of those days and she cursed Detective Sergeant Johnson for the start of a bad day. And there was the usual problem of communication, she could not safely ring Clarke and would have to wait until the evening when he came home. And that was no guarantee of a meaningful dialogue.

The previous evening Clarke had been both late

and uncommunicative, almost surly in his responses to her. At first she thought that something dreadful had happened but he eventually convinced her that it was overwork and tiredness and that he needed his sleep that night.

After the visitor had gone she had more time to think over the meeting with the sergeant and the more she went over it the less convinced was she that the sergeant was actually a police officer. Would she have come alone? She had made no notes. And she knew about Mirek and she knew that bloody shots had been fired. And that doubt made it much worse. If she wasn't police then who was she? And who the hell was Bykov? It was difficult for her to know which way to turn. Just who could she confide in? When she considered that she did not like the answer and felt very alone.

When she met Clarke that night the whole atmosphere between them had changed. They had entered their own private worlds and because it had happened to them both it was not so noticeable to either. They wanted to be left alone with their own thoughts and to sort out their own fears. Clarke still made the excuse of overwork and Anne the frustration of wasting time on a wannabe who had ideas of grandeur and surprisingly good contacts to have heard of the house which made her begin to wonder if he had represented the opposition.

Anne had mulled over the prospect of telling Clarke about the visit of the police. She still was not sure if the caller had been the police but in any event she felt that Clarke might panic if she told him. So each had their own secrets which they kept to themselves and the result was to separate them emotionally. Yet they had to give the impression that the feeling for each other was normal, set back only by fatigue and frustration.

Anne Corrie projected her thoughts beyond the present and wondered if Clarke would ever be up to the strain of coping with threatening situations. He could cope while everything went well but cracks were beginning to appear and she reflected that she might be better off without him. Or, if he remained, he was too unpredictable to stay with. She considered getting out. And then she considered getting him out. She had no direct contact with Mirek but felt the answer lay with him. There must be a contact number for Mirek somewhere on Clarke. She would have to wait until Clarke was asleep.

Having considered that she reflected that in spite of protests of over-tiredness neither would sleep very well and that was not good. She went to the bathroom and turned the key silently behind her. She took a bottle of Temazopan from the cabinet, opened two of the plastic phials and dropped the powdered contents onto a piece of toilet paper. She dropped the empty phials down the sink, ran the tap, screwed up the paper with the powder and slipped it into her waistband. She then flushed the toilet, ran the tap again and rejoined Clarke in the lounge. He was watching the late news on television.

Anne went to the drinks trolley and poured two stiff whiskies, slipping the powder into one of the glasses and stirring it thoroughly with her finger, making sure her body screened her actions from Clarke. She took the drinks over to him. 'After a day like this I think we both need one. Cheers.'

Clarke took the drink, thanking her quite warmly. He needed the drink to steady his nerves now he had started to play a charade.

Anne returned to her seat. There was something that had been niggling at her ever since the police sergeant had left and she did not know how to broach it but felt that she should. During the commercial break she said offhandedly, 'Have you ever heard of someone called Bykov?'

She was unprepared for his reaction. She thought he was going to drop his glass but he steadied it in time to lose only a few drops; his hand was tight around the glass and his expression frozen. His voice was unusually dry as he struggled to say, 'How do you spell it?'

She told him how she thought it might be spelled but explained that she had pronounced the name phonetically.

Clarke had recovered a little but he could still feel the bucket over his head and the disembodied, demanding voices. 'No,' he said at last. 'No.'

'It took a long time for you to decide.' Anne could have added that his whole reaction was alarming — he had heard the name all right and that worried her although she could not explain why. Why deny it if he knew?

He glanced over to her, sipping at his drink. What next? 'I was giving it some thought.'

'You almost dropped your whisky at the mention of the name.'

'Not at the mention but at the intrusion; I was miles away. It just came as a shock. It's the state I'm in. I'll see what I can do tomorrow to cut the workload down.'

'So you've never heard of a man called Bykov?'

'No. Nor a woman.'

'Very funny.'

He drank half his whisky and felt better. Then he said, 'What made you ask anyway? Who is he?'

'I don't know. I've heard the name somewhere and I can't think where. It's been niggling me. You know how these things do.'

'Yes.' He did not want to pursue it any more for fear of where it might lead. That was the second time the name had cropped up in as many days. He knew where he had heard it and was certain that so did she. And that worried him a great deal.

★ ★ ★

A satisfied North had got the whisky out. 'We've shaken the tree. Now we have to wait.' He raised his glass. 'Cheers. You both did a great job but I won't be satisfied until Clarke starts to ring you with useful information. We've sown the seeds. We have to be patient and see how they sprout. Sooner or later either Anne Corrie or Jeremy Clarke are going to start looking after number one. They can't be very comfortable just now.'

North took a good long look at them and thought they both appeared jaded. He was fully aware that his own men would not have coped as well with the thug in the basement in Northwood; it had taken the kind of training that these two part-timers had endured in their military days. Yes, they had shaken the tree but how effectively and which way the fruit might fall was unpredictable. It could very well go against them and he guessed they realised that without him saying anything. He had to hope that their effort worked as they wanted it to.

'You want to put a tail back on Mirek?' Paula asked.

'No. I've considered it. I think we should stick to the soft underbelly and stay with Clarke and the woman. Anne Corrie must have agonised over the bullet hole. By now she'll be pretty sure you weren't police and I believe that will worry her sick. It's a question of which way she jumps.'

Still talking to Paula, North said, 'Go to the Savoy and see what Irina Janesky is currently up to. I'm getting a little bit nervous of her and she could spoil the whole game.'

★ ★ ★

Anne lay beside Clarke and listened to his restlessness. She did not know how long the pills would take to work but he was far from being in a deep sleep. She turned to look at him in the subdued light coming from the street lamps outside. He was on his back, legs splayed, head back and strange noises were coming from his throat as if he was trying to speak. She leaned forward and placed an ear close to his mouth but his garble was unintelligible. It was difficult just to lie there because he had left her precious little room. Finally she swung her legs out of bed and gazed down at him. He was still fighting his demons, still stirring restlessly and still mumbling. He was trapped in his own nightmares by the drug which so far controlled him. But he was struggling against his terrors and she was concerned about how long he would remain out. She covered him up although with the central heating left on all day it was quite warm in the apartment. He was still restless but she decided she could wait no longer.

Anne went to the wardrobe and slid back one of the doors as quietly as she could, turning to see if he had heard. Clarke was meticulous about his clothes and she had no trouble finding the suit he had worn that day. She carefully unhooked the hanger from the rail and moved toward the lounge door. When she reached it she looked back but nothing had changed and Clarke was still murmuring. She carefully opened the door and went through into the lounge, closing the door behind her and switching on one of the lights.

Sitting down on the settee where she could spread his clothes out, she started on the lapels of the jacket in a way so thorough that it suggested she had done something similar before. She followed the stitching right round the edge of the jacket and then felt over the lining. She left the pockets until last believing they would be the most unlikely place to find anything useful. She then started on the turn-ups of his trousers; Clarke had always asserted that they would come back into fashion. She did not rush the search because if he had anything to hide at all it would be well hidden.

When she eventually finished she glanced at the wall clock and was disturbed to find that she had been there over an hour. She had found nothing. His wallet was an unlikely place for him to keep a secret and that was in his bedside table drawer. She put the suit back on its hanger being careful to ensure that it was facing the right way and crept back to the door. She switched off the light and opened the door, peering over to Clarke before entering the bedroom.

Clarke was now on his side facing his bedside table and his breathing was almost inaudible. He was quite still. Anne crossed to the wardrobe, hung up his suit and slid the door along. She turned toward the bed realising that by now she was really pushing her luck. She went round the bed and faced him. At first she thought he had stopped breathing but she picked up the gentle sound and guessed he had shed his nightmares for the time being. As she watched him she suffered the illusion in the poor light that he was watching her but it was the way the shadows were cast around his eyes.

She opened the side table drawer slowly, a bit at a time. Inside the drawer was his loose change, his wallet, his credit card case and a bottle of co-codomal to deal with his recent headaches. She removed the wallet and the credit cards, closed the drawer, crept back to the lounge closing the door behind her and sat on the settee again.

There was now a slight tremor in her fingers as she emptied the main wallet. Time was passing too quickly and now there was more urgency in what she did. Yet she could not be careless; if anything was not in its proper place Clarke would know. So as she emptied the wallet she laid each item out on the settee in order. Apart from club membership cards, money, a couple of small snapshots of her, there was little of interest. There were no bits of paper with telephone numbers on.

Anne was becoming increasingly frustrated. She was taking a high risk and knew she would never be able to give an explanation if he caught her. She placed the items back in the correct order but by the time she had finished was not satisfied that she had got it right. She was becoming increasingly nervous. She laid the wallet aside and picked up the credit card case.

There was an array of credit cards including two gold cards. And there were some more recent ones like Wild Life, Sky, RSPB, some that had more recently come on the market. She didn't know why he needed so many for basically he only used one as she did. But Clarke had always liked to impress. There were a couple for more recent causes — one she had vaguely heard of, the other was totally new to her. She examined them thoroughly, took them over to inspect under the light but they contained no hidden numbers and scratching might well have invalidated them through the machines.

She turned her attention to the card case itself and could find nothing inscribed anywhere. There was nowhere else to search unless he had the number at the office. If it was somewhere in the apartment it could be anywhere. Depressed, she started to put the cards back in the case, each in its separate plastic compartment, when she hesitated at the unknown one.

She held it in her hand. It was a blue card with a background motif of a dolphin leaping from the sea. The heading was initialled, S.T.D. Investment. There were so many of these cards these days that it became confusing. The number of this one was different from the rest. It was in silver colouring and embossed like the others but whereas the others had their numbers split into groups of three or four with a gap in between each, this was one continuous number.

She suddenly realised she had no pen to write it down; a stupid oversight which reflected her fears. She took the card to the kitchen and wrote down the number on the kitchen pad, tearing off the sheet. She was about to leave when she heard a noise outside and someone fell against the door. Clarke staggered in, eyes bleary, balance gone, the bottle of co-codomal in his hand.

Anne caught him before he fell and supported him against the kitchen counter. 'My wallet's gone,' he gasped, holding on to her to remain upright. 'Someone . . . stole my wallet.'

Anne ignored that and helped him onto a kitchen chair. He almost fell off it taking her with him. She saw the small bottle in his hand and said, 'What do you want those for?'

'Splitting headache. Something's happened. I can't wake up.'

She was not at all sure if he should take co-codomal after the sleeping pills but she could not tell him that. He wanted something for his headache and she had only to look to see that he was suffering. If she did not help him he would take them himself. She took the bottle from him and unscrewed the top.

He said with difficulty, 'What are you doing here?'

'I came for some water. Something must have upset us.' She poured water into a tumbler, put two pills into the palm of her hand and held them under his mouth. 'Take these and swallow the water. All of it.'

He did what she said, swaying on the chair. He swallowed but she was still worried about mixing the pills. 'Where's my wallet?' he repeated.

Anne reacted better under active pressure. 'Never mind your bloody wallet. You've been dreaming. Having nightmares. Can you hold on there while I get you an extra pillow and tidy the bed? Just steady yourself against the counter.'

She hurried out still clutching the credit card which she had tried to palm, and dashed into the lounge, slipped the card into its section of the case, grabbed the wallet and dashed for the bedroom. As she returned the wallet and case to his drawer she realised with horror that she had left the scribbled number on the kitchen counter. She was just about to dash back to the kitchen when Clarke staggered in, bottle of pills back in hand, and he stood glaring at her in a wild, frightening way. He tried to take another step forward, found that he could not and then fell forward still clutching the pill bottle as if it was his life line.

As she stood gazing down at him she was bombarded with a mixture of feelings, most of them bad. He was quite still. She did not know whether to call a doctor who would need some explanation and probably find one, or try to get him to bed and take it from there. The whole day had been a bastard and was still getting worse. As she gazed at his unmoving body she wondered just how worse. If he was dead her troubles had only just begun. But even then she managed to get her priorities right, stepped over his inert form and went to the kitchen to retrieve the piece of paper with the number on it.

18

Paula called at the Savoy Hotel the morning after seeing North. She was now living with Jacko as a matter of convenience but in separate rooms. It seemed to her to be a pity that Jacko's conscience over Georgie was so strong, yet she respected it although Jacko had not heard from Georgie, who was still in Cyprus as far as he knew, for some months and to most people that would have been a severance. But one of Jacko's charms, in spite of his ruggedness, his overall toughness and his acknowledged brilliance with a gun, was an underlying old-fashionedness, a strong sense of loyalty, that appealed to most women. Paula had to admit that if they ever got together she would hope that he would extend those old-world ideals to her. It would be a comforting feeling.

She had gone to the hotel on her own knowing that she at least got on with Irina Janesky. It was time to find out why she had not returned to Paris.

Paula checked at reception to find that Irina was still staying there but was not in her room when they called through. Paula produced her forged police ID and asked if she might wait in her room until her return. This caused some consternation with reception. They did not like the idea of anyone waiting in a guest's room in their absence and they liked less the knowledge that the police were involved.

They were all saved embarrassment as Irina crossed the lobby and Paula hurried towards her before the receptionist could announce her in a name she would not know.

'Madam Janesky.' Paula had come up from behind.

Irina turned, recognised Paula instantly but her reaction was guarded rather than friendly. She waited for Paula to speak, clutching her copious handbag to her.

'Could we talk? In your room?' asked Paula.

'How did you know I was here?' Irina replied with some concern.

'Oh, we've known for sometime. We might attract attention here. Wouldn't it be better if — ?' Paula motioned towards the lifts.

'If you insist. I don't like being spied upon.'

'Oh, Madam Janesky, we are not spying but we are concerned for you. Please, it will not take long.'

Irina had a suite with a pleasant view, the Thames beyond the Embankment's winter-bare tree line and the room was bright. Irina indicated a chair and Paula guessed that this would not be an easy exchange; there was a resentment in Irina which she believed she had dispelled in Paris. Now it was back but somehow different.

When Irina sat opposite Paula she still clutched her handbag which made Paula immediately wonder what was in it.

'Does your husband know you're here?'

'That is really not your concern.'

'I agree. I'm sorry. I wondered why you had

returned to London when the last time I saw you you could not leave it fast enough.'

'That is still no concern of yours. Why are you questioning me?'

Paula recognised that she was handling it badly but she was getting no help from Irina and she supposed that was the idea. She had made the early mistake of thinking that Irina would be helpful. 'When you left us you were sure that the man Mirek is not Vadim Bykov your ex-husband. Is it possible that you were not absolutely sure and wanted to satisfy yourself further without people like me harassing you?'

'I have not changed my mind about anything.'

'But did you speak your mind? To us? Or did you want to mislead us?'

Irina was about to retort angrily when she suddenly relaxed, took a few moments to collect herself then gave a resigned smile. She placed the handbag on the bed just in front of her. 'When I first met you I thought you were a persistent young lady. Perhaps I would be more positive if I knew exactly why you are here.'

'Supposing Mirek is Bykov — '

'He is not,' Irina cut in.

'Just supposing he is, for the sake of argument, wouldn't that place you in some danger?'

'Why?'

'Well, if he recognised you he would have to decide what to do about it, wouldn't he? He could not let it hang.'

'Following your unlikely fantasy would the reverse not be true?'

Paula said cautiously, 'Do you mean he would want to protect you or that you too, would want to do something about it?'

'Who knows? It's your fantasy.'

'If it's fantasy it makes your return to London much more difficult to understand. We are concerned for you, please believe me.'

'But you'd still like me to lead you to a positive identification of my ex-husband. That is your real concern is it not? I'm afraid I can't help you.'

'In that case it would be very wise of you to return to Paris.'

Irina gave an eloquent shrug. 'Are you then going to deport me?'

'Of course not.'

'So I am free to stay?'

'Naturally. If you have told me the truth you have absolutely nothing to worry about.'

'So I infer from that that you think I am lying?'

'Why else would you want to carry a gun in your bag?'

Irina's hand shot out to cover the handbag on the bed. It was an involuntary movement which she regretted making as soon as she had. 'Don't be absurd.'

'Would you mind if I examine your bag?'

'Yes I would. That is intrusion and police harassment.'

'Have you a licence for it? It would have been difficult to bring from France so you must have obtained it here.' Paula had taken a chance. She had seen a hump in the bag which might have been anything but she could see that her guess had turned out to be a good one. 'That would be grounds for you returning to France or worse still, face charges here. Guns are an increasingly sensitive issue here. How did you get it? And more to the point, why have you got it?'

Irina had taken her hand off the bag and was tight-lipped as she sought a way out.

Paula said, 'I have the power to make you empty your bag if I feel you have a dangerous weapon.' She was not at all sure that the police had such power but it sounded logical. 'I'd much rather you showed me yourself.'

Irina stood her ground. 'No. I have no gun. I would not know how to use one.'

'They are easy enough to use, it's accuracy that's the problem. Why would you want one?'

'If I had one it would be to defend myself.'

'Against whom, Madam Janesky? Bykov?'

Irina sat with her legs crossed and her long-fingered hands ran wearily down her face. She was tired, confused and quietly angry at falling into a trap. But she was again in control, not so positively as she had been in France, but sufficiently to stand her ground. She gazed steadily at Paula and there was a vestige of the respect she had felt for the Englishwoman in France. 'Why on earth is the Mirek-Bykov thing so important to you? Apart from a big mystery what does it matter? It means nothing to anyone but me.'

'It's important to us too. If it is one and the same man he is here illegally for a start. And if that's the case then we want to know what he is doing here; a man already dead. A ghostman. If Mirek is Bykov how did he escape the firing squad and who was the poor devil who was executed? You think that doesn't matter to us?'

'You are still making a fatal assumption. If I am satisfied, and I'm the one person who would know, then why can't you be?'

'For the same reason that you came back. I don't believe you are really satisfied. You want to be sure. It must be agony for you.'

'We are never going to agree are we? We will go round in circles. What do you intend to do?'

'Would you like me to look into the possibility of providing you with protection?'

'Against whom?' Irina mimicked. 'Someone long dead?'

Paula at last accepted that she would get nowhere but Irina's obstinacy convinced her she was right. Irina had an agenda. 'How long do you intend to stay?'

'I could be rude to you again but you are a nice person and mean well. I really do believe that you have my interests at heart. So thank you for your concern. I suppose I will be here another few days. No more.'

Paula nodded and then rose. She gazed down at the handbag which influenced Irina to say, 'You still haven't told me what you intend to do.'

'About the gun you mean? I haven't seen it, have I?' And then with a slight smile. 'I haven't exercised my powers of search. So I intend to do nothing. You clearly can't be persuaded to go home. But I must add that while my attempt to persuade you to go back was wholly in your own interest, my motive for accepting your refusal is not. You have decided to stay so I must view matters through more selfish eyes. There might be advantages to us if you stay; I can see absolutely none for you, only danger. Look after yourself Madam Janesky and I really do mean it when I say, I really do hope we meet again on much better terms. Watch your back.'

★ ★ ★

Anne Corrie had managed to get Jeremy Clarke back into bed but only after retrieving the piece of paper from the kitchen. She had prised the bottle of co-codomal from his grasp and put it in the medicine cabinet in the bathroom. Only then did she attempt to get him onto the bed and this had to be done in stages. He was a dead weight.

When she had finally got him in bed and covered up she knew she should send for a doctor. When he was on the floor she had thought he was dead. There had been no movement and still wasn't but a knife held to his mouth had picked up vapour and had misted. So he was breathing, if only just. But to call a doctor would probably be followed by an ambulance and hospital and the discovery of what he had taken.

Clarke was unaware of taking sleeping pills and he would have found out in hospital and so she left him in bed not at all sure whether or not he would survive. It was a catch-22 situation and she sat up all night, drinking endless cups of coffee and praying that he would come round. If he was

288

going to die she would rather it was not here and was done by someone else.

By daylight his breathing was distressed but audible and she took that to be a good sign. The irony was that while he was unconscious like this she could have taken her time going through his things rather than take the risks she had. As it was clear that even if he came round quite soon he would not be fit enough for work she decided to ring his office later that morning. Meanwhile she felt rather as he looked. It had been one hell of a night.

There were no appointments in Northwood that day, they were now tailing off and not for the first time Anne was interested in what would happen to the display of specialist arms in the basement. Would they close shop, and if so who would do it? Some enormous deals had been arranged in the innocuous looking house. Sometimes, even when visitors were not expected, she would go to the house to check that all was well but as things stood she was afraid to leave Clarke in the condition he was in. She belatedly reflected that he might be allergic to the sleeping pills; they did not suit everyone.

He began to come round mid-morning, and once he started his recovery was quite rapid. That he felt ill was obvious. When he struggled up on his pillows he barely knew where he was. When he saw the time he almost relapsed but Anne reassured him quickly, told him she had phoned in for him.

'What the hell has happened to me?' He was sitting up, gazing round the room. 'I've got a splitting headache.' He opened his drawer and gazed inside as if he could not believe what he saw. 'That's funny. My wallet was missing.'

'So you said in the night. When I checked it was there. You had been dreaming. Your headache pills are in the bathroom cabinet. But I wouldn't take them until you are sure they did not do this to you. It was after you took some that you collapsed. Something has clearly affected you. Did you have any snacks at the office?'

He shook his head still bewildered. He still felt strange. 'I collapsed?' he queried.

'On the bedroom floor just there. After taking co-codamol in the kitchen. I don't think it was them but we must be careful. I almost called the doctor.'

That startled him. 'I'm glad you didn't. Have you been awake all night?'

'I had to make sure you would be all right.'

'Thanks, Anne. You must have had a job getting me to bed. What would I do without you?'

It was a good question and one she had been asking herself. She was just beginning to feel a sense of relief. It would not have worried her had he died but coping with it afterwards would never have been easy.

He was coming round fast now but still had to hang on to Anne as he stood up and made for the shower.

'Take your time,' she said. 'Clear your head.'

Once the bathroom door was closed Anne picked up her mobile phone from the bedroom and went into the lounge. She had yet to dress herself but she sat down and took the piece of paper from her dressing gown pocket and rang the number she had copied from the credit card. When she heard the ringing tone she was overjoyed; it had been a very long shot but the result of perseverance.

Mirek answered. She knew his distinctive voice at once.

'Mr Mirek?'

'Who is that?' Suspicion was instant.

'Anne Corrie. There is something I think we must discuss.'

'How did you get this number?'

'With the greatest difficulty. I would like to meet you. I think it important.'

'I am seeing Mr Clarke tomorrow. You could — '

'Without Mr Clarke. Definitely without him but very much about him.'

'I see. Is it important enough for us to meet later today?'

'Yes it is. Have you any idea where it might be safe?'

'It might be better if I hire a car and pick you up somewhere. You must make sure you bring no one with you. That is vital. And this better be as important as you say. This is a risky business.'

'I'll be careful. Don't worry. Jeremy is not at work today; he isn't well so it will be a good time to meet.'

'I'll go along with you, Miss Corrie, but I hope you know what you are doing.'

When Clarke came out of the shower he was almost back to normal and was in the mood to go to the office after lunch. Anne decided not to stop him. She did not think he was fit enough but it would be better if he was out of the way. She knew he wanted to go because he was afraid of losing touch with his day-to-day work which offered some sense of normality.

She did not think she was being followed on a regular basis but knew that with Mirek involved she had to be extra careful. She prepared a light lunch for herself and Clarke and was somewhat relieved that he really was coming round fast. When he had gone she checked the time and left the building by the rear, where the huge dustbins were gathered, and the yard littered with loose paper.

She was not an expert on spotting people following her but was a great survivalist and had a basic cunning which coped with most dangers. The back streets behind the apartment block were a good testing ground and by the time Mirek picked her up a couple of blocks away she was quite satisfied that nobody was following her. The car drew in and she climbed in beside Mirek and was then alarmed to see Chaznov in the rear. So Mirek did not trust her.

Seeing her consternation Mirek said, 'Don't be alarmed. He is there to protect me. I don't really know you, Miss Corrie, although I do know of your efficient work. I'm just being cautious. It's the best way to survive.' He turned briefly and gave her a guarded smile.

Anne was uncomfortable with the big Russian sitting right behind her but saw the sense of it from Mirek's point of view.

Mirek was coping with the traffic quite adequately

but did not see the possibility of a meaningful dialogue in the London traffic. He said, 'We drive into the country. Not too far. But if what you have to tell me is as important as you say then we need to concentrate and we can hardly do that here.'

It made sense but left Anne with an uneasy feeling. She reflected that Mirek was covering his bets, that in the country he could jump either way especially with Chaznov in the car. She began to feel a little nervous.

He drove out on the M40, went beyond Northwood in distance but not quite in direction. She eventually saw signs for Little Chalfont but he turned off onto a quiet country road before reaching it and stopped on what was not much more than a farm track, the surface hard with frequent frost. He had pulled into a lay-by with high, denuded hedges either side of the track.

Mirek kept the engine running to retain the heat but the soft purr did not intrude. He turned to Chaznov, said something in Russian and the bodyguard climbed out without a word. Feeling the cold was nothing new to Chaznov and he wandered out of sight.

'Right,' said Mirek. 'We are alone so you should feel no intimidation. How did you get my number?'

Anne told him a large part of the truth because this man was no fool. She omitted the part about the sleeping pills.

He had swung round in his seat so that he could face her and she was very much aware of his scrutiny. When she had finished he observed, 'You are a very determined lady and an observant one. But why did you do it? And what made you believe Clarke would not wake up?'

'Because he was in a drunken stupor. I had to get him to bed and that was not easy. He's cracking up and I knew I must do something about it.'

'He's cracking up because he got drunk?'

'No, not because of that alone. He has not been the same since he was interviewed by the police about that man who was murdered; the one who happened to be in your hotel not long before he was killed. He's been looking over his shoulder ever since.'

Mirek inclined his head. 'I too was interviewed by the police. It was inevitable in the circumstances. They were just doing their job. You say this upset him unduly?'

'Yes. He's afraid. And the climax was the other night when your man discovered the bullet holes. He's not been the same since. A bundle of nerves. Did anyone find out what happened to the guard who was staying there?'

'No. He might have lost his nerve and run. In which case one day we will catch up with him. Continue.'

'Jeremy thinks it is far too dangerous to continue in Northwood.'

'Do you?'

She paused, knowing her answer was crucial to what she was trying to achieve. She decided not to tell him about the woman police caller. She had not told Clarke and she had left it too late to tell anyone and then explain the delay. But that was not her only reason for holding back. She was acting on impulse with the feeling that it might cause panic and this was a time for strong nerves. She did not believe there was real danger in the ommission; if there had been something would have happened by now and she was still convinced the caller was not bona fide. 'I think the time there is limited. But I don't see how the police can be involved when shots are fired and nothing further happened. Are there rival factions here?'

'There are always rival factions. Big money is involved. But it would seem that the basement had not been found. There was no sign to the contrary. It would appear that our man appeared at the right time. He was not the only one to flee and whoever it was would expect us to strengthen our presence which I have arranged and of which I would have informed Mr Clarke tomorrow and presumably he would have told you. But I agree with you that our time there is limited. There are two more important callers to come and then we close down or simply move somewhere else. We've done some very strong business there and you have coped exceedingly well.'

'Thank you. You are the first one to say so. But I still think Jeremy is fast becoming a danger. If the police ever interviewed him again I think he would crack up completely.' Anne knew there was truth in what she said.

'But aren't you lovers, you two?'

Anne looked him straight in the eye. 'As a matter of convenience.'

'So what is your real interest in all this?'

'Money. This is a good thing and I want to profit

by it. But we have run into the odd problem and that is when the men are separated from the boys. Some can take the strain and others can't. Jeremy is weak. He's okay when everything is going fine but in the type of operation we are running there is bound to be the occasional blip. I'm not concerned about the blips except to deal with them, but I am about him. And he's started to talk in his sleep.'

'I know he's a weak man; that's how he was recruited in the first place. But he has coped well under supervision.'

'He led me to believe he was running the show. That alone is now enough to make me nervous.'

'Well he has certainly supplied us with some good British contacts which will make it easier to get things abroad under a legitimate label. But the British side, although important, is only one aspect. It suits us to use Northwood because Clarke owns the house and it is convenient but as you point out it might not be entirely safe for much longer.'

They sat there for a while lost in their thoughts when Mirek said, 'Would you sleep with me?'

The question came as a shock, not for any reason of morality but because Mirek had never given an indication of being interested in her. His very presence so close to her in the car had not dismayed her in any sexual way. Now it did. She said, 'I take that as an enquiry and not as an invitation. You want to know how far I will go to get what I want?'

'You're discerning, Miss Corrie. Well?'

'If it will help me get what I want, yes. If that

sounds cold-blooded then isn't this a cold-blooded game we are all in?'

'I just want to know how I stand with you and how important it is to you.' He smiled briefly. 'Don't worry, Miss Corrie, I never mix business with pleasure and that is no adverse reflection on your undoubted attractions. I now know to what degree you are committed. So what exactly are you asking of me?'

Anne felt the warnings rise in her; she had to get this one right. 'I think we should get rid of Jeremy.'

19

'Get rid of him. Do you mean kill him?'

'Yes.' Anne had the sensation of digging her own grave yet it was too late to turn back.

'Then why haven't you done it if you feel so strongly?' Mirek sounded so reasonable as he spoke of potential murder.

Anne showed her unease and clutched her hands. 'I'd be no good at it. I wouldn't know what to do.'

'You're a sensible woman. You've already proved yourself to be efficient and strong under pressure. You could think of something. You managed to put him out last night while you searched his things.'

'I did no such thing. He got drunk.'

'And you didn't help him on his way? Did you try to stop him? Don't take me for a fool.'

'I'd hardly do that. I just think he has become a danger to us.'

'What about his contacts here? Have you got them? In order to carry on where he left off?'

'I thought you would have them. I don't think there are any more to come. What is left is administration and I think I am much better at it than he.'

Mirek sighed. 'So you want us to kill Clarke and then dispose of him?'

'I think it would be better. He's had his day.'

Mirek sat thinking it over; not just the removal

of Clarke but whether this very hard, very efficient woman, was not just trying to project herself regardless of whether Clarke was cracking up or not. In truth she confirmed something he had increasingly observed.

It was some time before he answered her. 'You think we are killers? That all you have to do is to ask?'

'No. No, of course not. But it is a dangerous game we are playing and a weak link like Jeremy can bring us all down. He's showing that he can't stand the strain.'

'And then you'll do his job and expect his profits?'

'Yes. I'm already doing his job and have been for some time. That is apart from his contacts which you must know about.'

'What about the house?'

'We go on using it until we've finished. He will simply have disappeared.'

'You've given a lot of thought to this, Miss Corrie.'

'It needed careful thought. What do you say?'

Again Mirek sat silently. He had shown no objection to a man being killed but had ideas about who should do it. 'I think you should kill him and we will dispose of him. That would be fair wouldn't it? That way we are all committed. Fair shares, I think you call it.'

Anne sat in the darkness of the car and suddenly the engine ticking over became a massive intrusion. It was as if it was inside her head. She had not expected this but it was difficult to answer. 'How would I go about it?' As she answered she realised she was in deeper which was probably what Mirek wanted. Recognisable commitment was everything to him.

'Well,' replied Mirek calmly, 'you won't want blood on the carpet. As his corpse is unlikely ever to be found again you do it in such a way that there are no signs in the apartment or wherever you intend to do it. What state his body is in does not matter as he won't be found once we have him.'

'When should it be done?' The roles had been reversed as she now asked him for advice. She had hoped he would see to it but Mirek wanted total and binding commitment and that meant involving her to the limit.

'You are the one who has stressed the need. As soon as you can.'

'Tonight? Will that be okay?'

'From that I gather you have already decided how. Don't make it noisy. You ring the number you stole when you have done the job and I will have the rest attended to.'

'I haven't got a gun and a knife is messy. It might be the middle of the night.'

Mirek offered a smile. 'I'll be on standby. You haven't got a gun yet you have been selling highly classified weapons with great knowledge of what they can do.'

'Jeremy taught me that much. It was not difficult to learn. I did not have to use them and I enjoy doing it.'

'I think you will be a bigger asset than hitherto.

I agree with almost everything you say. Having discussed Mr Clarke's lack of nerves we are now about to test yours. We'd better get back.' He touched the horn and Chaznov reappeared.

* * *

Clarke had initial difficulty in coping at the office. He felt infinitely better than he had but it was still difficult coping with routine work. He kept having little attacks of dizziness but as the afternoon wore on they diminished and by the end of the day his head was fairly clear.

During the whole time at work he had worried about his wallet. He was still satisfied that when he opened his drawer to find the co-codomal the wallet was not there. He acknowledged that at the time he must have been in a terrible state but it still stuck in his mind. When it was close to leaving time he decided to check on his wallet, took it out and went through the items one by one. There was nothing missing and everything was in order. With a sense of relief he put the wallet back and produced his card case. When he examined that he found two cards had changed places.

The revelation made his head throb again. How could that be and why would someone want to do it? Straight away he assumed that the change had not been done by himself, he was very fussy about keeping the same order. He went through them again. *The* card was in its right plastic pocket. But two others were not and he was worried sick. He could not accept for a moment that he had inadvertently made the change himself. That left Anne as the only person who knew where he kept them.

It was a crass irony that he had made the mistake himself under the recent strain he was still suffering, and that Anne had put the cards back exactly as she had found them. On the way home the whole thing played on his mind. What had made him feel so bad and for how long had he been out? Why was she in the kitchen? But against that she had nursed and looked after him and had got him to bed. He was suspicious yet confused. He really did not know what to do for the best.

When he reached home Anne was not there. There was no particular reason why she should be but he knew there was no need for her to go to Northwood that day and that the visits there were almost at an end. He would be glad when they shut it down. And then he considered the huge fees he was being paid for the use of the house, the commission he received for each sale done there and the fees he received for the introductions of the businessmen outlets. He was already in a good financial state.

He made himself some coffee, wondered what to do about a meal if Anne was late in returning and about how he would receive her. Should he challenge her or just keep a wary eye open? The big problem was that he really cared for her; she had worked on him well.

She arrived at the apartment about an hour later, apologised for being out when he returned after such a terrible night and promised him she would cook a meal he would remember. She also made a big fuss of him, showed her concern at his attack in the night. She could always dispel his doubts but was irritated when he finally said, 'Someone's been at my card case. The cards are out of order.'

She laughed it off. 'I know how careful you are, darling, but there's always a first time. Have they been used?'

'No. I don't think so.' That was where the logic fell down; why would anyone mess with his cards unless they wanted to use them? Except for the one card of really important value but no one but he knew it was there or what it meant. He had told no one, not even Anne.

'So what's the problem? You made a mistake; you are not infallible and haven't been yourself these last few days.' And that was her mistake.

'What do you mean? Apart from last night I've been all right. Overworked maybe but okay.'

She should have left it there but was in a state of stress; she had never planned to kill a man before. Until now she had always been able to manipulate people into doing her dirty work. 'You have been strange lately, darling.'

He was tired, confused and wanted someone to agree with him, to support him while he suffered his present depression. And it seemed to him she was now goading. 'What do you mean, strange? What the hell are you talking about? You're the one who's been acting strange.'

They drifted into a semi-heated argument and the words got sharper and tempers higher until they were both just hitting out with anything they could think of, right or wrong. Voices began to rise as the row intensified and it was doubtful if either had a real inkling of what was being said. He was provoked by what he saw as injustice but behind that was the increasing belief that she had been at his wallet and card case. And she was trapped in the knowledge that she had to kill him and this was not quite the time she wanted to do it.

Finally it became a straightforward slanging match, both losing control until Anne struck out with all the fury that had built up inside her. She hit him round the face so hard that he spun round, but as he steadied himself he struck back with a violent back-hander which caught her on the chin.

Anne went reeling and fell over the arm of a chair onto the floor. She was not unconscious but near to it. One leg was still draped over the chair while her head was on the carpet.

Whatever faults Clarke might have he had never in his life struck a woman before and could not believe that he had done so now. For a few moments he was stunned by his own action and then he stepped forward to help her.

He bent down, going slightly dizzy as he did and he groped to find her arms. Anne was still groggy and there was blood trickling down her face from a cut on her forehead where she had caught it on a side table. She had a hazy image of him bending over her. She kicked out and caught him on the shin and he yelled out with pain.

He almost fell on her but she was scrambling up as he dropped on one knee while holding his other leg in pain. She staggered to her feet in a blind rage and kicked him in the head as he was crouched forward. The head was a little high for a really good kick but he keeled over while she held her balance against the chair. A drop of her own blood fell on her hand making things look far worse than they were and she hurried to the kitchen after giving him one more kick.

In the kitchen she examined her face in a small magnifying mirror at the back of the counter and saw the blood oozing from inside her hairline. She cut some hair away and managed to get a plaster over it. When she had finished she held on to the counter and tried to calm herself down. It was not supposed to be like this. She had intended to give him a massive overdose of sleeping pills but rage still simmered in her. Why not now while she was in a murderous mood. She took a metal steak hammer from a drawer and returned to the lounge.

Clarke was on his knees holding on to the arm of the chair, his head cradled in the crook of his arm.

For a moment Anne stood in the doorway looking at him. He was obviously in distress but the only feeling she could rouse was of hatred and contempt. She did not realise until now just how much she had controlled her feelings while living with him. She felt no compassion; he had served his purpose.

She moved towards him, the steak hammer in her hand and as she neared him he must have heard for he raised his head and gazed blearily up at her. He gave a sickly grin and mumbled, 'What a bust up. I'm so sorry — ' He never finished as the steak hammer crashed down on his head. It was a fierce blow and the hammer was hard although light as hammers go. He was dazed and in pain but as he tried to raise his head again in a pathetic reflex action, she struck him again; and again, and again and was still striking him when he was prone on the floor and she had to kneel beside him to hit him and she could no longer recognise the messy pulp she was hammering. A single drop of blood fell on the carpet beside his body and she realised it had escaped from the plaster on her forehead. Her concern for that alone pulled her up.

She sat back on her heels, panting heavily and half crazed with fear and anger. She started to tremble. Sanity was slow to return and when it did came terror and fear of her own action. She could not recognise the features that had once been Clarke's. She did not have to feel his pulse to know that he was dead. Which was as well for her emotion had swung full circle and she was now trembling with fear at what she had done and the position it now placed her in. The overwhelming reaction now was self-preservation. Nothing could ever bring Clarke back in any form.

Anne Corrie rested on her heels for some time until she realised that she was still holding the steak hammer and when she looked down at it she retched, jumped up and ran for the kitchen. Her intention was to clean the hammer as soon as she could but she was violently sick first and had difficulty in thinking logically. When she did, to her horror she was still clutching the hammer as if afraid to let it go. But now she had the sense to clean it under the taps and to start to think of what to do next.

Mirek had said, 'No blood on the carpet.' She was afraid to go and look yet she had to. She left the hammer in the sink, sluiced her face with cold water, something she had never done, and then went back to the lounge with dread in her heart.

Her first thought was that Clarke had not moved, as if somehow he might have done just to spite her. She could barely bring herself to look at his head but she had to to see what mess was beneath it. By some miracle and the position of his head there had been no gushing of blood; his head was just a bloody mess, caved in mostly at the back. She reached for a cushion which she could later discard, pulled his head up by the hair and laid it back on the cushion. The only blood on the carpet she could see was the single drop of her own which had dripped from her forehead.

She straightened, feeling drained but without remorse for what she had done. Already, as she observed that the mess could have been far worse and that she had been lucky, a big sense of relief swept over her. It was done. Not as she planned but it was done. The thought kept passing through her mind and the few tears she then shed were for her own sense of achievement and a tremendous relief.

She sat on the arm of the opposite chair and heaved in great gulps of air. She still found difficulty in looking at Clarke's head but as minutes passed and she stopped to work things out, increasingly she found that she could. Her relief grew by the minute until she was able to take a long and sensible stock of the damage to the furniture and carpet.

Most of the blood was on the head itself but the shoulders of the jacket were heavily spattered and his shirt collar, once white, was now deep red. But as far as she could see without moving him the damage had remained on the body. Should she ring Mirek now? It was much earlier than he would expect. She thought it through and decided to make herself a strong coffee and then to contact him. He should be pleased that the deed was done.

★ ★ ★

About the time this was happening Mirek and Chaznov were crossing swords in a more friendly way than hitherto. Circumstances had drawn them closer and Chaznov had been flattered by Mirek's request to do a private job for him although he wished Mirek would get on with it. Now Chaznov was pointing out that Mirek had asked him to get a disposal team together at short notice when only recently he had bawled Chaznov out for killing the man he thought to be a threat to Mirek.

'Suddenly it is all right to kill? You've changed your attitude.'

'No. I still think that what you did was unnecessary. But this is different. Weaknesses are beginning to show in our own ranks and have to be removed. I have not asked you to do it but you can help by removing the body. Can you organise a helicopter at short notice?'

'No problem. We'll drop the body in the North

Sea. That's the easy part. Where do we pick it up and when?'

'I'm awaiting a phone call. When I have the signal I'll ring you. Keep your phone on standby. It will be at the girl's apartment.'

'You mean where Clarke hangs out? I know it. There's a fire escape and a back alley.' Chaznov gave a brief smile of approval. 'So it's him. Who's doing it?'

Mirek hesitated then accepted that Chaznov would know the moment his men arrived at the apartment. 'The woman Corrie. Just get the body out and we don't want it found again.'

'Good.' Chaznov approved. 'He's weak. The woman isn't. I hope she does a proper job. It will be up to her to clean up. We want in and out as quickly as possible.'

'We all do. Take the back roads to the airfield. We don't want the police stopping you with a dead body on board.'

Chaznov agreed though did not seem unduly worried. 'That would mean a shoot-out but I prefer not to kill the police until the whole job is over.'

Mirek was not sure whether Chaznov was trying to impress or not but he did know that Chaznov would not balk at shooting the police if they stood between him and escape. It was best not to press the point. 'I'll give you a ring.'

'Have you made up your mind yet about the woman you want removed?'

'Oh yes, nothing's changed. It's just a question of the right timing. Have you a plan?'

309

'Of course.' Chaznov grinned, something he rarely did. 'It looks as if the chopper pilot will be busy.'

'I don't want her hurt. A painless job.'

'There's no time to hurt targets; that causes problems. She won't feel a thing.'

'Just one more thing,' said Mirek. 'When you've done go to Northwood and stay there. I want someone to secure the place properly. You take what help you need.'

'What about looking after you?'

'Assign someone else for a day or two. But I'll rest easier with you at Northwood for the moment.'

★ ★ ★

Anne Corrie drank several cups of strong coffee but between each one she did some tidying up in the room, straightening things out where they had fought. It was a miracle that nothing had actually been broken so by the time she had finished the room looked normal apart from the gruesome centrepiece of Clarke.

There were times when she looked at him that she could not believe that she had killed him and at other times she felt an elation that she had managed it, not only that he was dead but that she had been up to doing it. For reasons she could not wholly explain she waited until after midnight before calling Mirek; it was as if she did not want him to know that the job had been rushed and was almost an accident.

When he answered she simply said, 'It's done.' He did not even acknowledge but switched off at once. She wondered if he had heard but realised he must have done. She now had to wait until someone arrived and that was going to be the worst part for she had no idea of how long it would take them to get organised.

The doorbell rang about two hours later which was the first indication of how they could work at short notice. Two men in boiler suits stood at the door. One had a coil of rope over his shoulder, the other was carrying what looked like a plumber's bag. The taller said in atrocious English, 'You have parcel for us?'

It was almost laughable and she had a job taking them seriously. She let them in, took them to the corpse. They stood gazing down at Clarke as if he was a specimen to be studied. Neither said a word but when they moved they were impressive.

They covered Clarke's face with wide bandages to contain the blood so that it did not drip when they moved him. They taped his arms to his side to avoid them flapping about the body and then loosely bound his feet. They then placed a blanket round his shoulders to contain the bloody mess on his shirt and jacket before lifting him up and going towards the kitchen.

Anne watched in amazement as they worked in silence and as if she did not exist. She could not help but wonder at how many times they must have done this. They moved as if they knew the whole layout of the apartment and with dismay realised that they probably did.

'Open door.'

At first she did not understand, the accent was so bad but then saw that they needed the kitchen door opened. The kitchen door opened onto the fire escape. They got the body onto the metal platform and bound it, threading the rope under the arms, and then lowered it down. Only then did she realise that there must be others waiting below.

When the two men were satisfied the body was in safe hands below they went down the fire escape, moving surprisingly quietly at a time when any sound carried through the night. It was bitingly cold and there was a stinging breeze. Anne went out onto the platform and gazed down. It was pitch black but she could just see a reflection on the roof of what might be a van. Then she heard the engine, the reflection moved away and she was alone. It was all over. Clarke had disappeared forever.

She stood on the platform until the biting cold forced her indoors. She locked the door and stood with her back to it for some time. She moved back into the lounge and viewed the spot where Clarke had lain — it was as if he had never existed. Then she saw the small blood stain but that was hers. It might as well have been his for it was a reminder of the whole bloody affair.

Anne sprawled onto the settee and put her legs up. She was drained, her mind going over events again and again. Reaction was setting in and she knew there would be no sleep for her that night. She had no idea what they would do with the body but judging by their efficiency she did not think there was need to worry. But the longer she sat there the lonelier she felt.

She was alone now. Really alone. Clarke had become a pain but he had been there. Someone to talk to, to argue with, to make love to when the need arose. And he spoke English. The men who had just left spoke none. She guessed that the one who had spoken at all had rehearsed what he had to say. And now she was in the hands of Mirek and suddenly that did not feel so good. She really knew nothing about him.

Anne Corrie was too tired to make more coffee, she was drifting from one thought to another, one conviction to several of doubt. Yes she was in the hands of strangers, foreigners at that and from what she had seen just now, highly efficient and very deadly strangers. Without fully realising it she was already missing Clarke, at least she had understood him. She was now on her own with these people she did not know and for the first time wondered what they might do to her once she had served her purpose.

She needed tears then but the tears would not come. She wrapped her arms round herself and shivered through the night as though she had a long bout of ague. She had sold her soul to the devil many years ago so why did she feel so badly now at a time she should be rejoicing? Right then she had never felt so alone and was beginning to understand the real sensation of deep fear.

20

News of Jeremy Clarke's disappearance was slow
to surface. When he had not arrived at the DTI
by mid-morning questions were raised and someone
rang his apartment. It was well known that he was
living with Anne Corrie and when she did not
answer it was assumed that they were somewhere
together and had been held up although that
assumption failed to explain why Clarke had not
rung in.

Anne Corrie, not yet ready for phone calls but
knowing they would come had put the answer
machine on. There was no need to go to
Northwood that day and she remained in the
apartment, afraid to go out. Daylight had brought
its own psychological problems but she was grateful
for it; daylight made thinking easier.

By late morning she knew that she must do
something and rang the DTI to return their call.
She told them that she had no idea where Clarke
was. He had left the apartment at the usual time.
She herself, with nothing particular on that day,
had lain in bed until late. She could not understand
why he had not arrived unless there had been an
accident.

From that point on the snowball was slow to
form. Nobody at first took it too seriously; as a
matter of course Clarke did spend some time out
of the office although his secretary would expect

to know where he was at any given time. It was not until mid-afternoon that the question of an accident was really investigated and when that bore no fruit Clarke's secretary rang the police. It was evening before the news drifted to the ears of Detective Chief Superintendent Matthew Simes and from that point things moved very swiftly.

Simes himself, with Detective Sergeant Andrews, called at the apartment late that night. By that time Anne Corrie was in a dressing gown, with no make-up, and geared up for the inevitable. She did not have to attempt to appear distressed, she had been stressed out since killing Clarke.

Simes introduced himself, stated his business and Anne invited them in. They sat down and Anne wrapped her gown round her legs and appeared ill with worry. 'So you haven't found him?' she asked quickly.

'Why do you say that?'

'Because it's bloody true, isn't it? Look at the pair of you, a picture of doom.'

'No, we haven't found him, madam. Just tell us what you know.'

'What happens every morning. I had nothing special to do today so I lay in for a while. I heard Jeremy get up and he brought me a cup of tea, I think it was about seven-thirty. I went back to sleep but I seem to remember the front door closing. By the time I got up he was long gone and I thought nothing of it until I checked the answering machine which he had thoughtfully put on knowing I was having a late morning. I rang his office in great surprise and that's all I know.'

'He hadn't told you he had somewhere to go before going to the DTI?'

'No. But there was no reason why he should; I'm not part of his business life. He simply left as he always does. It's frightening. Could he have been mugged?'

Simes shrugged. 'The area hospitals have been checked. Had you been quarrelling about anything? I mean was he upset?'

'We have the odd row as most couples do. But nothing serious. Last night was quiet; we even turned in early.' Anne suddenly shivered. 'You know I'm getting really worried about this. At first it was difficult to take seriously but there's a nasty feel about it now.' She gazed at the spot where the blood had been and was relieved that she had scrubbed it off and that it had dried.

'Well,' said Simes slowly, 'we've got a nationwide search on the go. After all, he is an important civil servant carrying a lot of knowledge some people would love to have. Can you cope all right on your own? Do you need to see a doctor?'

'For sedatives? You're talking as if you don't expect to find him. He's gone missing, that's all. He might have lost his memory or something. It happens.'

'Let's hope you are right, Miss Corrie. Do you know which suit he was wearing?'

Anne gazed at the ceiling. 'I don't know. Do you want me to go and look to see which one is missing?'

'It might help us with a description.'

Anne struggled to her feet and the men rose

with her. She led them to the bedroom and went to the wardrobe pulling back one of the doors. She rattled along the rail and found an empty hanger, mused and then said, 'His dark suit with the pale line. There are a couple at the cleaners but I'm sure that's the one.' She pulled out the tie rack and ran her fingers along the row of ties. 'He's probably wearing the plain light green tie.'

Andrews made notes and then they went back into the lounge. Simes remained on his feet as he said, 'You are understandably confused and worried right now but if anything useful springs to mind ring me at this number.' Simes handed over a card. 'Thank you for your help.'

Once outside Simes asked, 'Did you notice anything, Sergeant?'

'She looked pretty shagged out. It must be worrying for her.'

'She was wearing no make-up. She was far from looking her best. I'm remembering she has a record, a long way back but still a record. There was a cushion missing from the settee. There was one each end and one on the back at the far end but none at the near end. It looked odd.'

Andrews appeared bemused. This was a sudden shift of direction from accidents and mugging and lost memories. 'What are you suggesting, sir?'

'I'm not suggesting anything. I'm merely indicating that we should broaden our enquiries.'

★ ★ ★

North did not get to know about Clarke until late that night when Simes telephoned him. North was immediately alert, dressed and returned to the office after contacting Jacko and Paula and instructing his team at the Lewis house in Northwood to be extra vigilant. It was well past midnight when they met at North's office. Neither Jacko nor Paula complained at the late call; North was not a man to panic.

North made them strong coffee and they clustered round his desk but showed little reaction when he announced, 'Jeremy Clarke is missing. He didn't turn up at the DTI today and Anne Corrie said he left as usual. He's missing.'

There was silence as this sank in with all its implications. Eventually Jacko said, 'You think he's done a runner?'

'I doubt that he's that well organised. He always struck me as a man who operated best with support around him. I've never seen him as a loner and the girl's still there.'

'So what's the urgency? Why are we here?'

North smiled briefly at Paula. 'A fair question. I think all the obvious reasons are out and so does Simes. Accident, loss of memory, all that I think we can forget about. He's gone and my gut feeling is that he's not coming back.'

'You think he's been murdered?'

'Either that or spirited away to be out of the way. Either way that could mean he's become a danger, a weak link. It's a sinister development.'

'That could mean Northwood is on the point of closing down. Your blokes are still watching it, aren't they?'

'Yes, Jacko, they are. Nobody has been there for a couple of days. There's nothing unusual about that except the feel of it. Why has Clarke gone and how?'

Paula said, 'Do you think the woman has anything to do with it? Perhaps Clarke's usefulness is over. I would say that Anne Corrie is more adaptable, she's the saleswoman and she obviously knows her stuff. Clarke was a contact man, maybe he's run out of contacts.'

'And out of luck, too. He was never good under pressure, hated it when Simes and his team were asking him about young Jones.'

'So you think he's followed Jones?' Jacko said. 'Perhaps they found out we had nobbled him.'

'I don't think we'll ever find out. Some sort of move must be afoot. Perhaps they are closing Northwood down; feel it's too risky.' North turned to Paula. 'Do you think Anne Corrie would have reported your visit to Clarke?'

'Not if she thought he would panic. But maybe she did and maybe he did panic. I gather from the way you're speaking that the police have already interviewed her.'

'It was Simes who advised me. Well if she's still part of the game she'll now be answerable to Mirek. I wonder how she'll cope with him?'

'Do you think we should move in and close Northwood down ourselves?'

'That's what we need to discuss.' North faced them, his features drawn. 'You've been very good, you two, but the crucial information is still missing. I can close Northwood down any time we like.

No problem. We established that it's an illegal, highly-specified, gun-running showcase. But we've precious little else.'

North stared at his cup as if trying to levitate it by intense thought. He was quiet for a while and then stirred restlessly. 'We can close it down and stop further development, at least from there. But we have no direct evidence that Mirek is involved. We don't even know if he's been there. If he has it must have been before we placed it under surveillance. He might have gone there after the shooting. I strongly suspect there are people behind him. Anne Corrie might know if he's been there. Clarke is now out of the frame. At least we have the names of the businessmen he dealt with but that's only a fraction of the information we need. Who are the foreign buyers and dealers?'

'He didn't have a list as you know and we couldn't find one at Northwood,' said Jacko. 'Yet there must be one somewhere. Would Corrie have it?'

'I doubt it. I doubt that she knew who she met there. Appointments were made and people turned up but it's unlikely she knew who they were. Mirek will know. But there's another thing. Unless we raid while the stuff is still there and settle for a limited result, we have no factual evidence that the weapons are there. We have the word of you, Jacko, and Paula. I'm very sorry to say that might not be enough. We need actual samples.'

A deep, uncomfortable silence followed. Jacko and Paula exchanged uneasy glances and North watched them closely.

Jacko was studying his feet when he said, 'You want us to go back in and get some?'

'That would be the ideal. It could be very dangerous.'

'And it still would not produce Mirek and a list.'

'It might.' North let the possibility hang for a while. 'The place must be better guarded than before. We know that they know about the shots fired and they must still be concerned about their missing man. We've still got nothing from him but he's a foot soldier, he won't know anything substantial. They also know that the police could not be involved or there would have been a follow-up. They also probably feel secure in the secrecy of the cellar.' North gazed at Jacko. 'If you hadn't sat on that bloody desk in the way that you did and felt the slight shift the chances are that we still would not have known. Like the list, the cellar is not there. You say they could not possibly have known that you found it?'

'They'd have closed down for sure if they thought that. But like you I think they're close to closing anyway. But why do you think Mirek might pitch up if we go in?'

'I think he's been forced into a situation where he has directly to involve himself much more. He can't be all that happy with the way things have gone recently. He may have decided to clear out the weak links like Clarke. He'll probably use the Corrie girl still because it looks as if she's done her job well, but she's new to him. He won't know just how much she can be trusted. He's got a bodyguard, a deadly one if he killed Jones, so he might feel safe in taking a more direct hand.'

'Or he might be instructed to take a more direct hand.'

North nodded his assent. 'That's a fair observation, Paula. This organisation is not local to Britain; this is just a limb. Mirek has been used for a specific reason and the only thing I can come up with is that he had worldwide contacts like Clarke and has an absolute thorough knowledge of the arms industry.'

North let that sink in and then added, 'Bykov, when he was alive, was in the Defence Ministry before the old USSR broke up and up to the time of his arrest.'

'Now he tells us. You bastard, you've known all along.' Jacko felt his temper rising.

'If you are saying that I think Mirek is Bykov, I still don't know. Irina Janesky says he's not.'

'So why is she still here?'

'If she's not sure she's every reason to be here. It's a puzzling business.'

'Armed with a gun?' Jacko was not letting go and felt let down. 'Why don't we tail her? We might find out more that way?'

North shook his head. 'We've been over it. Paula knows. If we follow her our people will be spotted by Mirek's bodyguard and I want them in a state of confusion so that they don't really know what's going on.'

Jacko was still angry. 'That's assuming Irina is keeping an eye on Mirek.'

'What else would she be doing here? Armed? I

agree with Paula on this: Irina wants to be sure. If she was sure she'd have done something by now. If she's not sure why do you expect me to be?'

'Because it would be a helluva coincidence to have two different men looking the same and with the same kind of knowledge and contacts on outlets on arms. I think Irina knows bloody fine. But she won't find it easy to get near Mirek with his goon around.'

'Maybe you are right. But we'll get nowhere with this kind of talk. Never mind Irina, her possible aim is not ours. We want to wreck and arrest an international gun-running group but need more factual evidence than we've got. So we're back to the cellar. Well?'

'Well? Will we go?' Jacko had not quite calmed down.

North gave Paula a questioning glance before turning back to Jacko. 'Unless you can come up with something else.'

Jacko was more concerned for Paula than himself. It would be far more risky than before and they had come close to disaster last time. North knew it and this irritated Jacko again. 'You just don't bloody care do you? Get your own people to do it.'

North leaned back, hands clasped across his chest. 'You know that my people, whatever their training, are no match for the sort of training you two endured. I'll have men across the road at Lewis's. And round the back. There'll be plenty of back-up.'

'Do we know how many men are in there?'

'We don't know if there is anyone in there at

all. Nobody has gone in these last couple of days during daylight hours. They might have gone in by night'

'Do you mean you haven't surveyed the place at night? Jesus, I don't believe this.'

'We've been watching for visits of Anne Corrie and any callers for her. That happens during daylight. Image intensifiers have their limitations. They might well pick up images but they are not always identifiable as particular people. Passing traffic can play havoc with their lights and the actual path to the house is obscured as you know. The house can also be approached from the back over neighbouring gardens as you also know. We didn't know Clarke was going to disappear and force our hand. I'm giving it to you as it is, Jacko. I'm not asking you to go in blind.'

'That's exactly what you're doing. Paula should not even be considered for this.'

North ignored that comment and said, 'Naturally we will supply you with body armour.'

'That's very reassuring. I don't like it at all.'

Paula had said nothing during this exchange but Jacko now turned to her and said, 'This is crazy. What do you think?'

'I agree that we need the hard evidence. Why not raid it in force?'

North shrugged. 'I thought I explained. That's just closing it down as an operation. It is not producing the people and information we really want.'

'You mean you want Mirek, period. And that he might not go there and as sure as hell will not go after a raid. He'll scarper.'

'Mirek is all important. He holds the key to the rest of it. All you need bring back is one sample of the creeping terror and one of the high velocity pistol. Are the cabinets locked?'

'I don't think so,' said Jacko, 'although I didn't try them. They seemed to me to have sliding doors. The security is in the hiding of the cellar itself. The cabinet glass could always be smashed.'

'The mines in the cabinets wouldn't be armed would they?'

'No. Too risky. There was ammunition for the Five-seveN pistol but the guns themselves would be empty for safety reasons. It would be possible to take one mine and one pistol and shift the rest around a bit to fill in the spaces without anyone immediately missing any.'

'If that can be done it will be marvellous. It will give us time for Mirek actually to commit himself and tie in with the house. All we need do is wait and hope.'

It was late and they were all feeling weary and were tired of going over the same ground yet knew the importance of getting it right. Jacko could not explain why but felt something was missing and it was nothing they had actually discussed. He said, not knowing if he was heading in the right direction or not, 'What happens to the stuff if it is got out?'

'You bring it here.'

'We're talking of a highly illegal operation which would look dead dodgy in a court of law. Would you be comfortable with it here?'

'No. But hopefully it would not be for long.'

'You wouldn't be thinking of planting it on anyone for instance?'

'Good Lord, no. Why would I do that?'

'Because if you did,' Jacko went on remorselessly, 'it would be down to us who stole it. And that's what you want us to do isn't it?'

'Well, we know that it's an illegal operation. So is the one we're fighting.'

'Would I be right in saying that one of the reasons you don't want a full raid is because it would involve the police? They would have to do it for you. And you don't want the police in this at all?'

'I never want the police involved. Not if I can help it. We work in entirely different ways and usually have quite different objectives. They'd be quite happy closing down an arms operation. They'd get good publicity from it. Our aim goes way beyond that.' North held out both hands as if to symbolically embrace Jacko. 'Why am I telling you all this. You know damned fine.'

'I know damned fine that we're going out on a limb.'

North stared at each in turn. Paula was giving little away but had listened carefully to what Jacko had said. 'Do you think I'd pull the rug from under you? What on earth would that benefit me? Jacko, you're tired. We're all tired. You're not thinking straight. I want this over and Mirek in jail where he should be.'

'And I think I know how you intend to do it if things don't go as you hope.'

Nothing was said for a long time. With the heating system turned down the cold was creeping into the office. Paula pulled her coat around her and looked so tired that she appeared to have lost interest. Eventually North said, 'Anyone want more coffee?'

Nobody did. Jacko sat staring at North with a look of accusation and was still waiting for an answer to his challenge. North suddenly reached behind him, grabbed the coffee pot and poured himself another cup. He held the pot up invitingly but nobody responded. At last he said, 'You're accusing me of intending to do the dirty on you. Apart from the crass insult why would I want to do that?'

'You wouldn't want to do it. It would be one of your options if things went wrong. Someone to blame. An illicit operation from the start. The only part your men have played is as a surveillance team over the last couple of days.'

'You are not being fair, Jacko. I would not do that. Some might. I'll stand by you.'

Paula stretched out to place a hand on Jacko's arm. 'I don't think he'd let us down, Jacko. Really. We don't have to do it. He can't make us.'

Jacko felt the tiredness sweeping over him. Perhaps he wasn't thinking straight. North had always played it straight; well fairly straight. But something still niggled at him. He said to Paula, 'Are you saying that you are willing to go back in there?'

'Only if you are. I'd go with you but nobody else.'

North watched the two closely.

'You realise we might get topped this time?'

'It's the sort of stupid thing we were trained to do. We're good at it. And this time we'd be prepared.'

Jacko was still not happy, not so much about the dangers but of what he still saw as a hidden agenda. He looked at Paula and then at North and after a brief hesitation said, 'I'd want a final check out on your range, more ammunition, and fresh batteries for the StarTacs. And, of course, body armour. Okay we'll do it.'

21

They drove to Northwood in virtual silence. It was not just the danger of what they were doing but Jacko was still not happy and could not put his finger squarely on the cause. Paula, having got to know and trust him respected his silence and sat beside him trying to draw comfort from the car heater; it was bitterly cold outside.

They had been to the Security Service range, done some practice firing, checked their weapons, loaded up and collected silencers for each of their pistols. They had then strapped on the bulky body armour which was uncomfortable sitting in the car. Jacko drove within the speed limit as if needing the extra time to mull over what they would try to do.

They were nearing the outskirts of Northwood when Paula said, 'You're still not satisfied are you? Something's eating at you. Do you want to share it?'

Jacko cruised on, eyes on the road. 'I'd love to share it if I knew what it is. Something, somewhere has been left out and I can't finger it. It might be nothing to do with North but just a gut warning.' He patted her knee. 'It's too late to worry about it, we're committed.'

They drifted into a night-quietened township. Street lights were still ablaze on almost empty streets. Jacko performed his usual lap of honour looking for changes and finding none. If it was bitterly cold it was at least dry. When satisfied he pulled into his usual parking slot not far from the station and sat there brooding for a few moments before opening the door. Paula climbed out when he did. Jacko locked the car and they walked along, arms linked like lovers.

They reached the corner. The amber lights strung out in a double line like well-spaced oases, a pool of light playing with the thickening frost offering an illusion of movement. It was a peaceful scene, an appreciation which was not lost on either. Jacko made sure his gun was loose enough in his pocket to use quickly if needed.

They walked towards Clarke's house and wondered if North's men were in position across the road and had yet identified them. The frost was crackling under their feet. They reached the gate and stood behind the tall hedge lining the street. Then Jacko approached the gate, took a good look at all visible windows and motioned Paula to join him. The house was in total darkness.

Jacko worked as quietly as possible on the lock and was both relieved and surprised to find that it had not been changed. It suggested that Mirek and company were satisfied with things as they were. But on this sort of operation little was as it seemed. He swung the door slowly back. There was still no alarm although this he understood more; whoever controlled the house, and it was now unlikely to be Clarke, would not want the police round in any circumstances if it could be avoided. They slipped into the dark hall closing the door carefully behind them.

They stood close together, hearing each other breathing and not moving a muscle. They stood there for a while before producing their pencil lights which they held in their mouths. By now each was holding a gun at the ready, safety catches off.

No obstacles had been placed in the narrow hall and they slowly worked their way down to the study door. When they reached it they stood still again and waited, listening and hearing nothing but the creaking of cooling timber.

They switched off the lights and crouched either side of the door, pistols held ready. Jacko reached up and slowly turned the door knob, holding it still before putting pressure on the door which swung open slowly. The room, as they expected, was in darkness. They still crouched low and slowly worked their way into it until Jacko was able to close the door behind them. Only then did they slowly rise with their backs to the wall. They switched on their pencil torches and took stock of the room.

As far as they could see nothing had changed. The desk, carpet, chairs were all there. Jacko swung his torch round and located the chip in the door lintel where the bullet had embedded into the wall. It was all exactly the same.

Paula produced a roll of coarse cotton wool and ran a strip along the base of the door as she had previously done with her scarf. She packed it in tight and then plugged the key hole. Jacko switched on the room light and Paula continued to run strips along all the door edges although they knew that most light escaped from the bottom. Satisfied that no light would now show into the hall they moved to the desk.

They took one end each and pushed it back on a signal from Jacko. It moved without a sound. They tipped the desk over to reveal the entrance to the cellar but before going down Paula crept over to the door and put her ear to it, raising a thumb once satisfied. The fact that they had been before was saving them a lot of time but when the two glanced at each other there was a communication that suggested it seemed all too easy.

They used the same procedure as before and Jacko went down the steps to switch on the cellar lights. Paula remained at the top in order to warn him if she heard anyone coming.

Down in the cellar Jacko wasted no time. He pulled across the two hidden wings of the display cabinets, one each side of the room, and then found a groove to pull on and the glass panel slid back. He pulled out one of the creeping terrors and laid it on the floor. There had not been many the first time and now there seemed to be fewer. He spread them out on the glass shelf and considered that no one would know the difference at a glance. He closed the panel and then pushed the unit back into its cavity. So far so good.

He whispered as much up the stairs and Paula acknowledged. He crossed to the other panel and repeated the procedure and produced one of the new guns called the Five-seveN, the F and the N representing the initials of the makers — the most powerful handgun in the world. There were two boxes of 5.7mm ammunition and he opened one and put a fistful of rounds in a pocket. Again he spread the weapons around and then carefully closed the panels. He could not believe how smoothly it had gone.

Jacko pulled a heavy-duty carrier bag from one of his pockets and carefully placed the mine and the pistol and ammunition in it. He was ready to go up when the lights went out just before he reached for the switch. He stood completely still, gun pointing up the stair well. He whispered urgently to Paula but she either did not hear him or was too preoccupied trying to cope with the dark.

He moved to one side and called up again. Still no response. Then there was a tremendous crash as if the door had been torn down, men's voices shouting in what sounded like Russian, the sound of two silenced shots in quick succession and then a body came hurtling down the steps and there was a crash above as the cellar closed.

At first Jacko remained absolutely still. He could detect the soft sound of laboured breathing, then a groan of pain and he shone his torch immediately. Paula lay spread out at the foot of the stairs and was trying to move. Jacko knelt beside her, torch in mouth, trying to control the direction of the beam. She was lying face down and he wanted to establish that nothing was broken before attempting to move her. Paula stretched a leg and groaned again and then with immense relief to Jacko she said, 'It's my bloody head. Help me up.'

He managed to turn her with limited help from Paula herself and was then able to lift her body while her legs remained outstretched. He put his hands under her arms and pulled her to the side of the stairs, out of sight from above, and where she could rest her back against the wall. There was blood flowing down from inside her woollen cap. He pulled the cap off and guessed she had hit the side of her head against the stairs on the way down. He wiped the worst of the blood away.

Movement was difficult in the heavy clothing and the body armour. In the limited light of the torch he thought he could see where a bullet had struck her. He unbuttoned her coat and saw the ragged indentation on the body armour. It was probably the force of the bullet which had sent her crashing down.

'It's all right,' she said breathlessly. 'It's not the first time I've been shot.' A wavering smile appeared under the torchlight. 'I'm in shock and out of breath. I'll be okay in a minute.'

He buttoned her coat up again, the cold was creeping in. 'It was a good shot. But I heard two; did you get one off?'

'Yes. But I don't know whether I hit anyone.' Paula was still having difficulty with her breathing. 'I thought it was all too easy.'

'Yeah. We've got to find a way out of here.'

'The only way is the way I've just come. There are at least two goons up there. Pros. Their timing was perfect. I wonder why they didn't kill me?'

'They probably thought they had. I've seen where they hit you.'

'Shit, Jacko, you've no right to undress me while I'm in this condition.'

He leaned forward and kissed her on the forehead.

'You're in no condition to struggle.'

'Help me up.'

'You sure?'

'Of course I'm sure. Come on, give me a hand.'

Paula stood shakily against the wall but was rapidly recovering. 'I must have dropped my gun.'

'Stay there.' Jacko sidled to the foot of the stairs and shone his torch up. The top was closed tight as he expected and there was no sign of the gun. 'Have mine,' he said handing over the Browning.

Paula shook her head. 'You're a far better shot than I will ever be. I know all about you. You keep it.'

'I've got another one,' he said. He found the carrier bag and produced the Five-seveN and loaded it. There were still spare rounds and more in the display case.

He snapped off the torch, the battery must be conserved but Paula still had hers on her. They stood near the foot of the steps but to one side of them, armed but in darkness and trapped in the cellar.

'The next move has got to be theirs,' said Jacko. And as if he had been overheard the lights came back on. 'So they need light, too,' he added dryly. 'Let's move over to the far wall.'

★ ★ ★

Mirek listened carefully to Chaznov on his mobile phone. He was in bed and his expression grim. 'Is the girl dead?'

'She should be. But I don't know until I take a look. They are both locked in the cellar. They can't get out. If they try we can pick them off quite easily.'

'Thank God I sent you down there. This man you've delegated to look after me, is he any good?'

'Not as good as me but a pro, yes. You have no need to worry.'

'If I give him an urgent job to do, is he capable?'

'The woman? You asked me to do that.'

'That still stands. Another woman. A quick, easy job. I want it done now.'

'He can do it. No problem. Are you winding up?'

'It's worse than I thought. We'll have to close down there and I mean tonight. There is still some business to be done but we'll have to cancel it. No regrets, we've done very well.'

'Okay. We'll wrap up here.'

Mirek said, 'I want the two in the cellar killed. When that's done leave the rest of the stuff down there. We've got more and it's served its purpose. And then get out. Best by the back. Go along a few gardens even though it will take longer. Don't come out immediately opposite, they might have friends waiting. But make sure those two are dead first.'

Mirek switched off, considered his position and then dialled out again.

★ ★ ★

They had backed to the far wall facing the steps. Even if the trapdoor was opened they could not immediately be seen from the top of the stairs. Someone would have to come down, at least partially.

Paula produced her StarTac. Jacko reached out and put a hand over it.

'Hold on a bit,' he said.

She turned in surprise. 'Isn't it time we called in the cavalry?'

'There are at least two professional killers up there. They'd pick them off with no trouble. It's not the SAS North has out there. These hoods will shoot their way out without compunction. Besides our situation isn't desperate enough.'

Paula fell back against the wall. 'You could have fooled me.'

'Okay. Just establish contact. But I don't want these goons to see any movement from outside. That might just make them panic and do something really drastic like burning down the bloody place with us trapped in here.'

Paula punched out a number on the miniature phone. She obtained a crackle. She tried again without effect and then Jacko tried his StarTac with no better result. He gazed up at the ceiling. 'We are down in a basement in a confined space. And the chances are the ceiling has been reinforced and might even be leaded. This is no makeshift job.'

'Are you trying to reassure me, Jacko, because you're doing a lousy job?' And then more objectively Paula added, 'I suppose it's like being in a tunnel when reception is zilch. We really are trapped.'

They could hear no sound from upstairs but they did not believe the gunmen had gone. Jacko reflected that they were seeking instructions using their own phones with no trouble but he kept the thought to himself. There was nothing they could do but wait. To try the stairs would be suicide.

A few minutes later they had the terrifying answer. Shots from above started pumping into the room from all angles. But these were no ordinary shots. Whatever reinforcing the ceiling had received the bullets passed through as if they were paper and pierced the concrete floor to some noticeable depth. Splinters of concrete were flying around the room like lethal chips as holes started to appear all over the ceiling.

Jacko and Paula still stood by the rear wall and pressed themselves into it as much as they could. Some shots, coming in at acute angles, shattered the glass in the cabinets as slivers of glass joined the concrete chips and it seemed that the whole room was full of lethal debris. The sound of breaking glass and the pieces of concrete, which themselves often struck the glass, was terrifying in itself. Had the two been standing in the room and not against a wall they would have been hit.

All Jacko could do was to put an arm round Paula and for them both to make as small a target as they could. The ceiling was like a colander. The safest place was on the stairs which were partly protected by the trap and unless the top was opened were difficult to aim at. But the stairs were the opposite side of the cellar.

The firing stopped as unexpectedly as it began.

The sudden silence, not from the guns themselves which had sounded quite muted, but from the damage they caused, was almost as unnerving as the firing for neither Jacko nor Paula believed it would remain like that.

'Quick.' Jacko pushed Paula forward across the room to the stairs. From there they could take a better view of the extensive damage. They had been lucky and for once in the right place at the right time. The wall they had stood against had not escaped entirely but was the least affected by the barrage. It was difficult for them to believe that they had survived; their body armour would have been no protection against the incredible high velocity of the shots.

'You didn't fire back,' Paula said. 'And you have the same type of gun. My God, impressive.'

'Blind firing would have achieved nothing more than they managed. I'm surprised they did that, it's too chancy for a pro. There was a lot of anger in those shots.'

'Perhaps I did hit one.'

'Let's hope so. And let's hope they think we're dead. There's only one way they can find out.'

They stood either side of the stairs and gazed up to the trap. The central cellar light barely reached the top which was thrown in shadow by the angle of the light. And then the lights went out again and they were blind but could hear the faint movement of the trap and a rattle on the stairs.

Jacko and Paula switched on their torches simultaneously and saw one of the creeping mines coming down the stairs as if out of control.

'For God's sake get back.' Jacko reached across, grabbed Paula's arm and pulled her across the room to where they had been before. When they had their backs to the wall they shone their beams to the stairs but could only penetrate a part of the way up. They heard rather than saw the mine tumbling down the stairs. And then the lights came on once again.

'They want us to see what's going to happen to us.' said Jacko bitterly.

The mine came into view. It was taking the stairs with difficulty; its six legs moving stiffly forward until it reached the edge of each stair and then it would almost tumble forward and land on the next stair. Each time that happened it seemed to lose direction, straighten itself and then continue uncertainly but the nearer it got to the bottom of the stairs the more correct was its action.

'It's picked up our body heat,' said Paula quietly. 'Is there no way to stop it?'

'I could shoot at it but that will probably set it off. We can't escape the blast. Get behind me. Keep back as far as you can.'

'No. I'm not using you as cover. Can we distract it?'

'Only by supplying a heat stronger than our own for it to fasten on.'

The creeping terror had reached the last step and almost as if it could think it faced them before taking the final plunge down onto the cellar floor.

'Oh, God.' For the first time Paula showed her fear.

'Get on my shoulders. It's stupid for both of us to go.'

'No. Shoot it and take a chance.'

'Give me the Browning,' said Jacko as the mine inexorably headed towards them, slowly but deadly.

Paula did not argue; he already had a gun, but she handed him back his Browning.

'I'm more familiar with this,' he said by way of explanation. He removed the silencer and adopted a crouch position. He took aim as the mine headed unerringly for them. He fired, the noise deafening in the cellar, and the mine spun round like a wounded animal, one leg hanging loose but five still working.

The mine realigned and came towards them once more, trailing a front leg and with a heavy limp but moving forward just the same. Jacko moved to his right, took aim and fired again. The middle leg on the same side snapped off completely and the bomb fell to one side. But even then it crept forward at an agonising angle, its heat sensors still working and its good legs trying to compensate for the horrendous loss of balance.

Lopsided and moving like an injured crab it somehow managed to follow an erratic course towards them but was slowed down by its effort to cope. But still it came on in spite of its difficulties. Jacko fired again and missed as it stumbled. He cursed, kept his nerve and fired again almost amputating its rear leg. It keeled over and the remaining three legs kept moving but propelled the mine in tight circles.

Jacko and Paula watched it with horror as it tried to rectify the balance until Paula said, 'You've done it.'

Jacko shook his head. 'No. It's still between us and the stairs. Even if we try to jump over it it will explode and we can't get round it. I don't know how near we have to be for it to explode. We can't take chances.' There was something obscene in the way the three good legs still worked away pushing the mechanical mine round and round in an attempt to finish what it had been designed to do. The heat sensors were still working and the mine still primed.

Jacko wondered just how high they would have to jump to be safe but with the stairs the other side they could easily fall back even if they obtained the height which he did not believe they could. If was too dangerous to approach from any angle. It was stalemate.

Minutes dragged by, the mine was still going round in erratic circles and Jacko and Paula could not take their gaze from its hypnotic effect. They were not sure for how long they stayed there, afraid to move, when they heard rather than saw the trap door open.

Jacko's reaction was to run forward but the mine was in the way so he flung himself in a prone position to obtain some sort of sighting of what was happening to the trap door. He could see just the merest slit and needed to get nearer. Then he saw part of a foot. It was all he had to aim at and he fired.

There was an almighty yell from above and then a

body came crashing down the stairs. A sub-machine gun arched out and over the rotating mine and crashed near Paula who grabbed it quickly. Then a man, still yelling in pain, bounced down the last few stairs and rolled straight on top of the mine. Jacko flung himself back and yelled at Paula to flatten as the mine went off.

The explosion was partly muffled by the huge body which had engulfed it. The body heaved up as if levitating and was suspended for a moment before crashing down as pieces of flying metal escaped from under it. A metallic leg came sliding across the floor to spin to a halt. And then nothing but total silence.

Jacko and Paula were afraid to move and then realised they must. Jacko crept to the foot of the stairs and gazed up at the opening above. There was no one visible. He turned to look at the mangled heap beside him. He had no need to lift the body to examine the damage; no one would have survived that blast full in the chest. The grey face was partially turned towards him and he recognised the man he had seen in the taxi when following Clarke; he did not know his name was Chaznov.

Jacko turned to Paula. 'We've got to take a chance.' He slid his Browning across the floor to her and produced the Five-seveN. 'I'll go first. Keep close behind.'

He retrieved the bag carrying the sample bomb and then crawled silently up the stairs, slowing as he neared the top. He peeped over. There was a man propped against the wall by the door, his gaze blank, one hand partially covering a pistol by his side. His eyes blinked as Jacko emerged and Jacko almost fired then realised that the man could not move and had an ugly chest wound. He could only think that Paula must have hit him before she fell into the cellar. But he was alive.

Jacko crossed over to where the man was propped. He placed his gun against the man's head and then retrieved the pistol, pulling it from under the man's hand. There was no resistance. From behind Jacko, Paula said, 'We'd better call an ambulance.'

'There's nothing anyone can do for him. He's hanging by a thread.'

'Just the same I think we should.'

Jacko said, 'Let's get our priorities straight. First we get out of the place. Then we ring North and then we call an ambulance.' He looked down at the fatally wounded man and said, 'That was a bloody good shot of yours.' And then, 'Forget the ambulance. He's gone.'

The man's head had suddenly lolled forward and Paula felt for a pulse at the carotid artery. 'Yes. He's dead.'

'Then we leave the ambulance to North. Let's get the hell out of here.'

★ ★ ★

Mirek was packing his clothes as he waited for a call back from Chaznov's temporary replacement. His inclination was to leave now in the middle of the night but that could raise complications. He wanted his departure to appear natural and

344

that meant settling his bill in the normal way; to do anything else was to raise suspicion. He had faith in Chaznov and had no doubt that he had the Northwood situation under control which took the immediate pressure off himself.

The telephone call came through on his mobile and he was satisfied with that. Another job done. Nothing could be traced back to him whatever suspicions there might be. As he packed he was suddenly aware of the door opening and when he turned Irina Janesky was standing with her back to it, a pistol with a silencer attachment in her hand.

The sight of her shook him visibly. 'How did you get in and what do you want?'

'I had help. You should not be surprised. As for what I want, well I intend to kill you.'

'You're mad. Who are you?'

'Oh, you know very well who I am, Vadim. I have not changed so much. Nor have you.'

Mirek stood by his bed where a suitcase was open on it. 'Vadim? My name is Jan Mirek. I saw you before in the restaurant. You are confused, madam, and put that silly gun down before I call the police.'

'You try to brazen it out to the last. You really haven't changed at all. Still scheming, still cheating, betraying, doing anything to make money. Who was the poor devil who took your place for the Moscow execution? But that would not matter to you.' Irina raised the gun.

'I can prove I am Jan Mirek. Just one moment.' Mirek turned to the beside table, opened a drawer, put his hand round the butt of a pistol as Irina fired and missed and smashed the table lamp. He whipped the pistol from the drawer and turned as she fired again, and again until the magazine was empty. Only three shots hit him, the last to prove fatal. But he was not quite dead as he collapsed on the bed. He stared up at her, air-filled blood bubbling from his mouth. 'The police will arrest you for my murder.' The words barely gurgled out. 'You're crazy.'

He had dropped his gun and she put her head close to his as she replied, 'How can I be arrested for the murder of someone who is already pronounced dead? You cannot die twice, you bastard.'

He was just about alive as she opened his lids one at a time and suctioned off his coloured contact lenses. 'I just wanted to be absolutely sure,' she said with loathing. 'It was the one thing that puzzled me.' Vadim Bykov never heard her; he was dead.

Irina Janesky quietly left the room.

22

They were in Mirek's hotel room, Jacko and Paula having been cleared with the police by North. The alarm had been raised when the guest in the next room had heard the commotion the shots which had missed Mirek had made, like the smashed side lamp. The hotel manager had already been advised by North to contact him should anything unusual happen in relation to Mirek. North was actually informed before the police which did not please the latter. Finally it was all sorted out and the right people were there. Jacko and Paula were the last to arrive having come up from Northwood.

North took them aside and gazed round the room; the place was full of police. 'Let's go down to the restaurant.'

They took the lift down and went into a darkened restaurant which would not be opened to guests for a time yet. North found a light switch and they sat down at one of the tables already laid for breakfast. North said, 'We've found the list. It was in a coded notebook he carried on him. It's already on its way to the cryptography boys who will work through what's left of the night. The contents won't be of interest to you.' North smiled, 'Very well done, you two. Splendid work.'

'Who killed him?' asked Jacko.

'We don't really know. Whoever it was did the job and left. Lousy shot, most of them missed.'

'That doesn't suggest anyone to you?' asked Paula, still suffering reaction from the Northwood débâcle.

'Oh, yes. But she has left the Savoy. Probably gone back to France.'

'Where the Sûreté will pick her up,' Paula prodded.

North stifled a yawn. 'It's a strange situation. Almost certainly the dead man Mirek was Vadim Bykov. My guess is that as the Soviet Union was breaking up Russian gangsters were already well in place. Many of the KGB were looking over their shoulders and feathering their nests. Russia had huge arms stocks which are still selling today. Bykov's knowledge of arms was second to none. He knew where they were and how many, big and small. And he had worldwide contacts. To the far-seeing he was far too valuable to kill. But he needed to be controlled. It was quite simple to put a hood over someone else's head and shoot them.'

'Answer Paula's question,' Jacko insisted. 'We need to get to bed.'

Just then a waitress came in with a tray of coffee; she looked as if she had been dragged from bed. 'The manager thought you might like this.' She slid the tray onto the table and left. Paula did the job of pouring.

'Irina Janesky had already had her life disseminated by Bykov. In the end it turned out well for her as you know. She would not want that destroyed by his resurrection. And how can you kill a man twice? Bykov was already officially dead. Let the police continue with their enquiries. It's their job to find a murderer not mine. Personally I don't see it as murder but rather as a delayed execution.'

Paula was rubbing under her heart and seemed to be in pain.

'Are you all right?' North asked with genuine concern.

'She was shot,' explained Jacko. 'Even with the body armour it's still bloody sore.'

Paula seemed not to hear any of this. She said flatly, 'Irina deserves to be free of the bastard.'

'So you are not going to be particularly helpful to police enquiries?' Jacko found it hard to believe the compassion which had suddenly flowed from North.

North stirred his coffee thoughtfully. 'The police hate interference from us. I will respect their feelings.'

They sipped their coffee for a while. It seemed strange in the empty dining room with most of the lights off. It was dark and gloomy and they were tired. But Jacko was still puzzled. He said, 'How did Irina get into the room? And she must have known that Mirek's bodyguard signed off once Mirek was back in the hotel. That would be her only chance.' He looked North squarely in the eye. 'I wonder if she had a little help from you?'

North said, 'You're overtired. You're beginning to hallucinate. As if I'd do something like that.'

'It's saved you a lot of trouble though, hasn't it? No long enquiries, no dragged-out court case. I think my question was legitimate.'

'In view of your activities tonight that is a word

you are not qualified to use. I'd go home if I were you. There's nothing you can do here and Northwood is well under control.' He glanced at the carrier bag containing the mine that Jacko still had with him. 'In the event we don't really need that. We now have those in the cellar.'

Jacko held his tongue with difficulty, the memory of what he and Paula had endured to obtain the evidence still vivid in his mind. He felt Paula's hand squeeze his knee and he eased off. 'What about Anne Corrie?'

'She can wait. She was overambitious. Sights aimed high. And she got in over her head. Way out of her league. Her problems are over.'

'You're talking as if she's dead.' Paula glanced at Jacko as if he might know something that she did not, but Jacko shook his head.

North said heavily, 'She was killed before Bykov. Almost certainly on his instructions. Nothing fancy, one shot between the eyes. We might not have known for some time but the night porter at the apartment block tried to stop the assassin going up and was also killed. The porter was found lying in the hall by a late returning tenant.'

Jacko and Paula sat back trying to take it in. Suddenly there was nobody left. So far as they were concerned it was over. What was left was for others to sort out.

'Let's go to bed,' said Jacko rising. He took Paula by the arm. They barely glanced at North as they left the dining room. As they headed for the main doors Jacko said, 'I think we need each other tonight, don't you?'

'I certainly don't want to sleep alone.' She squeezed his arm. 'I'd have nightmares about who we might have missed and that bloody mine you are still carrying.'

THE END

McLEAN AT THE GOLDEN OWL
George Goodchild

Inspector McLean has resigned from Scotland Yard's CID and has opened an office in Wimpole Street. With the help of his able assistant, Tiny, he solves many crimes, including those of kidnapping, murder and poisoning.

KATE WEATHERBY
Anne Goring

Derbyshire, 1849: The Hunter family are the arrogant, powerful masters of Clough Grange. Their feuds are sparked by a generation of guilt, despair and ill-fortune. But their passions are awakened by the arrival of nineteen-year-old Kate Weatherby.

A VENETIAN RECKONING
Donna Leon

When the body of a prominent international lawyer is found in the carriage of an intercity train, Commissario Guido Brunetti begins to dig deeper into the secret lives of the once great and good.

A TASTE FOR DEATH
Peter O'Donnell

Modesty Blaise and Willie Garvin take on impossible odds in the shape of Simon Delicata, the man with a taste for death, and Swordmaster, Wenczel, in a terrifying duel. Finally, in the Sahara desert, the intrepid pair must summon every killing skill to survive.

SEVEN DAYS FROM MIDNIGHT
Rona Randall

In the Comet Theatre, London, seven people have good reason for wanting beautiful Maxine Culver out of the way. Each one has reason to fear her blackmail. But whose shadow is it that lurks in the wings, waiting to silence her once and for all?

QUEEN OF THE ELEPHANTS
Mark Shand

Mark Shand knows about the ways of elephants, but he is no match for the tiny Parbati Barua, the daughter of India's greatest expert on the Asian elephant, the late Prince of Gauripur, who taught her everything. Shand sought out Parbati to take part in a film about the plight of the wild herds today in north-east India.

THE DARKENING LEAF
Caroline Stickland

On storm-tossed Chesil Bank in 1847, the young lovers, Philobeth and Frederick, prevent wreckers mutilating the apparent corpse of a young woman. Discovering she is still alive, Frederick takes her to his grandmother's home. But the rescue is to have violent and far-reaching effects . . .

A WOMAN'S TOUCH
Emma Stirling

When Fenn went to stay on her uncle's farm in Africa, the lovely Helena Starr seemed to resent her — especially when Dr Jason Kemp agreed to Fenn helping in his bush hospital. Though it seemed Jason saw Fenn as little more than a child, her feelings for him were those of a woman.

A DEAD GIVEAWAY
Various Authors

This book offers the perfect opportunity to sample the skills of five of the finest writers of crime fiction — Clare Curzon, Gillian Linscott, Peter Lovesey, Dorothy Simpson and Margaret Yorke.

DOUBLE INDEMNITY
— MURDER FOR INSURANCE
Jad Adams

This is a collection of true cases of murderers who insured their victims then killed them — or attempted to. Each tense, compelling account tells a story of cold-blooded plotting and elaborate deception.

THE PEARLS OF COROMANDEL
By Keron Bhattacharya

John Sugden, an ambitious young Oxford graduate, joins the Indian Civil Service in the early 1920s and goes to uphold the British Raj. But he falls in love with a young Hindu girl and finds his loyalties tragically divided.

WHITE HARVEST
Louis Charbonneau

Kathy McNeely, a marine biologist, sets out for Alaska to carry out important research. But when she stumbles upon an illegal ivory poaching operation that is threatening the world's walrus population, she soon realises that she will have to survive more than the harsh elements . . .

TO THE GARDEN ALONE
Eve Ebbett

Widow Frances Morley's short, happy marriage was childless, and in a succession of borders she attempts to build a substitute relationship for the husband and family she does not have. Over all hovers the shadow of the man who terrorized her childhood.

CONTRASTS
Rowan Edwards

Julia had her life beautifully planned — she was building a thriving pottery business as well as sharing her home with her friend Pippa, and having fun owning a goat. But the goat's problems brought the new local vet, Sebastian Trent, into their lives.

MY OLD MAN AND THE SEA
David and Daniel Hays

Some fathers and sons go fishing together. David and Daniel Hays decided to sail a tiny boat seventeen thousand miles to the bottom of the world and back. Together, they weave a story of travel, adventure, and difficult, sometimes terrifying, sailing.

SQUEAKY CLEAN
James Pattinson

An important attribute of a prospective candidate for the United States presidency is not to have any dirt in your background which an eager muckraker can dig up. Senator William S. Gallicauder appeared to fit the bill perfectly. But then a skeleton came rattling out of an English cupboard.

NIGHT MOVES
Alan Scholefield

It was the first case that Macrae and Silver had worked on together. Malcolm Underdown had brutally stabbed to death Edward Craig and had attempted to murder Craig's fiancée, Jane Harrison. He swore he would be back for her. Now, four years later, he has simply walked from the mental hospital. Macrae and Silver must get to him — before he gets to Jane.

GREATEST CAT STORIES
Various Authors

Each story in this collection is chosen to show the cat at its best. James Herriot relates a tale about two of his cats. Stella Whitelaw has written a very funny story about a lion. Other stories provide examples of courageous, clever and lucky cats.